Broken Fairytale

By

Nikola Jensen

Dear Noeleen,

Enjoy, Though I may be slightly embarrassed ♡♡!

Lots of love, Nxx

(Ditto xx)

Published by Nikola Jensen

Createspace Edition
ISBN-13: 9781491284506
ISBN-10: 1491284501

Copyright 2013 Nikola Jensen
Song lyrics Copyright 2013 Nikola Jensen

All rights reserved. This book may not be reproduced, scanned or distributed in any printed or electronic form without permission from the author. Please do not participate in or encourage the piracy of copyrighted materials in violation of the author's rights. All characters and storylines are the property of the author and your support and respect for this is appreciated.

The characters and events portrayed in this book are entirely fictitious. Any similarity to real persons, living or dead, is coincidental and not intended by the author.

Cover created by Renae Porter at Social Butterfly Creative.

For more information please come and visit me at https://www.facebook.com/AuthorNikolaJensen

For the three loves in my life

I love you

Always

Prologue

Daddy's mad again. He's mad at Mummy and me. Most of the time he's only mad at Mummy, but he's yelling at me as well this time. I can't remember what I did but I must have done something bad or Daddy wouldn't be mad at me again. I think he's getting mad at Zack too 'cause he won't stop crying. I keep trying to hush him quiet in my lap but I don't think he understands. He is so little. I'm little too but I'm bigger than Zack. I'm so scared because Daddy is so big and angry and I want to make him smile again. He doesn't smile much. Mummy doesn't smile much either; she looks so sad right now. Daddy is dragging Mummy into another room, she keeps crying for him to stop, not in front of the children. I know I'm just a kid but I know he hits her sometimes because I can hear it and I see Mummy's bruises. No one else sees them 'cause Mummy hides them under her clothes. I've seen them though when she has baths and they look like they hurt.

Daddy has never hit me or Zack. He yells a lot and he says things that make me sad but he's never hurt me. He calls me stupid a lot and tells me I'm in the way. He should never have had me. If I wasn't here maybe he would smile again?

I can hear Daddy and Mummy in the bedroom so I tell Zack we have to quickly go to bed before Daddy comes out again. I take his small pudgy hand and he waddles with me to his room.

Zack crawls straight into his bed and under the covers. I pull his cover up so only his head is out and turn on his Buzz Lightyear night light. Zack is afraid of the dark. It makes him cry. Mummy's not here to kiss him goodnight or tell him a story so I pick up The Gruffalo. It's his favourite. I don't read so well yet because I haven't long been at school but I know this story off by heart cause Mummy always has to read it to him and I always listen in before going to my bedroom.

Zack has stopped crying and looks at me with his big eyes sucking his thumb listening to the clever mouse that took a walk in the woods. Mummy always stays after she's finished reading until he goes asleep. So I stay with him too. I don't want to leave him scared, and Mummy isn't here.

The yelling has stopped and Zack is sleeping. I try to tip toe my way to my room but I'm so scared cause it's dark with shadows and I don't know where Mummy and Daddy is.

I'm nearly at my bedroom door when I hear a loud slapping noise coming from Mummy and Daddy's bedroom. I don't know what to do. I'm scared and shaking cause I know it's not a good noise. I shrink backwards as quiet as I can but get my foot stuck in the runner on the hallway floor. Falling I grab onto the sideboard where Mummy keeps her glass figurines. One falls to the floor and smashes into a thousand pieces.

I start to cry; I'm gonna be in so much trouble. Mummy loves her figurines. I quickly try and brush the glass under the runner hoping no one will notice. My hand starts bleeding and it hurts but I have to do this quickly.

I didn't hear Daddy come so when he grabs my arm too hard. I yelp in pain. His face is red and purple that's how mad at me he is.

Daddy is hurting me.

It really hurts Daddy; please don't hurt me.

I make myself small against the wall, rolled into a ball. Daddy has a cigarette in one hand, grabbing my arm with the other. He is yelling so loud.

I'm so scared I tell myself the story of the big brave mouse who was so clever he never got eaten by the snake, the fox and the owl while Daddy hurts me.

Daddy leaves me on the floor.

I count to twenty real slow and open my eyes. It's still dark but I'm not scared anymore. Daddy has gone.

I can hear Mummy crying in her bedroom.

I go to the kitchen to get some baby wipes and wipe my hand and arm. There's not much blood anymore but I can't reach the kitchen cupboard to get the plasters I need. I think about climbing onto the kitchen counter but I don't want to make too much noise. Instead I take the kitchen towel and wrap my right hand in it. I think that will stop the bleeding.

I quickly run to Zack's room, I don't want to be alone and I don't want him waking up from a nightmare crying cause that might make Daddy even more mad.

Climbing into bed with Zack and pulling the cover over us both, I wonder why my back hurts so much. It feels like it's on fire.

Daddy scares me. I need to look after Zack now. I can't let Daddy hurt Zack.

Chapter One

I wake up with the sound of my alarm thinking here I go; this is where my life begins again.

I kind of wish I'd set it to some random alarm rather than the radio. Lying here listening to the lyrics of the song playing I can't help but feel they're an ominous prediction of how my day is going to play out.

Listening to Myles Kennedy asking who's going to watch over me when he's gone, who's going to ease my pain and who's going to save me. Who indeed, I'd love to know, I want nothing more. I can't think straight but I know I need to because everything's different now and I have to get out of bed and live again and be strong. If not, well that thought scares me too much.

I get out of bed and look at myself in the mirror. So much has changed. I don't even recognize me. I still physically look like myself but I don't see that, I see the fear in my too big blue eyes, I see the shadows and I see the hidden scars. I know the placement of my physical ones. I wonder how others will see me today. They don't know yet but will they see the fear?

I hope they'll see me as I was and want to be again, an outgoing girl with a sarcastic sense of humour, who is still kind of shy. I dread that they'll see me as I am now, marked and temporarily withdrawn.

I guess still shy but for very different reasons.

I know I want to revert to who I was before, bring it back to the surface. I refuse to be who I am now, a result of consequence, with all that's happened I wouldn't even know how to find the 'me' from before; she's gone, hidden and buried under layers of hurt and ugliness. I go turn off the radio before I wake the rest of the house up, I don't need an audience on my first day. Day one of my brand new life, without Zack to experience it with me as planned.

What do I wear on my first day back in the real world? I've always thought that the clothes we wear on the outside is a statement of who we are on the inside. Well mostly, because I'm a girlie girl but I like black. A lot. I was always told I wasn't allowed to wear black; it's the colour of death and rebellion. Well, not to me, to me the colour black has been the colour of freedom for as long as I can remember and now I can finally wear it without repercussion. I hope.

My room's one giant mess, I know Dad's going to kill me when he sees it, I stop what I'm doing and an involuntary shiver runs down my spine....wrong choice of words and I can't believe how easy that sentence came to me without actually thinking. Well if that isn't a sign that I'm beginning to deal. I don't know what is.

Right, I pull myself together; let's get back to the problem of what to wear. I wish I hadn't left this till the last minute but I always do and then I panic.

I settle for my black skinny jeans, a white fitted long sleeved t-shirt and my silver all-stars. I can't help but smile; this is me, who I was; still is. Start as you mean to go on right?

I tie up my long white blonde hair into a messy knot, put a bit of black eyeliner and mascara on, put my lip gloss in my messenger bag and go to the kitchen to get some breakfast.

The house is so quiet. You wouldn't even know anyone was here except me. I grab a bowl of cereal and quickly eat it while checking the bus times. I wish I had a car, but my savings haven't been topped up since before the accident happened and I know they won't until I get myself a new job.

There was no way I could stay working in the book shop. No one wants to go check out a book from a snivelling snotty mess of a sales assistant. Plus, Mum needed me and watching for signs of her impending slap dash attempts at killing herself from grief took up nearly all of my time. I suppose it took away my own life as well until now.

I finish off my breakfast and make sure I have everything I need before quietly slipping out of the house. I don't want to wake anyone up, I don't need any aggravation. Today's important to me, it's the day I leave the past behind and try and make my new life and create my future.

Pulling my parka hood up, I walk to the bus stop listening to my iPod, trying to remember what my story is going to be for the last eighteen months. I can't help but wonder if the rain is a premonition of the day to come. It's miserable, grey and stormy with rain pelting down.

As I see my bus pulling up I manage to slip in a puddle that's obviously hiding a hole, but just before my knees hit the floor I feel an arm wrap itself around my waist and pull me up into a hard body. I start shaking from fear as being restrained is not one of my favourite things but I turn around to say thank you and am met with a huge white smile. I can't help but smile right back, its infectious which surprises me.

"You okay?" asks this giant of a guy. I say giant because I'm small, in fact, I'm tiny. At five foot two everyone's pretty much taller than me, but this guy has to be at least six foot something.

"Yes...thanks to you," I nod and untangle myself from his arms feeling the heat in my cheeks from my clumsiness. I haven't got a clue what to say next so I just smile and run off to get on the bus. It's pretty full now and I have to squeeze into a seat at the back next to a young Mum and her little boy who's screaming his head off. I turn my iPod back on and try to psyche myself up for the next big step. As I get off the bus I try to remember where it is I need to go. This is my first day at University. Who would have thought? Finally, I get to start. I knew I'd always get here, one day; Dad wanted me to. As the first in the family, it was a status thing. He wanted to be able to brag about it. More so than wanting it for me, I'm sure. As I study the campus map I was sent in the post, I feel a tap on my shoulder. Tensing up, I wrap my arms around myself and turn around. It's the guy from the bus stop.

"Hi there, again....you ran off. I don't bite you know," he laughs, whilst looking me up and down. I smile back, see I can do this whole friendly thing, well I'm trying anyway.

"Umm...Hi," I reply as I start walking in the direction of the registrations office.

"Are you off to register?" he asks as he starts walking alongside with me.

"Yes....yes I am," I reply, feeling like a bloody idiot as I feel the blush.

"You don't say much do you?" he laughs, shaking his head at me.

What do I say to that? "Are you off to register too?" I ask him, mentally slapping myself for my inadequate conversation skills.

"Nope, I'm starting my second year on the mature student programme. See I tried to be a kick-arse rock star first but sadly it didn't work out so this is option number two."

I'm trying to figure out how old that makes him. But as I'm a mature student as well I haven't really got a clue.

"I'm late in starting too, I didn't try to be a kick-arse anything, boringly I'm signing up today as option number one albeit a bit late."

I go quiet wishing I'd kept my mouth shut. Looking at him I suddenly realise how gorgeous he is. His hair's kind of messy and slightly wavy, nearly reaching his chin. It's so black that in the right light I bet it looks almost dark blue. His eyes are big and warm, they're dark brown but with flecks of green and I think gold. Odd, I don't think I've ever seen eyes his colour before. His bottom lip is pierced and he's got a bit of a lopsided grin, but that could well be because he knows I'm checking him out…dammit. I quickly look down at my crumbled sheet of paper with my registrations details, all the while feeling my cheeks getting red hot. I look up again and realise the office is just to my left. Turning around I look at my guy…*my guy*? Seriously? He's still grinning at me knowing full well how uncomfortable he's making me feel right now.

"Right well, I have to go in there," I say, pointing to the office with a shaky finger. "So yeah, I'll see you around." I quickly walk off, actually I run off, before he can reply. I can hear him laugh as he walks off to wherever he has to go. Great, as a first impression mine properly sucked, a clumsy stuttering mess. Yep sucked. Oh well, this is a huge campus I'll probably not see him again, I think to myself, whilst chewing on my lip thoroughly embarrassed. The thought of that just made me skip a breath; I've got it bad, a complete butterfly in your belly moment. I mentally berate myself for developing a pathetic school girl crush on day one. This isn't me. I don't do crushes. Not anymore.

I walk over to the office and pick up my schedule and despite only taking five subjects I'm on campus every day. This makes me happy; I now have a valid excuse to leave home every day without having to lie and make shit up to avoid confrontation and pain.

I wish I was staying on campus or in town but that was never an option, I tried, but Dad refused to help, and seeing as I can't afford to move out on my own right now, it isn't an option. Not yet, one day soon though. I can't bloody wait.

I quickly walk to my tutor's office to sign in and get my reading list for my subjects. Looking for the door that says Dr McGrath I collide with another student. Great, this day is so not working out for me.

As I'm trying to pick myself up from the floor I see an outstretched hand and look into the bluest eyes I've ever seen. Mine are blue too, but these are seriously blue. I wonder if they're real or contacts.

"I'm so sorry, I'm not having much luck today," I say pulling myself together.

"No worries, I wasn't looking where I was going, in fact, I'm so lost I don't even care anymore." He laughs and sticks out his hand all formal like. "Right, I'm Aiden, and I should really know where I'm going but I don't and I'm utterly confused, so nice to knock you over."

I burst out laughing, shocking myself in the process, I can't remember the last time I laughed this easily. I decide to formally respond still laughing as I shake his hand.

"Well hello Aiden, my name is Izzy and I'm very happy to meet you, even though your methods are somewhat unusual."

He shakes his head grinning and proceeds to look at a crumpled piece of paper in his hand. "Dr McGrath," he mutters to himself. My ears prick up.

"That's the magic door I'm looking for too, before we collided, I think it's further down the hallway, I'll walk with you." I can't stop thinking how surreal this is, it's almost like the last year hasn't happened. Like I no longer need to run and hide. I can be myself. I used to be happy, I had a permanent smile on my face and I could give as good as I got. Can I do this again I wonder? Can I have this separate life, be who I was or would my two worlds collide? My thoughts are suddenly interrupted by a hand on my arm.

"I think this is it," Aiden says. The line outside the door is enormous. We take our place in it and I put my iPod on. One of my ear plugs is immediately snatched out of my ear and Aiden promptly puts it into his. Now, considering how short I am this is quite a feat. He has to stoop to fit it in.

"Black Stone Cherry? Really?" he says, laughing but not taking the headphone out. Laughing. Seriously. I don't even know how to take that.

"If you want to listen in buddy, I suggest you stop the snipes," I retort trying to look offended. "They happen to be one of my favourite bands, so if you don't mind I'll have that back," I say, yanking the ear phone out of his ear.

"Nah you're good I don't mind them, and you're cute when you get stroppy." He winks at me.

Now, I have to say Aiden's got one of those faces you can't describe as anything other than beautiful. No guy wants to hear he has a beautiful face, but that's what it is. His hair is a dark reddish brown, auburn I suppose and cropped, but not too short. He has a bit of stubble, like maybe he got up a bit late this morning and ran out of time to shave. His eyes, like I said, are blue and look like they laugh a lot, which I'm guessing they currently are when I suddenly hear him chuckle. Why can't I be subtle about staring at people, somehow they always catch me. I look away embarrassed and hope that I don't have to wait too long before Dr McGrath can see me. Aiden tries to get my attention again by asking me if I live on campus. I tell him I live nearby with my parents so will be bussing it in every day but that I'm eager to move out. I obviously don't tell him why, because no one needs to know the real reasons for why I still live at home and why I'm so late in starting Uni. I hope he doesn't ask me any more personal questions. I don't know him. Yet. I think I want to. By the time Aiden and I are next in line to go in, I tell him he can go first, but he refuses, so I go instead. I suddenly feel very nervous and feel a cold sweat break out on the back of my neck.

Dr McGrath is everything I expected a psychology lecturer to look like. Despite already being afraid of him, for what he can potentially uncover, I'm relishing the fact that I'm finally starting my Psychology degree. I've always been interested in helping others, especially kids. Now, more than ever, hoping I can be there for a child the way I wish someone had been there for me and my brother.

Clearing my throat to alert him to me being here, I realise that Dr McGrath looks slightly mad. He has completely white hair, which is crazy long and tied in a ponytail. He's wearing a crumpled old suit with a mis-matched shirt and a tie that has a huge coffee stain on it. But his eyes, his eyes are the kindest eyes I've ever seen. They look at me, so intense that I feel like he's reading me and knows.

"Umm…my name is Izobel, Izobel Jerome," I stutter, feeling completely stripped under his scrutiny.

"Yes, Izobel, I remember your application," he replies with a shrewd look.

I can't help wondering if that's supposed to have a hidden meaning? Does he know? Surely he can't, because I'm no longer seeing Dr Beckett and anyway, patient confidentiality and all that, there's no way he should know.

He starts rooting around the papers on his desk and finally finds my schedule. For someone who has eyes as perceptive as his, he comes across as the exact opposite. Almost Granddad like. Not that I know what one of those actually is. I never really had one. Well I did, but mine were not your usual stereotypical cuddly Granddads.

Mum's Dad never stopped living his youth. Yes he got older but he never acted that way. He still went to strip clubs until the ripe old age of seventy-five and he owned a porn shop. Yes, that's right…a porn shop, in which I used to sit out the back having my lunch when we went to see him during the day.

He lived in an apartment in the city centre in a nicer part compared to where his shop was. It was never what you could call homely, rather it was stark and cold. The only colourful room was the "clubbing" room. This room had a big dance floor, a bar and a huge disco ball hanging from the ceiling. On the walls were posters of half-naked women in various suggestive poses.

As kids we'd sit in there and think this is magic, watching the colours spark off the disco ball and listening to whatever Granddad had playing on the stereo. Mostly it was The Rolling Stones or The Beatles. As far as being a Granddad though, there was no way he'd ever qualify for that title.

My other Granddad was nice, I really did love him, but he never spoke, unless he had something important to say. He grunted, a lot, fiddling continuously with his pipe. My brother and I spent many weekends with him but he'd sit in his chair in the corner of the room and would only move when it was time to eat.

So yeah, when I hear about the amazing bond my friends have with their Granddads I can't help but feel jealous and like I've lost out somehow. I feel a lump in my throat at my thoughts. Silly really I suppose. Both my Granddads have now passed away, leaving me with just one Grandmother who I never speak to. My face must reflect my emotions as I get lost in the memory because I'm startled by Dr McGrath clearing his throat. I quickly pull myself together.

"Right Izobel, here's your schedule and a list of necessary books. You've also got my contact details and the hours I keep; contact me at any time for anything." He smiles at me reassuringly. I wonder what he means and if he says this to all his students. Shit, I really have to stop reading more than I should into what people say.

"Thank you," I mumble and just about run out of his office. Why I'm freaking out like this I don't know, but I'm adding this episode to the series of bad first impressions people have gotten of me so far today. So much for the confident new me I sigh loudly.

Aiden's in next and before I manage to run off, he grabs my hand and puts something in it. He gives me a wink and closes the door behind him. I look at the note; it has his mobile phone number on it with a funny face doing a *"call me"* sign. I burst out laughing. I think Aiden could be good for me. No one's made me laugh like he has in a long time.

I walk down the hill to the bus stop, take the bus back into the town centre and start browsing the second hand book shops hoping to find the books I need for my curriculum reading list. I could just ask Dad for the money for them, but I don't want to. I need to do this myself. I hate having to ask him for anything. Almost two years ago it wouldn't have been an issue, I had a good job saving up for Uni and things were a lot different.

I find what I need and walk to get the bus back home. As I get closer to my stop I see the guy from this morning. Great. He's standing there chatting to a really pretty girl, who must have said something funny, because he's laughing and not the kind to be polite, more like the proper belly kind of laughter. For reasons I don't want to admit my face drops and I feel unsure of myself.

I'm still a fair bit away so I automatically slow down so I can study him as I'm walking over. He really is too good looking, absurdly so, almost like he should be on the cover of a fashion or music magazine. He's wearing faded and snug worn jeans, but I'm guessing not the kind you can buy, these are worn to perfection. His t-shirt is fitted and white and has a very faded 30 Seconds to Mars logo on it, and on his feet are a pair of very beat up black all-stars. A guitar case is strapped to his back and is scrunching up the arm of his t-shirt which means I get a glimpse of a black tattoo.

Okay, now this is where I freak out on the inside. Whenever anyone's asked me what my ideal man looks like, I always answer with a much repeated and rehearsed answer; he *has* to be able to play an instrument, he *has* to have dark hair and he *has* to have at least one tattoo. Shallow me? Yeah, probably...actually most definitely.

But this is the kind of guy I continuously crush on, always have. I've read books about him, I listen to his music, I see him on the TV or in the cinema. I know he's what I want. However, he's not what I've had in the past. Don't get me wrong, they've all been great looking lads, sure, but none have made me feel like this, like I absolutely need to know who he is. I can actually count on one hand the number of boyfriends I've had that have lasted more than a week. Is that many or not? I'm not sure.

Compared to my best friend Sofia it's a lot. But then she met Taylor when we were all sixteen and they've been together ever since. Kind of sweet really, though they joke that they are in their seventh year which is always ominous, it's not called the seven year itch for nothing. Despite their relationship being on and off the first few years they still count the seven-ish as they're almost there. I've always been more of a, let's have fun for a few weeks and at the first sign of anything more I bail. I guess it's because I never wanted anyone to find out. I never let anyone close enough to the other *'me'* and the signs of my *'other'* life.

As I get closer to my bus stop I look down, I don't want him to see me, I want to slip onto the bus unnoticed. Fat chance of that, I should've guessed really. As soon as I get to the bus line a woman and her dog come out of no-where, literally. She's clearly lost control of her dog which is running off, dragging his owner along attached to the lead. The dog crosses my path, I trip over the lead and take a spectacular nose-dive. Ten out of ten for effort I'm sure.

Again, before I fall flat on my face I feel an arm grab me and pull me up against a very hard body. I don't even want to look, I know who it is. I hear the laughter first, then the voice that gives me goose-bumps for the third time today.

"So, is this you and me from now on? You fall, I catch?" he laughs.

If only, I think to myself. I open my eyes, look up and pretty much drown in those dark amazing eyes. I'm speechless. I'm sure my face is the colour of the bus that's just turned up to take me home. Red....

"Sorry about that," I laugh nervously while cringing inside. He's looking at me with a knowing smile on his face. That's it; I think to myself, no more, just let me go home with no more painful and embarrassing moments to share. But for some reason he won't let go of me and before I know it, the bus has closed its doors and driven off. It's just him and me left at the bus stop.

"Right, seeing as though I've now saved you twice from a face plant, I deserve your name in return." He still has me locked in his arm, looking down at me. I'm staring at his mouth thinking how it'd feel to kiss and taste it. I forgot what he said. What did he say?

"Sorry what was that?"

He starts laughing, never breaking eye contact. "Okay, I'll start then shall I? I'm *Declan*, my friends call me Dec."

I can't stop thinking about his lips on mine and I tremble slightly when I finally manage to stutter "Izzy."

"Well Izzy, you've obviously missed your bus so how about we go and get a coffee while we wait for the next one?" he says more of a statement than a question.

"Umm…okay." I drop my eyes and pretend to be mesmerized with my shoes. As we walk to the nearest coffee shop he takes my hand and looks down at me.

"Just in case you encounter anymore random dogs and puddles…right." He winks at me pulling me along. My hand feels so small in his, it makes me feel safe, which is strange as I don't even know this guy. His hand is warm, his fingers calloused from, what I'm guessing, is playing guitar. We order our coffee and go sit outside as the rain's stopped and it's now turning into an unusually sunny and warm afternoon for this time of year.

"So Izzy, let's play twenty questions, we each get to ask whatever we want, what do you say?"

I chew on my bottom lip in worry and apprehension at what he's going to ask me, but I nod, staring into his warm and friendly eyes.

"Don't look so scared," he whispers whilst tucking some loose strands of my hair behind my ear and very slowly freeing my lip with his thumb. Unfortunately at the exact time he does that I lick my lip and catch his thumb at the same time. I hear a sharp intake of breath and look into his eyes, eyes that are now staring at my mouth. My body suddenly goes on high alert and I feel every hair stand on end. The moment's rudely interrupted by the waitress arriving with our coffee. I'm both disappointed and relieved so I quickly pick up my coffee and take a sip as a distraction. Shit it's too hot. I stick my tongue out and chant, "Hot, hot, hot."

Declan bursts out laughing but it doesn't last long. Becoming all serious he suddenly reaches over, grabs my head with both hands and puts his lips to mine. All the while keeping his eyes open to gage a reaction. I'm stunned, I wasn't expecting this. His lips are firm yet so soft. His tongue licks my lip where I burnt it. It's so gentle, soothing even and it makes every inch of my body tingle. He moves away but keeps his hands on my face whilst looking into my eyes.

"Does it feel better now Izzy?" His eyes burn tracks across my whole face. I can't look away, I'm lost in his eyes.

I've got no idea what to say or do. I feel completely out of my comfort zone for the umpteenth time today. I just sit here, probably looking stupidly gobsmacked until he finally lets me go, perhaps sensing my embarrassment. He curses and looks annoyed when his mobile phone starts playing *'Different People'* by Biffy Clyro. Declan's got nice taste in music I think to myself with a smile.

"Aren't you going to get that?" I ask him feeling a bit awkward. He looks away and picks it up immediately becoming animated in conversation with whoever is on the other end, I really want to listen but instead I'm thinking of a way I can sneak off.

My heart is pounding and I feel like any minute I'm going to pass out, I feel trapped and strangely exposed. I check the time, *shit*, my bus is in two minutes; so I pick up my bag and run to the bus stop without looking back cursing my own stupidity.

Once on the bus I realise we've hit commuter hour and there's no seats left. I move as far back as I can and stand holding on to the nearest seat. As I'm putting my iPod on, the bus takes a sharp corner, the driver obviously thinking he's at Silverstone. I stumble and would've fallen but for a hand on my waist steadying me. Without looking I've got no doubt who that hand belongs to. I know it too well by now seeing this must be the third time today. But who's counting right? Yep, it's Declan; he's managed to slip onto the bus somehow unbeknownst to me. I wonder where he's going, he doesn't look happy, in fact he looks quite pissed off. Not knowing what to say I settle on a nervous stupid smile. I can guess why he'd be pissed though, can't say I blame him really. My stop is coming up soon and I have an inner debate with myself. Do I say something, but if I do, what do I say? I decide I've been through enough weird and embarrassing situations for one day so I press the stop button. Before walking to the front I take one last look at Declan and give him a genuine smile. After all, the butterflies in my stomach haven't forgotten their crush. He picks up my hand and places a cheeky kiss on it. Seriously, who is this guy? Blushing and feeling like a teenager, I step off the bus and watch it drive away catching one last glimpse of him.

Chapter Two

Standing out the front of our house, I feel so reluctant to walk inside. It's such a pretty house, clean and crisp white cottage style with a thatched roof. It looks idyllic, the garden at the front has that luscious green grass you normally only see at manor houses or golf courses. There are pots everywhere with luscious intentionally colour co-ordinated flowers. In spring and summer you can smell our garden from the road. Sweet, almost cloyingly so.

We've only lived in this house for eighteen months, we moved in after the accident. We had to leave our old house and town because of what happened and ended up moving closer to London. I stand looking in, not wanting to enter my *'other'* world but knowing I have to.

Unlocking the door, I'm met with silence. Silence scares me; it's always meant the calm before the storm. I check each room as I move through the house. The kitchen's empty and looks like how I left it this morning. The living room and lounge is empty too. This must mean Mum's still in her bedroom.

I slowly open her door and sure enough, there she is, sitting in front of her mirror. A mirror that reflects the naked truth whenever either of us looks in, catching the eyes of the other, she does this often. I wonder if she sees her truth or mine, or whether she sees our truth exposed by the deception that surrounds us? The deception he's caused us to embrace. Mum's brushing her hair and putting on her make-up in her own meticulous way. Her face is devoid of any emotion as she continues her daily routine; frozen as opposed to mine which looks upon her in sadness and defeat. It's very late in the day so I'm guessing she hasn't left the house today, she never steps a foot outside looking anything but immaculate.

"He'll be home soon you know," she says without looking at me; staring disconnected at herself in the mirror.

I go and sit down on the bed looking away from the haunting sight of detachment. "I know."

"I'm making fish pie for dinner tonight, it's his favourite after all."

I nod and not knowing what else to say I leave her. I walk to my room, close the door and lie back on my bed, annoyed and saddened by the fact that I don't know what to say to my own Mum anymore.

She never used to be like this. She was happy, fun to be with and always laughing, over silly stuff mostly. Everyone says I look exactly like her, I wonder if people still think so. I hope this isn't true anymore but I have a feeling it might be. Our eyes will always look the same because we've both seen pure horror and tragedy. I turn on my stereo, my hand stilling on the button. I hear Myles' voice again and I feel the tears before I realize I'm crying. What are the odds of Alter Bridge, my brother's favourite band playing twice today, of all days. I think it's a sign and I think it's telling me to get the hell out of this house before it's too late for me as well.

Time stops and I can't move. I used to love their songs before the accident, I think I still do but for very different reasons. I wonder whether I'll ever be able to listen to *'Watch Over You'* without remembering my brother from now on. I can still hear his voice every day in my head. I shudder. Just stop it Izzy, I berate myself. I'm not there yet, far from it.

I can smell the dinner cooking from my room so I go set the table in the kitchen. Laying the third plate and not a fourth still feels like a knife twisting in my heart, a heart that starts to pound as I hear Dad's car driving over the gravel in the driveway. I wonder which side of him is coming home tonight. It all depends on what sort of day he's had, whether he's been drinking or whether he just feels plain guilty.

I count to five, take a deep breath and as he walks into the kitchen, I greet him with a nervous smile as he starts to walk over.

"Izobel, how was your first day at University?" he asks me, putting his briefcase down.

"It was good Dad, I met my tutor, got my schedule and books, ready to start my first term in a couple of days." The straight to the point ramblings of a nervous and intimidated daughter who knows to stick to the relevant facts only, yeah I learnt my lesson at an early age.

Mum has by now placed all the food on the table and asks us to sit down and eat. The seating arrangement is odd. It's been like this ever since my brother left us. Mum and Dad sit on one side, I sit on the other. The pressure is intense. I feel like I'm sitting by myself as my parents sit in judgement across from me. The silence is heavy, uncomfortable even and I squirm in my seat. Mum's eyes never leave her plate whereas Dad always has that stern calculating look on his face as if wanting to find fault in someone or something. Another typical dinner time. I've never lost the nervous fidgeting that started when I was little, even now in my early twenties I have it, it's a habit, a nervous tick I suppose.

"Will you sit still for God's sake, eat the meal your Mother's cooked and stop annoying the hell out of me," Dad yells.

I cringe and taste bile in my throat as his hissing words spit at me. I immediately try and do just that, but know it'll only get worse as I now know which side of Dad has come home putting my nerves immediately on edge. The only way I can get out of this unhurt is if I placate him with meaningless questions that stroke his ego, then I'll be safe. I decide to concentrate on my food and wipe all emotion of my face, it seems to work for Mum. Who knew that despite being in my early twenties, I'd still feel like a child under his roof? As soon as I walk out the front door of our house I become me, I feel confident, well as much as is normal for me. But at home, not so much, I'm like a scared child, I hide in the shadows and I know an innocent remark can have dire consequences. My confidence gets knocked out of me almost daily and I've read enough psychology reports to understand my behaviour and the home I live in.

Dinner ends with everyone and everything intact for once. I take a deep breath, a breath I feel like I've held since we sat down; my insides finally cease to shake. Dad retires to his office as usual while Mum and I clear up.

Once we've loaded the dishwasher and the kitchen is again restored to the OCD state of cleanliness Mum wants it, I go to my room and change into my sleep shirt and shorts before grabbing my kindle. If I don't join them in the lounge, I know I'll hear Dad yelling for me in a minute to declare family time. His definition of family time is very different to anyone else's.

Mum and Dad are already in there. Dad's watching TV, Mum's knitting so I go and curl up on the chair in the corner of the lounge. Nothing changes; this has been the pattern for as long as I can remember. Not a word is said, all I can hear is Dad's crime thriller and Mum's knitting needles clicking. I get lost in my book. Actually, I've been lost in a book since I was five years old. It has and always will be my escapism. I get completely lost in the fictional lives of others, escaping from my own life for hours at a time. Dreaming of what could be if my life was different, living in a fantasy world. Dad's programme ends which signals time for bed. Family time's officially over. The exact opposite of quality time really but I'm not complaining. I suppose in my world quality time is synonymous with no pain, so I'll take it. I say goodnight and go to my room climbing in under the duvet. Tonight, for the first time since the accident I don't read in bed. Instead I touch my lips and think of Declan until I fall asleep with a smile on my face.

Chapter Three

I wake up feeling great; I remember dreaming of Declan last night. My happiness lasts for about five minutes until I hear them. It's Saturday and I know this is going to last all day. They'll be screaming and at each other's throats, Dad vicious with it and Mum will be trying to please and pacify. I can't wait till I have enough money to leave. It breaks my heart that I had enough once. Then after the accident I had to spend it all, trying to pay my way, feeling under obligation and love, to stay and look after Mum.

I'm determined that today's all about finding a new job. I haven't worked in eighteen months and I'm beyond ready now, I need to get out of this house. It's pathetic that I'm in this position, but it was out of my control. My hands were tied.

I get out of bed and sneak to the bathroom to shower and get ready. It's a warm day today, unusually so for September, so I decide to put a dress and summer sandals on. I leave my hair down and put a bit of make-up on. This way I'm ready for my job hunt and that important first impression, which yes, I clearly sucked at yesterday, but am determined not to repeat today.

I try to leave the house without anyone noticing, I don't want to get caught up in what's currently going on in the kitchen, not today, not ever if I can help it. Not again.

Taking the bus into town with my CV's burning a hole in my bag I look for notices of help wanted as well as pop into a few Recruitment Agencies. By the time I'm done I'm absolutely shattered and my face hurts from the forced smiles.

I walk to the nearest coffee shop and buy a sandwich and a drink. Instead of eating it here I decide to walk to the park, finding a nice shady spot to eat my lunch while reading my new book. I'm startled awake when I feel something annoying me on my nose, I hadn't realised I'd fallen asleep.

When I open my eyes, I see a grinning Aiden, down on his hunches tickling me with some grass.

"Hey gorgeous, sleeping in parks is dangerous you know, anything could happen, you could wake up being ravaged by a savage beast looking like you do."

I smile at him and roll my eyes at his remark. "I didn't even realize I'd fallen asleep. What are you doing here?" I ask him as he lies down next to me, stretching out, closing his eyes all content, like a cat.

"I've been at work since seven am this morning. I had the early breakfast shift at the restaurant I work in at weekends so I'm going to go home, have a shower and a snooze," he says. "I don't live far from here, in a shared house just on the other side of the park. I share it with my two mates, so I was nearly there when I saw you drooling in the grass."

I smack Aiden in the shoulder and go all Miss Marple on his arse asking him all sorts of questions; there's something about him that I instantly love. We lie in the grass talking for what seems like hours about nothing and everything. I think he reminds me of my brother, not to look at, but his personality. And even though this makes me sad, it's also comforting in a way.

Aiden tells me that he moved into the house with his mates who he's known most of his life and that the three of them are in a band called *'The Standards'*. They still play for fun but know it's not something they can make a living out of.

"Will you ever try and take it to the next level up from pubs and clubs?" I ask him.

"Nah that ship sailed a long time ago," Aiden laughs, but I hear a hint of regret in his voice and his smile fades.

Apparently there's still a spare room waiting to be filled in their house as the last guy graduated from Uni this summer. They've decided they need a girl so the house doesn't fall into depths of grime and disorder. I smack him on his shoulder again for the sexist comment but can't help laughing.

"So, are you looking to leave home, and willing to come be our domestic goddess?" he teases with a grin on his face.

"Seriously Aiden?" I feign a look of disgust.

"As fun as that sounds I'd love to, but I can't afford rent right now…I lost my job eighteen months ago and am trying to find a new one."

He gives me a penetrating look so I start to awkwardly pick at the grass not knowing what to say next. I'm guessing he can read the shame and anxiety that's written all over my face. Aiden suddenly puts his hand in mine and changes the subject. Yep he got it.

"Right, so tonight I'm going to the pub with the boys, fancy coming along?"

I haven't been on a night out in ages. Not since Sofia moved abroad on a foreign exchange programme to teach. Shit, I miss her so much it hurts, not only for the nights out, I miss her in every way

I had her, I just miss my best friend. I force a smile on my face, I'm good at those.

"Sounds good, what time shall I meet you?"

Aiden stands up and gets ready to walk off. "Meet me around eight-ish on the corner of Brook Street and we'll walk there together."

I stand up and give him a brief hug to say thank you. Looking at his back I can't help but smile because I know that Aiden's a decent person and I've found someone who could most definitely become a good friend. On the bus home, I start to think about what Aiden said about the room that's standing empty. I'd love to move out from Dad's clutches so I mentally calculate what I've got in savings and what I'd get if I hear back from some of the places I went to today.

I think I could just about do it but it leaves nothing for a car. To be honest I actually think I seriously want to do this. Sod the car, the bus works just fine and it's in the centre of town so I can walk most places. Shit, I'm going to do this. I'm an adult, of course I can. I prepare myself for the reaction when I tell Dad, it'll be completely different to Mum's, I know, but I can't feel responsible for her anymore. They thought moving to a new part of the country would erase the memories, maybe it's worked for Dad but it sure as hell hasn't worked for Mum or me.

As I open the door to the house I'm met with silence. I walk straight to my room and gather everything I own, hoping Aiden meant it and that I'm not taking liberties; that I can actually have the room going spare. I also hope the other blokes don't mind that it's me who takes it.

I don't want to waste any more time, who knows how much I have. I haven't got a lot to pack though, most of it got burnt in the fire. I shudder involuntarily and feel like I want to throw up. Every memory from that night brings along the smells, screams and feelings. It makes me feel weak and that is one thing I don't want to feel anymore. I need to take charge of my life and sever the hold Dad has on me. Feeling a sense of self-empowerment, I begin to pack. Despite feeling strong, a part of me is still cowering, making me feel nervous and scared of the consequences of what I'm about to do.

Two bags and lots of psyching myself up later I walk to the kitchen. Mum's in there cooking dinner. She's all dressed up, her hairs coiffed to perfection, her make-up perfectly applied to match. I've got no idea why she feels like she needs to do this. But this is what she does; she knows it's what Dad expects and she knows the verbal abuse that'll undoubtedly follow if she falls below his standards.

Thinking back it all began when he became this hot shot at work. Suddenly his family didn't look right; I guess he didn't think we fit into his new life. Dad set about re-modelling us, re-inventing us into something acceptable to him and this new image he wanted to uphold.

"Mum," I hesitantly call out. "Is Dad home? There's something I need to tell you both."

Mum turns around and looks at me fear in her eyes as they begin to well up with tears.

"You're leaving aren't you, leaving me alone with him?" she whispers while clutching at her apron with shaking hands. This must be where I get my fidgety hands from I think to myself, staring at them whilst mine do the same. This is huge and every bit of me knows it.

"Well I knew the day would come Izobel but I don't want to be in the same room when you tell him, I don't want to see his reaction."

As she turns back to the cooking she mutters about loss and her broken heart. Mine is breaking too and it hurts that she doesn't realise this. I've no idea how to reach her and I feel an immense sense of guilt, even if I know this is the right decision for me.

"Mum, you should leave too you know, it's not healthy, especially with what happened," I try and get through to her, my reasons for leaving.

"Too late for me." She shakes her head avoiding any eye contact. "I wouldn't know how Izobel, it's been too long and I haven't got the energy. I'm so tired."

She suddenly turns around and looks me straight in the eyes before surprisingly enveloping me in a tight embrace as though she's changed her mind. As if she saw something in my eyes. In a way I hope she did, I hope she sees the pain and guilt that's eating at my insides every time I leave the house; leaving her alone with him.

Pulling herself together she nods in the direction of Dad's office. "Go on darling girl." She takes my hand and gives it a squeeze before letting it go. "Good luck my love." Her back slumps as if the world is once again resting on it and turns, getting back to the cooking. Gathering my strength I close my eyes and stay here pulling myself together and trying to set aside this emotional moment.

As I walk out of the kitchen I feel like I'm walking the green mile. As Dad's office gets closer and closer I fill with a sense of dread. My hands feel clammy and my head starts to hurt. My heart is pounding as if high on caffeine. I knock on his office door and open it slightly.

"Sorry to disturb you Dad, is it okay if I come in? I need to talk to you about something...run something by you I mean."

Dad grunts and motions me in with his hand. On shaking legs I walk over to his desk and marvel once again at how huge and imposing he is despite sitting down. His physique coupled with his piercing eyes has always filled me with fear and apprehension. It should have made me feel safe growing up but ironically, it didn't. Dad looks at me over his glasses and puts his papers down, his eyes immediately narrowing in anticipation, yet he says nothing. He doesn't even ask me what I want; it's as if he already knows what's coming.

"I think it's about time for me to move out Dad, I need to be closer to Uni and umm...work and stuff." Bollocks, why does my brain disconnect from my mouth every time I try to speak to him? Why does my nerve always fail me when I most need it? Dad's expression doesn't change much except his frown lines get deeper and he looks down at me with a scowl.

"Can you afford that Izobel, because I'm not helping you fund a move. I told you the minute you turned eighteen and became an adult, you had to make your own way."

Of course he isn't, he could though, it'd be nothing to him, small change. But then I don't want his money anyway because it binds me to him even more, which I definitely don't want.

He steps out from behind his desk and my walls instantly come up. Crossing my arms, I shrink and feel myself going numb and rigid already. He walks straight past me though and down the hallway towards the kitchen. I've got no idea what's just happened here. I feel dizzy. This isn't the reaction I was expecting. I return to my bedroom, sit down on my bed trying to catch my breath. The anxiety has caused an adrenaline spike and my body begins to shake. Taking deep breaths I realise looking around my room that you wouldn't even know this room was lived in. I guess we haven't really been in this house long enough for me to personalize it with accessories and posters, maybe I knew subconsciously I wouldn't be here long.

"Izobel, dinner's ready, can you come sit down please." I hear my Mum yell.

I pull myself together and go join them in the kitchen. Dad and Mum are already sitting down waiting for me. I take my seat and begin to eat as expected, despite not feeling hungry at all. I can feel the food growing in my mouth with every bite. I'm unable to swallow, the food suffocating me and stifling my breathing. Even though I keep my eyes on my plate, I can feel the burning of his on me throughout the meal. I'm scared to look up. My crossed legs are shaking. My foot taping the floor incessantly. There's no doubt that Mum's trying to diffuse the tension by making small talk with Dad, I realise what she's trying to do. Dad's going on yet another business trip it seems. He goes on these a lot. Deep down I'm sure Mum knows there's more to these but is afraid to voice her suspicion. Voicing it makes it real and there'll be no going back then. Ignorance is bliss and all that bollocks.

Listening to this suddenly makes me angry. I can't understand why but all of a sudden, I have this urge to poke the lion that's ready to roar. I want to lay it all out there, I want to take a chance, no time like the present. So I swallow and take a deep breath…

"I'm going out tonight with a friend I've met at Uni and hopefully I'll be able to sort out my accommodation at the same time. They've got a room standing empty, so if it all works out, I'll move out tomorrow. Oh and this works really well because that way I'm ready for when lectures begin on Monday."

I pause as I've run out of breath. I feel lightheaded and I can see black spots forming at the corner of my eyes. Before I get to say anything else Dad's cutlery drops with a loud clang on his half-empty plate, managing to splatter his dinner all over the pristine white linen table cloth quickly bleeding into the fabric like an ugly growing stain. Mum and I freeze and I mentally berate myself, I should've known better. I automatically cower as the loud buzzing starts in my ears. I've got no idea what Dad's shouting, my ears feel like they're stuffed full of cotton balls. I think I hear ungrateful, just as I feel the sting of his hand, then the numbness, followed by a loud rushing sound in my ear, almost like that sound you get when you go to the beach and put a seashell up to your ear. They say it sounds like the waves of the ocean, but to me, it's merely the white noise of despair and pain. Another hit quickly follows, this one catching the corner of my eye which immediately starts welling up not only with tears but also something hot and sticky. I'm guessing his wedding ring caught me again. A wedding ring that symbolises so much more than its true meaning.

I stand up swaying and feel the room spinning from the pain and lack of oxygen as I half-run to my room. I'm shaking uncontrollably but rather than feeling knocked down I suddenly feel something snapping inside me. As though I've been wound up so tight, like one of those brown elastic bands, which in the end snaps with a sting. Everything implodes. Standing in front of the mirror looking at what he did, I open a pack of baby wipes and try to clean up my face. This time needing them to remove more than make-up. As I clean myself up I realise that only I can end this. I need to be the strong one. I can't rely on anyone else, on him changing, or even on Mum leaving. I need to save myself.

Picking up my cases I walk out of the front door without a parting word or even looking back at what I'm leaving behind. I know full well what I'm leaving behind and it's been a long time coming. I'm trying to set myself free.

There's still over half an hour till I have to meet Aiden so I walk slowly to the park, enjoying the feeling of breathing without the invisible restraint, and go to sit down on a bench. My arms feel sore from the strain of my cases but I welcome the pain because of how I got it. I pull out a mirror from my bag and wince at the cut on my face. How the hell do I explain this to Aiden? I dab some concealer on the cut and the worst of the bruise hoping he won't realise what caused it. I'm a good liar but this time I can't hide it.

The efforts of leaving suddenly overwhelm me, making me feel exhausted as I slouch into a comfortable position. The park is still lush and green; the Indian summer has brought all the families out, playing games, couples laying in the grass showing each other affection. So much togetherness surrounding me. I swallow the lump in my throat. I miss my brother, I miss Sofia, I miss normal. Perhaps it's coming; perhaps I just took that first all important step. I suddenly see Aiden crouched in front of me by the bench.

"What happened to your face Izzy?" He's looking at me with both concern and anger all rolled into one expression as he places his hand on my knee in comfort.

"Nothing really, I got hit by a door…you know how clumsy I am right? Do you not remember how we met?" I nervously reply trying to sweep some of my hair across so that it covers the evidence.

"Izzy, that's bullshit and you know it." He clenches his fist at his side and looks away from me as if counting to ten in his head before he says something he might regret.

Looking back at me he opens and closes his mouth a few times. I know I am betraying how I'm feeling because I feel the heat in my face.

"I'll let it go for now Izzy," he finally says. "But don't think that's the end of it." He looks pissed off as he eyes my suitcases, then looks back at me before taking my hand and pulling me up off the bench.

"Right, you're coming with me, no arguments I told you us lads were in dire need of something pretty and sweet in our house." His tone is almost jovial but he can't hide the intense anger his eyes are so clearly showing.

Looking frustrated, he picks up my suitcase and as my left hand is still firmly gripped in his, I pick up the other smaller one. We walk to the other side of the park in silence, cross the street and stand in front of a red bricked townhouse. I stand there looking up at the house feeling like an abandoned stray who's been picked up through sheer pity and compassion. Yeah, I feel every bit as little as my height symbolises, standing here with my small hand engulfed in Aiden's.

"No one's in Izzy so don't worry, they're all down the pub already, so we can get you settled in then we'll talk."

When he says that, he looks at me with so much emotion I almost burst out crying, but I don't, I refuse to give in. Instead I just nod and smile. I think he knows because he hurries me into the house and up the stairs.

"Right, so this'll be your room, it's not much, but do what you like with it and feel free to do the same to the rest of the house." He winks at me.

"Yeah alright....I got it Aiden, *'a live in housekeeper'* at your service," I sarcastically respond laughing at him. The room isn't overly big but it has a bed, a desk, a small table and an armchair by a huge bay window with views of the park. The room's painted a fresh subtle green with a darker accented wall where the bay window is. It's perfect and I can't help smiling as a warm feeling rushes through me. I put my suitcases in my new room and Aiden shows me the rest of the house. There are three bedrooms and one bathroom on this floor...yikes only one bathroom...and there's a bedroom in the attic.

He shows me his room, it's next to mine and it's immaculate, just like Aiden himself.

"The room next to mine belongs to Max, who's our drummer and the manager of the City Vintage Record shop."

Max's room is something else; if it has a floor I can't see it.

"The fourth bedroom is in the attic and belongs to our esteemed lead singer and guitarist Declan, who I've known forever. We let Declan have the attic seeing as he's a bit of a male slut and we got tired of having to listen to the girls giggling and fawning all over him."

I can't breathe and must look like a rabbit stuck in a pair of headlights. Declan…..my Declan lives here. How *small* is this world? That's if it's the same Declan, there must be loads of Declan's out there right? And apparently he brings a lot of girls home. Can I deal? I can't help but wonder about what happened at the coffee shop less than two days ago.

Aiden's looking at me quizzically. "Izzy girl, breathe…come back to me."

"Sorry…I umm…so show me the downstairs?" I manage to calm myself down. I'm not sure I should be here, what if this is the same Declan and he doesn't want me to live here, how awkward is this going to be. I shake my head to as Aiden and I walk downstairs. The kitchen's in a right state. You can definitely tell that only blokes live here. The lounge isn't much better. Aiden's actually got the decency to look quite embarrassed. Running his hand through his hair he mumbles "Yeah so…uh this is it, and believe me I do try to keep it tidy but the other two are slobs and one man cannot be expected to do this alone."

With a smile on my face I look around the parts of the house I can see from this room, but even though I can't see beyond the mess and the walls, I can see my separation from my past; I see my escape and I bloody love it. Aiden looks searchingly at my face as if waiting for me to either break down or completely flip out so I put my arms around his middle and squeeze him in relief. "It's perfect Aiden, thank you."

I both hear and feel Aiden clear his throat "So umm anyway…do you feel like going to the pub or shall we have that talk now?" He pulls away, looking down at me with a frown replacing his smile.

Thinking about it I have a feeling that tonight's not the best night to go to the pub and try to be social. In reality I can't think of anywhere I'd rather be than there…but no. The less people who see my face the better, I haven't got the energy for lies upon lies tonight. I shake by head at Aiden and he looks at me with a reluctant acceptance. I feel his hand on my face, it still stings…I can't help but flinch and he wraps me tighter in a warm and gentle embrace. I'm not sure how long we stand here for, but I know I haven't felt as safe as I do right now, in a very long time, probably since before my brother left us.

"So…" Aiden breaks the silence pulling away from me.

"I think I'd like to go to bed, it's been a long day and I'm knackered. But about the rent, I can start paying as soon as I've been to the bank on Monday…"

I don't get to finish what I want to say because Aiden's already dragging me upstairs, silencing me with his actions. He leaves me in my room and makes me promise to get him if I need anything; apparently he's staying home too, which makes me feel guilty. I know I'm the reason he's staying in and yes despite feeling guilty, it does make me feel less alone on my first night here. I go through my night time routine and climb into bed but even though I'm shattered I can't fall asleep. All I can think about is what happened at home and the fact that I'm now under the same roof as Declan. Possibly….

Just as I'm about to fall asleep I hear laughter…yeah definitely his, followed by giggling…nope definitely not his. I quietly creep to the door and open it slightly without drawing attention to myself. I can just about see Declan, he's swerving with one hand wrapped in long dark hair and his mouth attached to some lucky girls neck. Both of her hands are down the back of his jeans. I'm pretty sure it's the same girl who I saw at the bus stop with him.

I can't watch this, I go back to bed, but no matter how hard I try to block it out, all I hear is Declan and the girl and the subsequent moaning and giggling. It suddenly all goes quiet and not long after, I feel myself drifting off.

Chapter Four

I wake up Sunday morning still tired after a shitty night's sleep where I once again, had the most unpleasant and recurring dream of Zack. The house is quiet so I put on my ratty old Pearl Jam t-shirt that Sofia bought me when we went to see them at Wembley Arena. It's shrunk quite a bit, but it's a favourite, I team it with my black joggers that have also seen better days. There's no point in wearing anything more appealing or feminine, I'm not really trying to impress anyone. I've never met Max; Aiden I'm pretty sure bats for the other team and Declan…..well Declan I'm sure made some kind of mistake with me on Friday afternoon, so there's no need to try and impress him. I wash my face and brush my teeth wondering whether or not I should try and cover up the small purple bruise and cut before I go downstairs. I decide to leave it to heal without covering it in gunk. Tying my hair up in a messy knot I walk downstairs to the kitchen, I'm in desperate need of coffee before I start transforming this house into a semblance of cleanliness. It's the least I can do for Aiden after coming to my rescue. As I wait for the kettle to boil, I jump up and sit on the kitchen counter closing my eyes as I lean back up against the kitchen cabinet.

"Izzy...what are *you* doing here?"

I freeze and my eyes snap open in shock. It's Declan in all his morning glory, well almost. He's wearing a pair of loose black running shorts, but that's it. He's got total bed hair that makes me want to run my fingers through it and his body...well I can't look away no matter how hard I try. He's got one of those bodies you only see in magazines or when you google hot guys, which yes I admit I do sometimes, who doesn't? He's lean but nicely muscled where it counts. Stop staring I chant in my head, but I can't. I want to run my fingers over his defined abs, grab his broad shoulders and amazingly defined and powerful looking arms. I actually have to restrain myself from touching him right now. His right shoulder is covered in an intricate tribal tattoo, which spans across the right hand side of his chest. He's got another one, a line of italic writing down the inside of his left arm. I quickly look down at the floor because I know I've been caught, but I can't stop the smile; he's gorgeous.

"Izzy sweetheart stop staring. Now, answer my question, why are you here and what the hell happened to your face?" He comes closer lifting my face up gently with his hand.

Oh yeah, he asked me a question, oh and he called me sweetheart. I think I just melted. I catch his guarded look so I jump off the counter and quickly turn away to continue making coffee seeing as the kettle boiled a few minutes ago.

"So yeah, Aiden helped me move in last night, I...umm needed to leave home...hope that's okay with you and Max? Oh and my face it's nothing, just me being clumsy again." I close my eyes hoping he buys it.

"Were you here last night?" he asks me, jumping up and sitting on the kitchen counter next to where I'm standing.

I know immediately that he's wondering if I heard or saw him coming back with that girl. I really don't want to admit to that so I just shrug, "Yeah," as I continue with my coffee. I refuse to look at him, actually I suddenly can't see straight, he kisses me on Friday, then Saturday he's all over someone else. I should be pissed off right? I have to bite my tongue before I lash out at him. Had this been a few years ago I would've given him shit and what for. But now…well it just takes too much effort, though I have to admit to being all kinds of angry.

As I stir copious amounts of sugar into my coffee I can't help thinking that I'm nothing like the girl he brought home last night. I can't possibly compete so why should I even bother trying? I turn back to face him gripping my cup tight to the point of burning my fingers.

"Look Declan, whatever happened well, it was nothing and I really need a place to stay so how about you just do what you do and I'll try and stay out of your way yeah?"

Shit, where did that come from? I mentally give myself a high five for sounding so cool and calm about the whole thing when I feel anything but. Actually do people still high five or did the cool factor just get null and void? I have to stop myself from laughing manically because this situation's so bizarre. This calm and collected me is a façade that completely belies the fissured storm inside.

Declan looks at me with a frustrated look on his face. "You ran off on Friday…I wasn't sure if you regretted what had happened Izzy. I don't know what it is but there's something about you, you're different…..I…..it wasn't nothing…not to me. Shit I don't know. Now tell me the truth, what the fuck happened to your face?" He rakes a hand through his hair and looks down at his feet, probably counting as he looks on the verge of exploding, the anger clearly rolling off him in waves.

I just look at him conflicted but there's no way I'm giving him any idea of how I feel, I don't need that rejection and I definitely don't need to tell him about anything. I feel like I've been put on the spot so I try to run off into the other room. He watches me stumble like an idiot trying to come across unaffected and reaches his hand out but I manage to dodge him. With a sigh he holds his hands up giving me a smile that looks both troubled and sad as he walks out of the kitchen. Me staying here is going to be so awkward. My shoulders slump in defeat as I hear him pounding up the stairs. All I really want to do is run up after him. But I don't. I look around the kitchen and know I need to do something to keep me busy. So I decide to get the cleaning stuff from out under the sink and make an attempt at cracking the grime and forget all about the guy upstairs who's quickly taking hold of my heart. But before this I need music. I find a radio and turn it on. Its classic eighty's hour which makes me smile. Ultimately, I'm an eighty's rock chick at heart, which will never change. I start on the washing up and fly through the kitchen until I've got to say it's pretty bloody sparkling. All the while I'm singing along to the radio, which has now moved on to Whitesnake's *'Here I go Again'*; another classic.

I look round to see if I've missed anything when I notice I have an audience. Declan and Aiden are standing in the doorway grinning and begin to applaud. I can feel the heat in my cheeks and I can't look them in the eyes.

"Yeah so kitchen's done guys…so umm I'll be moving on to the lounge next, but if you think I'm touching *your* rooms, you're very much mistaken."

I tuck a stray lock of hair behind my ear still refusing to look at them. Instead I take the radio with me ignoring their laughter from the kitchen and get on with tackling the job of finding the furniture under goodness knows what. Once I'm done in there I finish with the bathroom and realize most of the day has gone as the evening autumn sky's here. I decide that it's now safe and hygienic enough to have a shower and stand under the warm jets of water and think up a plan of action for dealing with Declan, I can't ignore him. I know I'm probably using all the hot water, I've been in here way too long, but I don't care. I think I've earned it and as I'm rinsing the shampoo out of my hair I hear Aiden shouting through the door.

"We're off to the Dew Drop Inn round the corner for a few pints Izzy…you fancy joining us girl?"

"Go ahead without me and I'll join you in a bit," I shout back, as I finish off with my shower. I think I need to get out and get some normal back into my life but not only that, I need to get normal back with Declan if we're going to live in the same house. This means I'll also get to meet Max.

I walk to my room in just a small towel as I'm sure everyone's gone by now. As I get to my door I hear pounding feet coming up the stairs. I freeze on the spot when I see its Declan. He stops in his tracks and I feel his eyes travel from my face down to my feet. It's as if his eyes are burning a trail down my body bringing on shivers. Walking over he trails his finger along my jaw as his thumb frees my bottom lip, I must've been chewing on it again.

"I'll see you down the pub Izzy?" he winks at me with a knowing smile.

Speechless, all I manage to do is nod lost in that look in his eyes. He walks upstairs but I can't move, so like an idiot I'm still standing here as he comes back down again, wallet in his hand. He shakes his head at me, smiling as he leaves. Walking back into my room, I collapse on my bed. What the hell just happened? He's the most confusing guy I've ever come across. I know that he's a bad idea and the last thing I should be doing is acting on how I feel about him. Actually I'm not even sure what it is I feel, except total lust right now.

In the first year after my brother left us…when I've felt like this, I'd just get drunk, find a good looking bloke and just go for it, I'd get it out my system and move on. No problem; no broken hearts.

No overlapping between needs and the truth. Alcohol and guys became an escape, but I knew if I didn't stop my destructive pattern of behaviour, it'd become an addiction, a way of forgetting, too easy a path of self-destruction that could lead to yet another early grave. So I stopped and it's now been six months since I've been with anyone like that. I quickly start to get ready as I try and pull myself together and forget. It's still quite warm outside so I put on my short denim skirt, a fitted tank top, a fitted black cardie and shuffle on my ballet pumps. I decide to leave my hair loose to dry naturally. Unfortunately, I'm one of those girls who's got no kink whatsoever in my hair. It's straight as it can be; it starts off straight when wet and it dries straight too. So I can leave it to dry without having to worry about waves or curls. If I had the choice though, I'd love to have this worry. I've always wanted curly hair. But then we all want what we don't have, never satisfied. I put a bit of make-up and concealer on, trying to cover up my injury. It doesn't look too bad really. I pick up my messenger bag; put my iPod on and leave for the pub. As I walk up I can see them sitting outside at a table laughing. They look so happy and care-free. I used to be like that and want to be again. I wonder if I join them, can I pull it off without having to fake it? Aiden must have seen me coming because he whistles suggestively…

"Hey gorgeous get your arse over here, I've got a pint for you," he says, smiling encouragingly at me.

Ah no excuses not to drink now. I sit down in the empty seat, which just happens to be between Aiden and Declan. Aiden immediately introduces me to Max.

"So Izzy meet Max…Max meet Izzy."

I look at Max and I'm floored, he's huge, in the tall and muscled sense. Short cropped black hair, and the biggest chocolate brown eyes. He has a pierced eyebrow and a pierced nose with a tattoo running up his neck. He's scary looking but stunning too. Can you call a man stunning? Well he is, and he's making me blush, not sure why…but wow. Shit, I have to compose myself before I make a complete fool out of myself, so I take a huge gulp of beer and try to deflect from my obvious embarrassment.

"So how did you all get together then, I mean end up in the same house really?" I know Aiden already told me bits of this story but right now my mind is blank and I don't want to sit here gawking like an idiot. Instead I'm trying to prevent an awkward silence. Max is staring at me with a wild look on his face. His eyes are working overtime taking in my bruised face and sizing me up. I get it. He's under no illusions on how I got this. I end up having to look away over at Declan instead as I can feel his eyes on me. Uh hold up there buddy, I think to myself, when I see his eyes are on my legs not my face. I give him a stern look but get a smile in return when he realises. Aiden answers my question with a sigh and a faint shake of the head, I think he noticed too.

"Dec and I've known each other since school, we used to play about with our guitars in my Mum's garage and Dec would sing. Dec's older brother Finn used to hang around in there too with Max, his best mate. Long story short, crazy Max ended up on Dec's drum kit."

I notice Max has a pair of drumsticks which he's repeatedly tapping on his thigh. Those drumsticks just hit Aiden squarely on the head after that comment and the guys start bickering about who's crazier. Aiden looks back at me and continues his conversation, batting off Max at the same time.

"Right…anyway, so when Dec and I finished school we took out two years to travel and work, well busking around really, before we had to get back to the books. We roped Max in and started doing pub gigs when we came back from Europe, playing at least one gig a week." He stops talking and downs what's left of his pint before handing his glass over to Declan.

"Well I can't wait to hear you play," I say, smiling at him. He really is absolutely adorable…shit…I giggle…I can tell I haven't been drinking much recently. This one pint has gone straight to my head and it doesn't help forgetting to eat properly today. I realize Declan's put a new pint in front of me and I know I shouldn't really have any more.

"What's so funny Iz?" Declan whispers at my ear. His arm's snuck onto the back of my chair, his long fingers playing with my hair.

"Nothing…just a passing thought," I reply quickly, picking up my pint glass and drinking it to avoid him sensing my embarrassment. He keeps his hand in my hair as the conversation across the table continues. I really should tell him to stop, but I can't. I'm enjoying it too much. We stay here for hours talking and laughing, it feels so good, so natural and it's been too long coming. I'm enjoying every minute of it when I suddenly realise I need the loo. As I stand up I know that I'm way past that invisible line of merry to almost bloody bladdered.

"You alright there Izzy girl, you want me to walk you to the ladies?" Aiden puts his hand to my arm getting ready to stand.

"I'll be fine Aiden." I bend over and give him a massive cuddle and kiss his cheeks. "You are so much like my brother," I whisper to him before it occurs to me what I've said. I quickly run to the toilet, find an empty cubicle and the tears begin. What the fuck….why did I suddenly say that, where did that come from and why did I direct it at Aiden? Aiden isn't Zack. No one can ever take Zack's place. Zack's gone; taken from me. I'm not sure how long I've been in here. I'm standing in the cubicle wanting to magically wish myself back to my new bedroom; when I hear Declan shouting, I guess I've been in here a while.

"Izzy, you still in there sweetheart?"

I wonder if I can ignore him and whether he'll go away if I do? No such luck, I hear him come in checking under the doors, I'm so busted.

"Izzy are you feeling sick? Come on out sweetheart so I can take you home," he says just outside the door I'm hiding behind. I can hear the concern in his voice and despite my drunken state, I know I've got to face him sooner or later so I open the door but can't look him in the eyes. Instead, I look at his black scuffed biker boots that look like they need a good clean, or is that what they're supposed to look like? Who knows. He tilts my face up with his fingers.

"You've been crying Iz…why beautiful? What's going on in that head of yours?" His face is so close I feel his hot breath on my cheek, his worry frown deep; his eyes full of concern.

"Can you take me home Declan, I need to go home to bed," I say as I find myself leaning against him. Thoroughly embarrassed, emotional and totally shattered. I feel my legs give out and he quickly moves in and wraps his arms around me.

"Let's get you out of here," he whispers in my ear.

"Not to my parents' house that isn't home. Take me to my new home, the old one can never be home again. Home is where your heart is….isn't that how it goes? Well my heart hasn't been there in a long time, it left when Zack did." All those fucked up words just come out on a rushed breath. I never meant to say them; I'm immediately regretting the unbearable honesty that comes with drinking.

"Who's Zack?" Declan asks as we make our way out of the pub.

"My brother…. Zack was my brother," I answer, nodding my head at the others in a silent goodbye. They all look at me with soft pity. It's embarrassing. Declan tightly holds me against his side on the walk home. Neither of us says anything and he never lets go of me. When we get into the house I bolt up the stairs and jump into bed trying to get away from Declan who stops when Aiden calls to him. He must have followed us home.

From under my duvet, I can hear Aiden and Declan outside my bedroom. I can hear their raised voices through the crack in the door; I mustn't have closed it completely.

"No Dec, you're not going in there, you're the last thing she needs right now."

"What the fuck is that supposed to mean Aiden…I'm not going in there to fuck her man, I'm not blind or stupid, I can see she's hurting."

"Well stand down then Dec, okay…. because I've seen how you look at her and I know what you do…don't go there. I realise this girl is pretty fucking special and I don't want her hurting any more than she clearly is now."

"Swapping sides are you mate?"

Lying in my bed I don't hear what's said next but I do hear the punch land. Shit, this is entirely my fault; I feel the tears and curl into a ball, making myself as small as I possibly can. I hear the door open and feel the bed dip as Aiden climbs in behind me. Turning around I put my head on his chest. He rests his on mine giving the top of my head a sweet kiss.

"Want to talk about it?" he asks, but I shake my head.

"Okay…but know that I'm here Izzy. Anytime okay," he says giving me a reassuring squeeze.

"I'm sorry Aiden. I feel like I've brought a heap of shit to your front door. You don't need or want me and my drama's here." I don't know what else to say so I stop there. I'm so tired I can't even keep my eyes open any longer.

The last thing I hear is him whispering, "Never be sorry Izzy."

Chapter Five

I wake up Monday morning and feel like crap. My first lecture starts today, so checking my alarm I realize I've still got two hours before I need to be on campus. I get all my things together and go take a shower, I can't help but feel a bit weird about sharing a bathroom with three guys; but I'm met by silence so I think everyone's still asleep. Once I'm ready to go I sneak quietly out of the house to catch the bus into Uni. I'm standing at the bus stop, lost in thought when I see Aiden jogging up.

"Hey Izzy girl, how you doing today?" he asks me as he puts his arm around my shoulder giving me a reassuring squeeze.

I look up at him and smile all embarrassed. "Sorry about last night Aiden, I umm haven't had a drink in almost six months; guess I'm out of practice," I shrug.

"Well, take it steady and slow next time hey," he laughs checking his watch.

"Actually, there's a new band playing at the Student Union tonight if you fancy it?"

"Yeah that sounds good, what time do you finish your lectures?" I ask checking my schedule to make sure I have the right time and block number.

"Not till three pm, so if you want, I'll see you at home tonight and we'll go together?" he asks, while adjusting the strap of my bag across my shoulder.

"Okay, sounds like a plan." I mentally tell myself that I won't be drinking tonight.

Aiden and I get on the bus and once we arrive at campus, we have a quick hug before I go to my first lecture. I can't wait to get started and get buried in books again. After three hours of lectures, I'm done in. Throughout two of them, I was so lost I realize I'm going to need to do some extra work. I turn my mobile phone back on and see I've got missed calls from Mum. Shit. I ring her back and it goes straight to answer phone. I know I have to go check on her now or I won't be able to relax. Taking the bus back to the house, I can't help thinking the worst. From the outside it looks dark and quiet. Getting my keys out I unlock the door sticking my head through first, nervous of what I might find.

"Mum...are you in?" I shout out, closing the door behind me. I walk round the house, which is, as always immaculate. You wouldn't even know anyone lived here, it looks more like a show home. Mum's always been a cleanliness freak. I find Mum in her room. She's sitting on the floor with photos of Zack everywhere.

"Mum..." I fall to the floor and hug her like you would a child, tears beginning to stream down my face, just like on hers. Seeing your parent cry is such a heart-breaking sight. There's not much else as frighteningly upsetting as that.

"I miss him Izobel....so much; so very much," her voice breaks and she closes her eyes from sheer pain. "My heart just won't scab over and scar. It's still cut open with my love for him and losing him; our loss, I don't think it'll ever heal...." She takes a deep breath as if to calm herself. "I just...I just don't know what to do?" Mum's face crumbles on a heart-breaking sob.

"I know Mum…I know." I start crying as my face mirrors hers. I take her shaking soft hands in mine. "The pain will lessen though Mum," I say trying to make her feel better, though how the hell do I do that? "We'll learn to live with the agony of it. If we stay drowned in the depths of it, I don't think we'll find our way out and somehow, we'll get lost in the sorrow," I say as I squeeze her tight, trying to give her some strength even though I daresay I haven't much to give. "And Zack wouldn't want that, I know he wouldn't and you know this deep inside too." This is so hard and my voice breaks from the pure weight of my emotions, but I need to get through to her. I have to help her. Mum hugs me back and I feel her physical strength, which is so unlike her mental state right now. She understands.

"What do you say we tidy up the photos? Have you got any albums to put Zack in?" I ask her.

"No, I've always put it off, I thought I'd do it one day but I never got round to it."

"Okay…" I say trying to keep it together. "Well why don't I pick some up after Uni tomorrow and come round so we can make a start, what do you say?" I'm starting to lose it, slowly but surely. The need to get out of here is intense, my insides are shaking and I feel a lump forming in my throat, pressing at my airways making breathing damn near impossible.

"Yes Izobel, my lovely girl, I'd like that very much." She puts her hand on my face, almost cradling it.

"Right, I need to go now Mum. I don't want to be here when Dad comes back so I'll see you tomorrow okay?" I start to stand up on shaking legs and hate that I'm leaving her sitting in a heap on the floor, all alone and surrounded by memories. But I can't stay. I'm about to explode from my pain and memories. Everything is too overwhelming right now. I give her one last hug and run out of the house. I feel as if I'm trying to escape my memories. I can't breathe,

I feel hot and cold and all I can hear is static noise. A fire begins to take hold of my heart, I know nothing will be able to put it out it's too far gone. Just like that day. I'm running off, scared. I need to forget. I want to numb myself to the point where I don't miss the piece of my heart and soul my brother took with him when he died.

I somehow manage to get the bus back without breaking down and once I'm in my room I act without thinking. I'm on autopilot; it comes all too easy, as if it never forgot. I shower, put on my black halter neck dress and my silver heels. I brush my hair out until it hangs straight half-way down my back. I transform my face into that of a welcome stranger from the past with dark smoky eyes. Grabbing my purse I leave the house again. I need to forget. Shaking my head I marvel at the ease with which I've slipped back into the role of a fucked up grieving sister. I walk to the pub we went to last night and order a large glass of Rose, sitting down at a vacant table in the corner. I decide to try calling Sofia. It goes straight to voicemail. "I miss you…I need to hear your voice…um when you've got a minute please call me, love you hun." I hang up and start thinking of my best friend as I chug down my wine.

The first time I met Sofia I was five years old and I thought she was an angel, an honest to God angel. She had the curliest white blonde hair that went all the way down her back and she was wearing a white summer dress and fairy wings. She always wore some kind of dress and her fairy wings. Her Mum later told me it was one of the battles she chose not to fight. Sofia didn't leave the house unless she was wearing her wings. She used to say it was so she could fly off in a second if she needed to leave. Sofia was *my* angel. She knew everything. Even though she tried to convince me over and over again to leave home the minute I turned eighteen, she never judged me for staying. She understood. She's still my angel albeit a foul mouthed one. I smile to myself at my memories of growing up with her. She's got a crazy arsed zest for life.

I stayed home for Zack. When Zack left us Sofia was there, all through the shock, the investigation and after. She hated having to leave me but she'd worked too hard to get on the exchange programme to give up her place at the last minute. She would have though; she'd do anything for me which is why I told her to go. I couldn't live my life so I wanted her to. I told her I'd live mine through hers because I didn't know how to continue mine as it was. I shake myself out of my thoughts, I don't want to remember, I'd rather forget. This day is getting worse by the minute so I know what I need to do. I go up to the bar, order another glass of wine and send a text to Aiden saying I'll meet him in the Uni bar instead.

Me: Hey you, I had to go out so I'll see you in the bar xx

Aiden: I'm home now, what time? x

Me: I'll just see you there, oh and there'll be dancing lol xx

Aiden: I don't dance!

Me: Can you be the drinks dispenser then?

Aiden: Really? You're back on it tonight? Brave! x

Me: Yep see you there in a bit xx

I finish my wine in one big gulp and walk to the bus stop to get the bus into Uni. There's a huge crowd on campus. Everyone's turned up for the live band who's supposed to be great. The band isn't coming on till later tonight so right now there's a DJ playing and people are drinking and dancing already. It's not a big dance floor but it's big enough to get lost in the music and forget. Which is what I intend to do. A copious amount of wine later I'm on the dance floor dancing with anyone and everyone, getting lost in the music, just what I love and need. I suddenly feel a hand on my back; my dress is completely backless so I feel the heat of the palm. I turn around and see a guy I recognize from one of my lectures.

"Izzy isn't it?" he mouths to me with a grin.

I smile up at him "That's right...you're Matt?" I ask as he puts his other hand on my waist. Now, Matt's pretty fit and obviously knows it too, but he's just what I need right now and I know there'll be no messy ending or secrets shared. We dance through who knows how many songs. Suddenly he pulls me really close and bends down to tell me something.

"Fancy a drink and some fresh air?"

I nod at him, so he takes my hand and we walk up to the bar to order another round.

"Hey Izzy...you okay there?" Aiden steps up next to me and gives a suspicious head nod to Matt.

"I'm great Aiden....just perfect." I smile at him trying to convince him that all's good.

"I'm here, just so you know, come get me if there's anything you need, and promise me you won't do something stupid," he says as he looks at me with a worried frown on his face.

I feel a bit pissed by Aiden's remark but I'm not that drunk that I don't realise he's looking out for me. I give his hand a squeeze and a cheesy wink. I know I'm near my limit but bloody hell do I feel great right now. Mission is slowly but surely being accomplished here. Matt and I take our drinks outside. He lights up a cigarette as his eyes roam all over me.

"Bloody hell Izzy you look good tonight," he groans as his other hand pulls me to him. Throwing his cigarette away he grabs the back of my neck and instantly his mouth is on mine in one hard kiss. So Matt's kisses are hot, I make a mental note of this, but I feel no spark. That being said, I'm not going to deny that I'm enjoying this. I press myself up against him and feel his other hand sliding down my back. This is not a sweet romantic snog fest; this is rough and slightly frantic. His hand grabs my arse and firmly presses me against him letting me feel just how hard he is. He spins us around so my back is pressed against the wall and moves his hand down the front of my dress. Right at that moment I open my eyes and see Declan standing not too far away, watching us and looking like he's going to blow any minute. I wish it was him, here with me, but then my heart would be involved and this needs to be meaningless. That's how it works; this is how I can forget. I try to shut him out and concentrate on Matt, but I've got nothing, Declan's broken the moment. There's no point now. It's not going to work.

"Matt you've got to stop…you *need* to stop," I say, trying to push him off me.

"Izzy….shit…why?" he breathes against my neck still running his tongue against my pounding pulse.

"I don't feel so good…I need to go." I try to push him off me again.

"You sure about that?" he continues to kiss me not listening.

"Matt stop…please." I slump against the wall giving up.

"You heard her Matt, get the fuck off her now," Declan shouts, suddenly right next to us.

"What the fuck Dec….I'm not forcing her to do anything…take it easy." Matt doesn't sound happy. Can't say I blame him really.

"Declan this is between me and Matt…. just go inside," I try to calm everything down as I feel a headache starting.

"I'm not leaving here till Matt gets his fucking hand off your tits Iz." He looks at me angrily.

Matt looks down at me all serious, "I'm really sorry Izzy. I'm not sure what's going on here, but if I hadn't thought you were up for it, I wouldn't have started anything," he says looking all contrite.

"Shit Matt…I'm the one who's sorry…we're all good, I wanted it…it's just…I need to go now," I try to make him see this is all on me. I started this. Giving him a quick peck followed by a shaky smile I run off into the night, wishing I could click my heels together three times and be home already.

"Izzy sweetheart slow down…where are you running off to?"

Bollocks, Declan's still here.

"Just piss off Declan, I need to be alone, go back to the bar, do your thing and I'll see you later," I shout back at him.

"Not gonna leave you like this so you can either slow the fuck down or walk with me, I'll be following you right the way home anyway," he snaps back at me.

I slow down, my feet are killing me, I've never been able to run in heels. People make it look so easy but it's not, well not for someone as clumsy as me anyway. We continue to walk in silence as Declan's insists on walking me home. He suddenly breaks it sounding like he could punch something or someone.

"Seriously Izzy,….Matt? You picked Matt?"

"What's that supposed to mean Declan. I picked Matt? I have no bloody clue what you're doing or saying, I'm out having a bit of fun and now it's over and I want to go home to bed."

"You're not that girl Izzy," he says shaking his head.

"How the hell do you know Declan? You've known me all of however many days…you know nothing at all about me," I snap back at him picking up speed.

He pulls me to a stop and starts trailing his fingers down my face. "I knew you the minute I looked into those big eyes; beautiful but very sad eyes." He suddenly looks at me, puzzled. "I've never seen eyes like yours before Izzy, eyes that change from one shade of blue to another, one minute to the next."

I'm starting to lose control of this situation; I need him to stop saying things like this to me. "Declan, please let me go…" I whisper.

"Why Iz, why do you get like this when it's just you and me?" he implores.

"Like what Declan?" I can't look at him. I'm so fucking weak.

"Scared, nervous…wanting to run off…" he trails off, tucking my hair behind my ear.

I know exactly what he means and I know why, but no chance in hell do I want him to know how he affects me. I push away from him as hard as I can and start walking off. Once we get to the house I lock myself in the bathroom. I feel like shit so I have a shower and get ready for bed. Climbing under my duvet I curl into my usual ball trying to make myself appear small so I can go unnoticed. I hear a knock and the door opens slightly.

"Can I come in Izzy?" Declan whispers hesitantly.

I don't answer, I want him to think I'm sleeping and go away, but he comes in anyway. He lies down next to me and moves me across his chest. He doesn't say anything; he just lies here stroking my arm. I feel so relaxed and safe that I can feel myself actually going asleep. I'm nearly there…

Declan

I'm lying here with Izzy in my arms wondering what it is that pulls me to this girl. There's no doubt that Izzy's beautiful. She's fucking gorgeous. But, it's not just that. She's also vulnerable but with a real feisty strength when she needs it, which really turns me on. I've tried to stay away but it's damn near impossible.

I've never met anyone like her, I feel like I need to be wherever she is. I don't know what it is about her, but the moment I met her, I saw through her. Her eyes had me wanting to pick her up and fight for her, take out anything or anyone who'd hurt her. Her eyes are so familiar; I know where she's been. I recognise that look. It's a look of terror and hurt, I've seen it enough times in the mirror to recognise it.

"What is it about you that makes me want you so much?" I whisper to her, knowing she can't hear me as she's asleep.

I've got no idea what I'm supposed to do. I'm scared if she sticks with me I'll make her miserable and somehow end up ruining her life. If I do that, I have no doubt I'll ruin mine in return when she leaves, which she will…

"What the fuck am I doing?" I whisper hearing my words, torn with guilt. I slowly move her off me and gently kiss her on those soft sweet lips before going back to my room trying to ignore how I feel about the sleeping girl in the bedroom below.

Chapter Six

My first thought when I wake up is whether I dreamt Declan in my room last night or not. I'm still thinking about it in the shower when I'm interrupted by Aiden coming in. I'm so thankful right now that the shower screen is too dark for him to see me properly.

"Aiden get the hell out, I'm in the shower," I shout, wanting to throw something.

"You should've remembered to lock the door then girl. Anyway I can't see you and I want to brush my teeth," he shouts back at me rustling near the sink. At least he's not interested in perving I suppose so I continue shampooing my hair.

"So Izzy, I want to know, what happened last night, tell me all about it," he says, as he begins to brush his teeth. I'm not sure what to tell him, so shockingly I decide to tell him everything. I obviously have no filter when it comes to Aiden. The only thing I don't tell him about is that Declan stayed in my room for a bit last night.

"You know Izzy, I'm not sure what's happened to you in your past, but I'd have to be an idiot not to know it's something big." He spits out some toothpaste, which makes me gag.

"So when you feel you can put your trust in me and tell me, I'm here, that's all. Oh, and as far as Declan goes, he's my best friend but you've got to be careful there Izzy, he's never had a serious relationship. The girls love him and he loves the fact that they do, if you know what I mean." He rinses his mouth out and moves on to the mouthwash, carrying on as if this situation isn't extremely uncomfortable for me. Unfortunately I know exactly what he means but this is a conversation I don't feel like having while I'm naked in the shower.

"Right so Aiden, you need to leave because I'm turning into a prune." I want his arse out of here.

"Okay, fine…we'll save that one for another time Izzy. I'll see you on campus later, just text me if you want to meet for a coffee," he says sticking his hand round the screen, giving me thumbs up.

"Just go," I laugh at him and wait till he's closed the door behind him. I quickly get ready and make my way into Uni looking forward to getting lost in something other than my own dramas. My second lecture of the day drags, I'm squirming in my seat because I know Mum's waiting for me. I finally hear the bell and literally run out of the lecture hall while texting Aiden to say I'm leaving to go pick something up for Mum so I can't meet him. I haven't heard from her since I found her on the floor. It worries me, I should be there for her, but I'm sure she knows why I can't. Well I'd hope so, although her avoidance trait is worse than mine.

I take the bus into town and manage to find three gorgeous photo albums. It takes me ages to choose; they're for Zack after all, so they have to be perfect. Once I'm back on the bus I text Declan, I have to; it's going to be too awkward if I don't. I try to keep it light so he doesn't know how he's left my heart, literally burrowing into the shadows of him trying to catch his light. I still have to live with him and no matter how I feel about that, the alternative is beyond worse.

I put my phone back in my bag when I see my stop coming up. I warily let myself in and don't bother checking the house, I go straight to Mum's room and sure enough there she is, knitting. I think there are two kinds of women who knit. There are the women who knit with purpose, with an end result in mind if you like; scarves, jumpers, mittens...whatever. Then there are the women who knit for therapeutic purposes. I do wonder if they just keep going until they run out of yarn or whether they suddenly just stop, unravel and start again?

"Are you okay Mum?" I ask her, wondering whether or not she actually realises I'm here. "I got the albums for Zack's photos, shall we start putting them in?"

She looks up at me and smiles, putting her knitting down. "Yes Izobel, yes I'm ready, let's document Zack's life as it was," her voice breaks at her own words and I feel the tears threaten, my eyes welling up.

His life. I miss him so much the pain never goes away. It never becomes any less than it was. We sit here for hours reminiscing about Zack, how handsome, loving and funny he was. Even though it hurts, it feels comforting at the same time. Zack was crazy, but good crazy. He was always everyone's favourite in the family, he had this endearing quality of 'little boy lost' no matter how old he got. He was funny too, more so when he didn't mean to be, his wit was sharp, bang on time in any situation. I loved him with all my heart and always felt very protective of him even though he was over a foot taller than me.

"How's University going Izobel?" Mum asks whilst she's stroking her thumb across a slightly wrinkled and tear stained school portrait of Zack. He can't have been more than ten years old in it. So adorable, gap toothed with that wonky smile. I have to take a deep breath before I answer.

"Good Mum, slightly more out of my depth than I thought I'd be, but I've made an appointment with my tutor Dr McGrath next week to get some extra material to help me," I say, unable to tear my eyes away from the photo in Mum's hand.

"His name sounds familiar Izobel....where have I heard that name before?"

"Not sure, I don't remember him ever being mentioned." I look at her picking up her knitting and frantically clicking those needles, lost in thought by the look of her frown lines.

"When's Dad coming home? I want to make sure I'm gone in time."

"Not till late love, I *am* sorry you know Izobel, so very sorry, but I've never been able to control his temper and putting myself in between you two," she trails off looking away. "Well I always did wonder if it would make matters worse." The tears start streaming down her cheeks. It breaks my heart but I know I need to be the strong one now.

"I know Mum, but it's over, he can't hurt me anymore, I won't let him and I don't need his love when he treats me like I'm nothing. I can't live this way, you shouldn't have to either. After all, he's the reason we lost Zack," I say with anger I didn't know I was capable off.

"Shhh Izobel don't." She looks at me and her expression makes yet another crack in my heart. My heart has so many now I know it'll take more than love to mend it.

"I need to go Mum, I'm sorry…I really am." I feel numb again. I should be used to it by now. I hug her for what seems like ages and on my way home, I question yet again why she's still living under the same roof as him. It's like she lives in a room with no windows or doors, not realising there is an outside world – trapped. Living with someone she used to know, someone Zack and I never got the chance to meet, in love with the past. I think there's two ways of looking at it, she's either showing great strength or great cowardice. I prefer to think its strength because the other option breaks my heart.

Once I'm back at the house, I make myself a cup of coffee before going back to my room. I sit in the big comfy armchair by the bay window as it really is the most perfect spot. I pick up my kindle and try to lose myself in the fictional world to escape the ugliness of mine. I nearly jump out of my chair from the loud buzzing when I get a text message from Aiden saying they're playing a gig in some pub on the other side of town. He wants to see if I want to join them as I still haven't heard *'The Standards'* live. I reply back saying I'm staying in tonight, but to enjoy and wish them good luck. I check my phone to see if I've got a reply from Declan to my earlier text but there's nothing. I have to admit this not only upsets me, but puts me in a bad mood. So I decide, as the house is boy free, to have a pampering session. There's nothing like it to feel brand spanking new and revived.

I have a long bath with a face mask. I wax, I manicure, pedicure, moisturize till I literally shine by the end of my session. I feel brand spanking new on the outside. I put on my strappy short nightdress, it's black and simple but most of all it's comfortable. I sit myself back in the chair by the window and return to my book feeling all refreshed.

I must have fallen asleep because the sound of the lads returning startles me awake in the chair. From where I'm sitting, I can see them out the window. I can also hear Declan singing, his voice makes me shiver and tingle in places, like he's done since I met him. He looks up at my window and I know he can see me. I can't look away no matter how hard I try, he stands there for a while just looking up at me, then he smiles and comes into the house. I can hear him pounding up the stairs and then suddenly, here he is in my room. I can hear Aiden turning the radio on downstairs and I hear the beginning of one of my favourite songs; *'I don't want to be'* by Gavin Degraw. It's as if the song sets Declan off, he takes two long strides into the room with a fierce look on his face, his jaw clenching. He slides his hand into my hair and grips it tight to the point where it's almost painful, but not quite. He bends over and his lips are just about touching mine, when he whispers at my ear, "When I met you Izzy, you crawled under my skin, you hit me so hard and I can't stop you, I can't stop thinking about you. I can't leave you alone."

I'm not quite sure what he means but the next minute his lips are on mine so I don't get a chance to ask him. His tongue roughly forces entry and invades my mouth, giving me chills all over my body. I slide my hands eagerly under his t-shirt finally touching and exploring the hard ridges on his stomach and his lean defined pecs. As he moans into my mouth, I feel a sense of triumph. I want him to feel just how I feel every time I'm near him. I knew he would feel amazing but the way my body is reacting to his, the way my heart is pounding right now. Well, I had no idea. I literally feel him *everywhere.*

He lets go for a second to pull his t-shirt off, then he lifts me up and I instinctively wrap my legs around his waist. He walks me to my bed and literally drops me following me down and ending up on top of me between my legs. I can't even describe how it feels having his weight on top of me, his warm skin, the hard muscle. I'm literally melting in his arms. His mouth is still on mine, his tongue touching and teasing me; his teeth grazing and nibbling on my lips. Shit this guy can kiss. I have never felt so turned on in my life. I slide my hands down his back and under his jeans and arch against him gripping his arse with my hands. His tongue is making a trail along my jaw, down my neck, across my collar bone and the tingling soon turns to fierce burning. I feel dizzy and out of control.

"Declan please…." I whisper, wanting him so bad I can't stand it any longer.

He stops what he's doing and looks searchingly into my eyes wanting confirmation. "You sure sweetheart?" His voice is so deep and husky, I'm left in no doubt of how much he wants me and this makes me even more desperate for his touch.

"Please…" I tell him pressing myself into him, feeling his hardness against me, wanting him inside me. He slowly pulls off my night dress, groaning as I'm left more and more exposed. The way he's looking at me with pure lust in his dark molten eyes makes me feel bold and desired rather than embarrassed. Kissing his way down my body leaving no part of me untouched he removes my knickers slowly. I moan loudly, my head falling back as I close my eyes from the onslaught of pure fucking desire. Declan slides his hands up my thighs kissing, licking and biting them as he makes his way back up again. I feel him everywhere and my mind is scrambled as my body trembles. I want him so badly now so I fumblingly try to undo his belt and push his jeans down as far as I can, followed by his boxers. His fingers are working me to the point where all I can feel is him, I can't breathe. But this lost breath is the good kind. Capturing my mouth in a burning kiss his hands leave my body and I hear the tear of a foil packet. As he settles himself between my legs, he suddenly stops and cradles my face with his hands, leaning on his elbows.

"Are you sure?" his hot panting breath whispers against my lips.

I'm nervous and scared because this is a huge step and I know I won't only be giving him my body here, it'll be more than that. But I want this. I need this. I want Declan.

"I'm sure," I whisper shyly, thinking that even if this isn't a good idea, there's no bloody way I can stop it now. I wouldn't want to. Declan's eyes are burning into mine, I nod again and his body tenses, his breathing becomes erratic as he slowly pushes his way inside. I can't breathe, I have no words, this is beyond anything I dreamed.

"Fucking hell Izzy….So. Bloody. Perfect," he groans, his thrusts getting harder and going deeper. He captures my mouth in another deep and all-consuming kiss and I grab his hair pushing my fingers through it, trying to get him closer even though it's physically impossible. I'm so burning hot I can't get enough of him, I can't taste him enough, touch him enough, get him deep enough. The muscles in his arms are flexing as his rhythm picks up. I turn my face and trace his tattoo with my tongue and he makes a noise that sounds a bit like a growl. Then suddenly, his hands are all over me, I cry out as he hooks my leg over his arm and he loses all control. The pounding is frantic, rough and hard, we've both lost ourselves completely to the moment. I forget to breathe as the waves wash over me and I'm pretty sure I shout his name over and over like a chant. I knew it would be amazing with Declan but this…this is something else and as I feel and hear him fall over the edge as he shouts my name, I feel a satisfying warmth, spread through me. As our breathing tries to return to normal, he gently places kisses on my face and lips rolling to his side and pulling me with him.

"You okay Iz?" he smiles at me stroking my face with his fingers.

"Mmm…" I can't speak, I'm scared I'm going to blurt out something stupid that I might regret later. This is how huge this moment feels to me.

"You know… you smell like cookies and sunshine Izzy, it's addictive," he whispers against my skin.

"You know…" I say smiling at him, surprised by the fierce look in his eyes. "I'm not sure how I feel about being compared to a cookie."

"Oh well cookies are my weakness so it's good Izzy…real good," he says before he starts to kiss me. Bloody hell I'll say it again, this man can kiss, I feel him all over me and I need and want more. Declan suddenly moves me to the side after a brief kiss and gets off the bed. I shiver at the sudden loss of warmth.

"I'll be right back, do you want a glass of water or anything?" he asks me.

"I'm okay thanks," I reply, burrowing under the duvet wondering what will happen now. I look at him pulling on his boxers and can't believe that he's mine, or rather *was* mine tonight. Who knows if this'll go anywhere, Aiden did warn me, so I know there are no certainties. Why should I be any different, I'm nothing special really. And my dramas are not something anyone in their right mind would want to take on. Suddenly I freeze, thank God the lights are off, he couldn't have seen them, could he? He never mentioned that he felt anything. There's no way I want to explain why I have scars that shape…like that. I quickly pull my night dress back on and slip to the bathroom to wash up.

When I come back into my bedroom Declan's lying in my bed, he has his arms behind his head and is staring up at the ceiling. I lose a breath, he's gorgeous absolutely mouth-wateringly gorgeous. I feel all hot and tingly again just from looking at him. He smiles at me all crookedly having caught me obviously.

"You look as if you want to eat me Izzy, why don't you get your arse over here and have a taste?" he cheekily asks, crooking his finger at me.

I feel myself blushing and giggle like an idiot as I get in next to him. He moves me so I'm on top of him and tucks some of my hair behind my ear.

"Izzy sweetheart you drive me bloody crazy. I don't know what's happening here and I certainly can't deny who I am, but fuck…I want to give us a try." As if frustrated, he pushes his hand through his hair and goes quiet. To be honest even though I know this may break my heart I know it's what I want and need too. I lean down and put my head on his chest while he wraps me in his arms. I feel tiny, well I know I'm pretty small but this, this makes me feel safe and protected. I don't know where I belong, but right now that makes me the lucky one considering where I started. We lie together in complete silence; I can hear his breathing slowing down and looking up at him I know he's fallen asleep so I try to do the same.

Chapter Seven

When I wake up, Declan's gone. I have a sudden moment of panic when I realise I'm on my own thinking up one conspiracy theory after the next. Why did he leave me, did he regret what we did? Serious to the banal thoughts run through my head, I wonder, did I snore, dribble or worse... talk rubbish in my sleep? The one thing I do know though, is that for the first time in a very long time, the nightmares didn't come and consume my dreams. I've actually woken up feeling great. I can still smell Declan in my bed and I'm reluctant to get out, instead, I want to stay and get lost in the replay of last night in my head. Bloody hell, listen to me. I check the time and realise I still have another hour before I have to get up so I stretch to get comfortable and somehow manage to fall asleep again.

My alarm wakes me back up in plenty of time but I get so lost in my thoughts as I'm getting ready that I've made myself late. As it turns out I'm not the only one running late this morning when I meet Aiden at the bus stop. He smiles at me but it doesn't reach his eyes. He's worried and not happy about something, that much is obvious and I'm pretty sure I know why.

"How's my Izzy girl doing today?" he asks me giving me a hug.

"I'm good Aiden, and listen please don't worry...I'm walking into this with my eyes wide open okay." I let him go and grab his hand squeezing it to reassure him.

"I know love, but I've also known Dec like forever and I know what he's capable of or even incapable of..."

I interrupt him stopping him from saying any more. "I know Aiden….to be honest I've no idea what we are or *'where'* we are together but I like what we could be, if that makes any sense?"

"Well if you need someone to take him down a peg or two for anything go ask Max, not me, 'cause he'd knock me out with one punch. I'm pretty sure Max would at least get one in before Declan went down," he winks at me flexing his muscle.

I burst out laughing and link my arm with his as we get on the bus. We both share a lecture today, which I love and whilst in class we revert to childhood days of passing silly notes. Just before the bell rings I receive a note that says:

'Fancy going down the pub and getting pissed? It'll be after 12 by the time we get into town, put a cross in either the yes or no box.'

I tick yes and slide the note back. Aiden reads it and looks at me with a massive smile and gives me the thumbs up. Childish? Yes, but I bloody love it!

We pack up our stuff and start walking to catch the bus when I see Declan talking to a girl by the Uni bar. I'm pretty sure it's the girl from the other night, I recognize her voice. His back is turned to me so he can't see me, which makes me feel less bad for staring. It looks as if they're arguing about something. She turns her face away from him in anger and his hand turns her face back so she can't help but look at him. Although they're arguing, it looks intimate, way too intimate. Like they know each other completely inside out and feel comfortable in each other's space. I look at Aiden who's looking at them as well, a frown on his face.

"Who is she Aiden?" I ask him, trying to catch his eyes so I don't miss the truth.

"Lina….She's been on and off with Dec for the last two years. They get together and everything is good then it all blows up in spectacular fashion and they split up. Then they'll get together again in an equally intense way. I'd go crazy if I tried to explain their relationship to you Iz, but I do know, and they know too, that they're no good for each other. Lina's a childhood friend, she was part of our gang growing up," he answers looking back at me; away from the scene in front of us.

I feel a bit sick as I watch Declan pulling Lina into his arms. I look back at Aiden and try to seem unaffected. Well I say try, I'm pretty sure he reads me perfectly clear.

"Pint?" I ask him as if that will solve everything.

"Pint!" he replies and takes my hand as we start walking off down the road.

It's started raining...not a soft drizzle but the hard pounding rain that hurts when it hits your face. Aiden and I are soaked by the time we get to the pub. We order our pints and miraculously find a table in the corner by the fire place. At least we'll dry out quickly sitting here, as the bar staff have stoked the fire.

I ask Aiden about his childhood as I have this perverse need to hear how people grew up. Waiting for the day I find someone who experienced what I did, I guess to make me feel like less of a freak and to convince me that I'm not the only one who's had to grow up living as an actress in her own family show.

"I grew up in a tiny village just outside of London. Everyone knew everybody and their business, which made it hard at times. Declan and Finn started at the same school as me a few years in;

they were transferred over when their parents moved. Finn started hanging out with Max and Declan and I hit it off straight away," he pauses to finish his pint.

"What was your family like?" I ask him, hanging off his every word.

"Dad was a copper and Mum stayed at home. I think Dad's the reason I got into criminal psychology really. Whenever we used to role play as kids, I always chose to be the Old Bill," he laughs at his memories and I feel the love coming off him in waves. He tells me stories about pranks him and Declan used to get up to as kids. They were a right pair. This makes me miss Sofia even more. I had loads of friends growing up but only one best friend. Sofia's the only one I let in, the others I kept at a distance which made them drop off along the way. In the end most of them thought me aloof and not worth the effort. That was fine by me, I had Sofia. Besides, I found it tiring having to keep making up excuses and hiding the bruises. You can't deny who you are. Somewhere the truth slips out.

Set Fire to the Rain' by Adele starts playing, shit, as if this day couldn't get any worse. Don't get me wrong I adore Adele, love her, she truly is beautiful, but she makes me cry, she makes me *feel*. She reminds me that, at times, I think I'm addicted to my own sadness. I look over at Aiden who seems really busy with his phone all of a sudden, despite me being worried he's caught me getting lost in my own thoughts. I compose myself and walk up to the bar to get us some more drinks. It's getting busy in here so I have to squeeze in between two lads, one of them moves sideways and lets me in by putting his arm around me. I nod at him in thanks and decide on not only getting two more pints but a couple of chasers for each of us. I try and shout my order to the barman over the noise and punters but not only am I a short arse, I also can't shout. Everyone laughs at me when I try to shout, they call it the girlie squeak. The guy next to me, who on closer inspection is gorgeous starts laughing. "I think that's the cutest thing I've heard in ages, you've got no chance love, let me get your order in for you."

I smile and tell him what I want and he shouts the order out. I can't help but stare at him while I blush, I can feel it. Yes I know how that makes me sound, I know for sure that my heart wants Declan, even though I've only known him for a short time, when you know, you just know right? However, this guy is so attractive. Yes I'm pretty sure I'm blushing now because I can feel my face is on fire as he catches me staring.

"You're adorable," he whispers as he leans down. The bartender puts the order on a tray for me; I pay for it and look up at my saviour.

"Thank you, you're quite a handy bar prop and I'm forever in your debt, especially if you're a repeat performer," I say winking at him.

"Ah, so you're not only adorable you're also cheeky, an intriguing combination." He bows dramatically in front of me. "You're very welcome and next time I see you I'm going to have to insist on having a drink with you," he says smiling at me.

Suddenly my feet become a very interesting diversion because I can't look at him. My bravado lasted about three minutes, but who's counting. He stops talking for a second then leans down and says, "I'm guessing that guy over there is going to come have a go in a minute the way he's burning a hole in me with his eyes."

I look around and sure enough Aiden doesn't look happy. "That's okay," I say. "He's just a mate and very protective." I pick up the tray of drinks wanting to get back to Aiden. "See ya," I shout back at bar guy, making him laugh. As I'm walking back to the table I mentally kick myself for not asking him for his name. I've no idea why I have this need to know, maybe it's because I don't actually know what's happening with me and Declan. Especially after the Lina scene. I'm so confused.

"Do you know that guy Izzy?" Aiden asks me as I get back to our table. He keeps staring at him not breaking eye contact.

"Nah, he just helped me get the drinks in, I got us a couple of shots each and another pint," I say as I place the drinks on the table. These drinks are going to my head way too quickly, damn I must remember to eat more than breakfast every day. While I'm talking drunken shite, Aiden's phone keeps going off.

"Who keeps texting you? Whoever it is sure is persistent," I ask him with concern. I just have a bad feeling but I can't explain it.

"It's Declan, nothing important just checking where we are and stuff," he says trying to dismiss it. Now I know I'm in that happy tipsy place but I can't help but think Aiden's hiding something here. As we finish off our pints and shots, I have this sudden urge to leave the pub and am getting really fidgety.

"Hey let's have another one for the road," Aiden says sounding almost panicky as he rests his hand on my bouncing leg.

"Nah, I'm done, can't you hear the drunken lisp is getting more pronounced, than it was one shot ago?" I say, getting more worried by the second here. I stand up and start walking out of the pub trying to shake off this weird feeling I have. It almost feels as if something's going on that may break me and I know without a doubt it's about Declan. I can hear Aiden trying to catch up with me, his fast footsteps coming up behind me.

"Hang on up Izzy," he pants, taking my hand as I start walking faster. As we get closer to the house it's as if Aiden doesn't want me to go in, I think I know what's going on, so fuelled by anger, fear and tequila, I storm into the house checking all the rooms as I go.

My palms start to sweat and I feel that ice cold fear on the back of my neck. When I get to the top floor, there's only the attic room left to check. I take the steps two at a time and burst through the bedroom door. I stop abruptly, still in shock at what I see. Declan's sitting on the floor with Lina sprawled across his lap. Besides wearing jeans, he's stripped of any other piece of clothing and crazily my first thought is of how utterly fucking gorgeous he is. Every one of his black tattoos on his olive skin emphasizes muscle. Lina's got all her clothes on, but seeing as she doesn't really wear much to begin with, except for a tiny skirt and tank top, that isn't really saying much. Declan has the decency to look away embarrassed when he sees me, Lina on the other hand meets my eyes with a smirk on her face….what a bitch. My face must be a real picture…disbelief, despair and realisation playing across it. Aiden grabs my arm.

"Come on Izzy let's go downstairs…Declan I'll talk to you later." Aiden sounds pissed off as he drags me out of Declan's bedroom.

Funnily enough I don't cry, shout or show any emotional outburst at all. I feel numb. I think I knew all along I was way out of Declan's league and I stupidly gave him a small piece of my heart. I gave him some of me. He didn't know this though, to him I was probably more like some kind of step off his usual much travelled beaten track. His 'Izzy detour' obviously didn't offer him much so he returned to what he knew best. In his defence, and I can't believe I'm admitting to this, we never defined ourselves. I think women don't need the spoken confirmation; we take a situation and define it with actions. Guys; perhaps not so much. Unless the word relationship is spoken out loud it could be anything. Then again, maybe I'm generalising, maybe this only refers to blokes like Declan. Who knows? I think I'm trying to rationalise what I just saw in Declan's bedroom and cutting off any emotional reaction in the process. I actually feel numb and my eyes can't focus on anything. Aiden pours me a glass of water and I down it in one, holding my glass out signalling at the half empty wine bottle on the kitchen table.

"I'm fine Aiden, don't look at me with those sad puppy eyes, Declan and I...we don't make sense, we're two completely different people." I refuse to let this hurt me. I have enough of that already inside me to last a lifetime.

"I'm not so sure about that Izzy, I think you're too similar, that's the problem here. You're both running from something in your past. I know what Declan's running from and unfortunately his avoidance tactic is what's destroying his relationships but he doesn't know how to stop. I was hoping you were the one, I still think you are, but he'll no doubt do too much damage and ruin what he's got with you." He shakes his head in frustration as he tops up our glasses.

I have no clue what Aiden's going on about, I never got the chance to dig too deep into what makes Declan who he is or his past for that matter. Thinking about it, what do I really know about him? Besides the fact that he makes me revert to a puddle on the floor with his looks, he makes me laugh...he's funny in that sarcastic way that I love. So that aside, is Declan, 'the man' I know. Well besides studying Humanities, his true love is everything music related and if he was any more laid back, he'd be lying down. I actually laugh out loud, how the hell could I possibly think that just because we slept together once, this means I know him and we were starting something. What does that make me, other than incredibly presumptuous and naïve? I've done the same thing in the past, but not this time. This time it's different. Aiden's looking at me like I'm crazy with a worried look on his face.

"You've gone somewhere hun, talk to me Izzy," he says reaching over to tuck a stray piece of hair behind my ear.

"You know what Aiden, this thing with Declan, I can't live like that….live in this way. I'm screwed up enough as it is without the doubt and the fact that he's oblivious to what I've given him. I'm better than that, I have to believe that I am, otherwise, I'm back onto the path of self-destruction again. This is good…yeah what happened here is good, it really is," I say, as if to convince us both.

"Whatever you say Izzy, but I really do think he wants and needs you…the thing is, that in it-self, is probably what's scaring the shit out of him." He leans over to give me a hug.

I hug him back and reach up to whisper in his ear, "I don't believe in much but I do believe in you and I thank whoever or whatever orchestrated our collision that day, I really do." I sneak a quick kiss in and run upstairs to my room. I get ready for bed and crawl under the covers, again curling myself into a ball trying to make myself as small as I feel right now. Always the same, this is what I've always done.

I wake up with a start and it's dark. Something heavy is lying across me. I look down and wonder if I'm dreaming. Declan's in my bed, his head on my chest with an arm across my stomach. What the hell's he doing in here and like this? I'm so tempted to shove him off me, but instead I start stroking his hair. I have no idea whether he's awake or asleep until I hear him speak, startling the shit out of me.

"I've started to fall apart here Izzy," he says before moving his head back, kissing my neck and rubbing his nose gently across the pulse beating out of my skin. I can hear myself breathing as it speeds up to match my pulse, but I don't dare respond.

"You've made me realize I need to start appreciating life and stop trying to let the past catch up with me all the time, fucking my life up. But love is absolute bollocks…I don't believe in anything *'love'*…all love ever does is whisper empty words which have the ability to break me and break everyone around me," he sighs in almost desperation as he lays his head back to rest on my chest. "I'm making no fucking sense here, am I? I sound like a right fucking pussy. But that's all I've got for you Izzy. Right now…that's all I've got."

    I don't know what to say to that, the shock of his words playing in my head. Every emotion possible is running through me. So instead, I say nothing at all but continue to stroke his hair. Stupid right? I could kick myself. He doesn't say anything more and his breathing becomes slow, deep and even so I slip out of bed trying not to wake him up and walk downstairs. Lying down on the couch I pull a blanket over me and try to get comfortable. Sleep doesn't come easy though and I see every hour until four am.

Chapter Eight

I wake up sore and stiff from a night on the couch to Aiden spraying water at me with a water pistol. What the hell?

"Very grown up Aiden," I shout, bolting off the couch soaked through.

"I know right? Classic," he laughs, still squirting water at me as he chases me into the kitchen.

"Stop it you arse," I laugh back at him. "What's the time? I didn't get much sleep last night, I'm bloody knackered. Am I late for the ten o'clock lecture?" I ask him, as I dry my face off with some kitchen towels.

"Nah, if you hip hop and scoot we'll make it," he winks at me with a stupid grin on his face.

"Hip hop and scoot…how old *are* you and what did you have for breakfast? I laugh at him.

"Twenty-three, Lucky Stars and they were yummy, thank you very much for asking." He starts packing up his bag getting ready to go. I burst out laughing at him.

"So why did you sleep on the couch last night Izzy?" he asks and looks at me quizzically.

"Long story and we really don't have the time for it now, let me just run upstairs and get ready so we don't miss our bus," I hastily reply and run off.

I sneak into my bedroom but Declan's gone. I wonder how he feels this morning, if he's as confused as I am. I quickly get ready so I can walk with Aiden to the bus stop. Aiden and I are sitting on the bus on our way to Uni sharing a bag of liquorice wine gums. Okay, so Aiden's not the only one who's playing the child card today, but I didn't have time for a grown up breakfast and I'm starving and this is all I've got.

"So, Izzy.." Aiden suddenly breaks our silent liquorice munching. "*'The Standards'* have a gig tonight, are you up for it or will what happened last night make it too weird for you?"

"Aiden, it's all good, of course I'd love to go," I say. Actually I'm really excited to hear them play. Pretence is such a wonderful thing though isn't it. I've done it before. I can do it again with Declan. Close guard yourself and no one will ever know. I learnt that early on in my childhood. I still have the scars to prove it.

Later that day I decide to go and see Mum, a reminder of why I shouldn't let everything get to me, I still have a double life to lead. I feel relieved that the front of the house still looks immaculate; this means she hasn't gotten any worse. I know gardening for her is almost like therapy and keeps her busy. Once again I find Mum in her bedroom. I wonder if she sees this as her safe haven, her cocoon where he doesn't enter. I wasn't that lucky, but maybe she is. Who knows?

"Izobel, I didn't hear you come in darling. I wasn't expecting you, are you hungry? Shall I make you something to eat, what about a drink?" she trails off and starts worrying her hands on the bedspread trying to flatten out the non-existent creases.

This is Mum in a nutshell, the one who aims to please others for fear of rejection. I believe she thinks if people are full and sated, they refrain from anger and spite. Maybe so, but I'm guessing this is what placates my Dad not the general population. I notice she's knitting again; the colours have gotten slightly brighter. Do I read something into that or not, I'm not sure. I still haven't got a clue what she's making but I reckon if you stretched it out, it would serve as a great runner. I shiver and look back up at her.

"I'm fine for food, but it's a nice day outside, why don't we go sit in the garden under a quilt and share a bottle of wine?" I ask her trying to get her out of her room. She needs some fresh air to blow the cobwebs away I decide.

"Yes, that sounds perfect Izobel, I bought a new red to try at the shops yesterday," she smiles and we walk into the kitchen, where she gets out two glasses and the bottle.

Stepping out into the Indian summer we sit down at the patio table. The afternoon goes so quick, Mum's almost 'normal', we even manage to laugh about memories of Zack, which believe me is quite a feat for both her and me. My phone suddenly rings making us both jump. It's playing *'I'm sexy and you know it'*; I burst out laughing in surprise and check the display. Yep it's Aiden, I should've guessed. He must've gotten hold of my phone and set a new ringtone to his number. Accepting the call I say, "Don't lie Aiden, there's no way you work out, if so, can I suggest asking the gym for a refund?"

"Hahaha when did you become a comedienne? Just checking you're still coming to the gig tonight. We have to leave in an hour and I have no clue where you are right this minute."

"I'm in the garden sharing…" I count. "What looks like two bottles of red with Mum." Oops how did I not realise, I look over at Mum who's sitting with a stupid grin on her face and it makes me smile. "Right, so, yes…what was the question?" I've forgotten what he asked me, the sudden serenity in Mum's face has stumped me.

"How much of those two bottles did you have?" he laughs.

"Oh yeah, I know. I'm not quite the alcoholic yet Aiden. I'll be with you as soon as I can, if you have to go, just go, and I'll see you there, oh and I promise I'll be there."

Aiden tells me the name of the pub and I hang up looking over at Mum.

"Sorry Mum I have to go now, I really enjoyed our afternoon; promise me we'll do this again very soon okay." I stand up and lean over to kiss her cheek. She stands to hug me and I almost cry. When you haven't seen a smile or pure happiness on your Mum's face in a very long time it melts you to the bone when you do. She sits back down and I leave her sitting in the late summer sunshine. I stop for a minute and watch her closing her eyes turning her face up into the sun. My heart skips a beat and the pain is so intense I almost stumble. There really is beauty in pain. Until you've loved someone you don't realise how painful love really is.

When I get back to our house, Aiden's left already. I have a quick shower and stand in front of my closet wondering what to wear. I decide not to dress up, it's only a night down the pub after all. I settle on my short denim skirt, a black fitted V-neck t-shirt and my black glittery flip flops; the weather still hasn't turned that chilly yet but I bring my black poncho just in case. I dry my hair and add a few small braids in it, put a bit of make-up on; grab my purse and run out the door.

I haven't been to this pub before but it looks packed. I can't believe this is the first time I'll hear *'The Standards'* play and as I get closer, I can hear the music through the open windows. I walk in and head to the bar, scanning the pub as I do. The guys are up on stage mid-song and bloody hell, they look and sound amazing. I have to admit that I get chills and literally swoon, bouncing up and down clapping my hands like some sort of freaking weirdo fan girl. I mean the guys look hot up there, the song they're playing rocks and the punters clearly love them. I wonder how many cool points I get for this. I check myself, reign myself in and shyly look around to make sure no one saw me and my inappropriate 'moment'. Unfortunately I'm so busted, by the good looking guy from the other night. He's looking at me with a raised eyebrow and an amused expression. I give him a little wave and manoeuvre myself into a small space at the bar to get a drink. Same story, no one sees the short girl squashed between the big blokes. My saviour from the other night muscles his way in and I'm not surprised, he really is huge. I think he's a good deal older than me too. Perhaps late twenties or even early thirties.

"So, I promised I'd be there for you when you needed me right? What are you having tonight and how many are you buying for?" he grins at me with a proper cocky expression.

"I need to get you a cape," I laugh at him, before I reel of my order. "I'll have a pint of orange lemonade and it's just me, because my housemates are up on that stage right now knocking the roof off this place," I beam up at him.

"They're great; I've heard them play before," he nods looking back up at the stage. He turns to me smiling cheekily. "So can we tell each other our names yet or is it more fun if we don't?"

"As exciting as that sounds, I'm going to tell you mine if you tell me yours," I laugh. "I'm Izzy and I'd be mortified if you guessed something horrible as it would make me want to question myself," I smile at him and look back at the stage where the lads have just started a new song.

"Izzy, well that's a perfect name, it suits you. I'm Connor."

He passes me my drink and we move closer to the stage, chatting as best we can considering the loudness of the set being played. Every so often I sneak looks at Declan. Shit, he looks and sounds amazing up there. I notice he sings with his eyes closed, I wonder what he thinks about or whether he's just in a musical trance doing his thing. I look at Aiden on the bass, he catches me looking at him and gives me a wink and an exaggerated pelvic thrust. Some drunken girls near him start shouting obscene sexual things at him. Poor them, they don't know they don't stand a chance. Or maybe they do and they think they'll be the exception to the rule, as if that's at all possible. Gah! What do I really know; I don't even know what the hell I'm doing with Declan. I must stop analysing everything, but that's what happens when you're the poster child of therapy. I look back at Connor and instead of looking at the stage he's looking at me. The way he's looking at me; I think, actually I know, I'm in trouble. Remembering last night, I decide that as Declan's laid no claim on me, flirting is completely okay. In fact whatever's going on or has gone on between us, it's no-where near anything that resembles a normal relationship. So yes, flirting's okay. I also don't want anyone to be so important to me that without them, I'd feel like nothing, and right now; how I feel about Declan, I have no doubt this would happen. So, I rationalise that it will not, and should not, stop me from having a bit of fun and some excitement in the meantime. I'm not an instigator; I would have to wait till Declan tells me it's me he wants in no uncertain terms. I'm not going to wait and live like I'm taken despite my heart knowing that's the path it's already on. If Aiden's right and Declan's as messed up as me it's probably not a good thing anyway. We'd be a mess together. But a beautiful mess…bollocks I can't help myself. Now, I do realise that starting something when I feel like this would not in any way be fair on anyone. But it's not going to stop me from having a bit of fun, and if it looks as though it may be turning into more, I know to get out. In that respect I still have enough of my heart left to recognize that.

Connor leans over and puts his empty beer bottle on the shelf next to me. He never leans back again, instead he shifts even closer. I find I don't mind, I don't feel crowded which can only be a good thing. It means that there's a chance for me. We chat about the music we like and find we have quite a few bands in common. I'm a huge Biffy Clyro fan, these Scottish boys are geniuses and Connor agrees much to my surprise. Sofia and I are fanatical fans and haven't met anyone else who's as obsessed as we are. I explain to him how much music means to me. That there's a song for every emotion and every situation. Our actions are spurred on and feelings are more intense, all of which is enhanced by individual songs. Music is life. Life without music would be unbearable. I couldn't think of many things worse than not having music as a big part of my life.

Connor tells me about his job as a football coach at a private school nearby and how it was meant to be a stop gap until he found something else. He enjoys it too much to leave though so he figures he's in the right place in life. Seriously, this guy is so good looking and has this passionate way about him, that I can't stop smiling. When he goes to get us another drink my eyes wander up to the stage again. They're starting another song and I immediately miss a breath and feel the chills travel down my body. Declan's staring straight at me but I can't read his expression, his eyes have frozen me to the spot and I can't look away even though I want nothing more. How can he make me feel so cold yet so hot at the same time from just one look. I feel trapped in his gaze. The expression on his face is intense and I wish I knew what was going through his mind.

"Hey…..earth to Izzy," I hear Connor say, he must've come back with our drinks. I tear my eyes away from Declan and look up at Connor.

"Fancy going to sit outside for a bit?" I ask him. I need to get away from the intensity I feel coming from the stage.

"Sure thing Izzy."

Connor follows me out as we go and sit in the pub garden to talk. I can still hear Declan's voice drifting out through the open windows. It's bizarrely comforting now instead of feeling awkward, I think the distance is helping. After a few more songs it sounds like *'The Standards'* are wrapping up their set and the pub bell rings for last orders.

"I think I'm going to walk home now Connor, I've had a really nice night, so thank you, make sure you apologize to your mates for abandoning them for me." I stand up and get ready to leave.

"I'll walk you home Izzy and don't worry, they're big lads they can look after themselves." He takes my hand and walks along with me. Walking in silence back to the house I suddenly get all nervous and haven't got a clue what to say. So I say nothing. My confidence is obviously going to take a while longer to rebuild.

"Right….well, this is me," I say as we reach the steps outside the townhouse. I look up at Connor and smile, a smile he returns. This guy has a blinding smile.

"So Izzy," he asks. "When can I see you again?"

I'm not sure what to answer here because the way he's looking at me right now, I know I could be in trouble. A complication I don't need, then again maybe I do. I pull out my phone. "Give me your number; I'll ring it now and then you'll have mine."

After we've swapped numbers he leans down and gives me a kiss on my cheek and waving him off, I walk inside. I leave the light off in my room, put some music on and sit in the comfy chair by the bay window. My mobile vibrates alerting me to a new text message.

Connor: I know it's not cool to be this eager but are you free on Wednesday?

Me: LOL I think so

Connor: Great. Dinner at 8?

Me: Yep, come pick me up

Connor: Look forward to it. Night Izzy

Me: Night night, don't let the bed snakes bite

Connor: No danger there, only got one and he's a close personal friend of mine

I burst out laughing at Connor's crap joke, put my phone down and go to bed. I'm not sure how long I've been asleep for, but I wake up when I hear some noise outside the window, the boys are back. I don't want any confrontations; I feel too happy and sleepy right now. I don't want this feeling ruined and taken away from me. I curl up under the covers and try to go back to sleep. A while later I hear my door creak open and footsteps coming over to my bed. I know its Declan but I don't open my eyes. He stands there for what feels like ages, I can feel his eyes on me. I'm fighting the irresistible urge to open my eyes, which is proving extremely difficult. Just before I lose the fight, I hear him whisper softly to me while he places his hand on my hair, stroking the tips of his fingers down my face.

"I wish I had the guts to put my faith in someone else, but I don't even trust myself, so how can I put my faith to the test with you? You deserve everything Izzy, everything good; you deserve that pedestal more than anyone I know. I knew it the minute I met you. I saw it in your eyes."

He lets out a deep exhale before he leaves. I've never had to fight this hard to pretend at being asleep. Seriously, this guy needs to come with more than a warning. I lie here for ages thinking about how Declan makes me feel before I fall asleep; wondering what he meant by those words. I've got a feeling I know, but I daren't believe it. I'd hate to be wrong.

Chapter Nine

The next day I'm sitting in my last lecture of the day and I realise I haven't taken any notes at all. I've spent almost a full hour thinking about Declan and Connor. Polar opposites, one's a good uncomplicated choice, the other not so much…I think. I can't believe I've only known Declan for just over a week. It feels as if I've slotted into a life that's been mine, unbeknownst to me, running alongside the one I was living. I don't even know how to explain how I feel about this or what words to use. Two parallel lives, but only one with an escape route. I know which one that is and there's an empty slot for me to fill, but first I need to extract myself from the one I've known. The world and the words I want to forget. I pack up my stuff and walk to Dr McGrath's office. It's my first appointment with him since starting my course. My first of the appointments I'm supposed to keep with him every two weeks. I hesitantly knock on his door and hear him shout for me to enter. He's standing in front of a massive book case. It looks as if he's frustratingly looking for something specific on his shelves. Once again I note his dishevelled look but his kind eyes find mine and he looks at me knowingly with a smile on his face. It makes me feel as if I'm standing in a spotlight but I feel a sense of relief at the same time. As if he understands.

"Take a seat Izzy." He points over at one of the comfy looking armchairs. I sit down and look round his office. The closest thing I have that can compare to how this room makes me feel, is the memory of the cave my brother and I used to make with chairs and blankets. On bad days we would place four dining room chairs together and gather all the blankets we could find in the house. Zack and I would drape them over the chairs making sure not a sliver of light would enter our safe haven. Well, we liked to think it was safe. Most of the time it was, sometimes we weren't so lucky.

Our next task would be to gather all our favourite things in our cave. Our pillows, a torch, my books, Zack's Superman magazines and finally a small picnic of treats because who knew how long we'd be in there. Sometimes we'd spend the whole night in there, taking turns in keeping watch on what was going on in the other room. Sometimes we'd fall asleep in there holding hands. The memory makes me sad and I feel myself shiver. A slight cough takes me away from my thoughts and I look over at Dr McGrath. He's sitting in the other armchair facing me at an angle, his hands firmly clasped, his eyes examining me, looking straight inside me. I feel a sudden chill. I know I'm missing something, a piece of a puzzle. Mum recognized his name. There has to be a connection. I wish I knew for sure.

"So Izzy, how has your first week been?"

"Good, although I feel a bit out of my depth in one of the modules," I say feeling relieved that we are on a safe topic here.

We have a chat about what I need to focus on and go through the list of extra reading and I note down the useful articles he suggests.

"Anything else you'd like to talk about Izzy? How are you settling down in your new accommodation?"

I suddenly wonder how on earth he knows I've moved, but then I remember that I had to change my details as soon as I moved in with Aiden and the others.

"Yeah it's good, I feel happy there....safe I suppose." I miss a breath, I shouldn't have said safe, that's like offering candy to a child. I know this when I catch the look in Dr McGraths eyes.

"Safe? You didn't feel safe before?" He looks at me questioningly wanting to obviously move this conversation somewhere new.

I have no idea how to answer his question; he'll be like a dog with a bone now. I've given him an *'in'*, I recognize the signs, after all, I've not long finished my sessions with Dr Beckett.

"Well, I live with three guys now so…umm they make me feel safe, you know, not like living on my own I mean."

"Did you live on your own before Izzy?" he quickly fires back not wanting to give me an out. I shake my head at him but say nothing; instead I turn my head to look out the window. "I believe I may have met your mother once, Izzy."

And there we go. I knew it. He knows or has suspicions.

"I of course cannot divulge in what capacity, but I want you to know that I'm here for you. But I believe I've told you this already," he says, and I immediately feel like he's drawing me out.

I want to change the subject but for some reason, maybe the way he looks at me, I feel like I need to affirm what he's said. I maintain my silence though. The door is staying firmly shut on the accident. Even if I wanted to I don't think I could open it. I look down at my hands. I can still see them desperately trying to get to my brother, searching for the way in, to save him from life but wanting to give it to him too. Suddenly I can smell it, smell the despair and I start to shake. I know I'm about to fall apart. I feel hot and cold at the same time, I hear the ocean in my ears and my heart is about to burst out of my chest. I know what's about to happen and it fills me with panic and dread. I look up at Dr McGrath and I'm sure he sees how scared I am because his face looks worried.

When I come to, I'm lying on the couch. I know that I just fainted; I recognised the signs just before I passed out. Even though it's been a while since the last time; I remember it as if it was yesterday. You never forget what it feels like once you've fainted from anxiety and panic or even a bad memory for that matter. I turn my head and see Dr, McGrath sitting on a chair next to me.

"How are you feeling Izobel?" he asks me as he hands over a glass of water.

Sitting up I grasp the glass and chug it down saying nothing. Emptying the glass in one go I try to steady my breathing and gather my strength so I can run the hell out of here.

I think I'd actually managed to separate myself from the accident. Taken what happened out of the equation of my new life, creating a battle-line. I guess I was wrong. I've been dealing with what I had to endure, for as long as I can remember but the moment it affected my brother and it resulted in him being taken away from me, well, I fell apart.

Dr McGrath's sitting there, hands clasped in his lap, gentle caring eyes that are willing me on, encouraging me to open up to him, wanting me to know I'm safe in here, safe with him. I know I have to say something, I want to say something, but I'm finding it really difficult to find my voice.

I struggle to explain, "You know how hard it is to hold onto something by a thread, hold on so tight you can actually get away with it, then for a freak situation to upset the balance with such disastrous consequences? Now that….*that* I cannot hold onto," I say weakly hoping he'll understand that I just can't, not yet. He nods at me in understanding and I feel a sense of relief.

I get my mobile out of my bag, finding Aiden's number and quickly send him a text asking him to come pick me up. I'm scared to speak, I'm worried everything will come tumbling out and I'm not ready. Not ready at all. I need to be prepared for that day. Dr Beckett got as far as he could with me before I stopped seeing him and I thought I was dealing, but obviously not. I'm guessing the door to what happened is still closed, but what's behind it has started seeping out through the gaps and cracks, like a cloud of black smoke thickly cloying and suffocating me, crossing the invisible line. The scars of my love for my lost brother have still not healed but are flashing in bright neon colours, like beacons in the dark. All through my morose and depressing thoughts Dr McGrath is still just sitting there quietly looking at me....those eyes terribly busy; analysing and seeing straight through me like I'm a transparent shell covering a multitude of swirling emotions and scenes playing in the background.

I want to be brave, I need to be brave and I know if anyone can help me, he can. I can tell it from looking at his eyes and how they're looking straight through me right now. Oh well...here comes the rain, the rolling clouds followed by the thunder, hell any analogy fits this freak of nature situation which I'm about to bring into the warmth and cosiness of his office. I look at the kind and age-lined face in front of me. I hope he's ready for it.

"Izobel?" he says encouragingly with a slight nod of his head.

I take a deep breath, close my eyes and return the nod. Here we go, I look down at my hands. "I've been here before," I whisper as if in pain. "So...I'll go to the beginning, where it all started. I'll begin with my Dad and what it was like at home," I say, knowing I'm opening up a can full of pain and anxiety.

"Why did you not feel safe at home? What was different and how old were you when you understood this?" he asks me gently.

"I think I was seven the first time I realised Dad was different," I tell him on an exhale. "Different to other Dads I knew, anyway. Whether there are more like him I don't know, but probably, yeah I'm pretty sure they're out there. You wouldn't necessarily know though, I don't think, because they're not the kind you brag about or want to show off, right?" I pause, and look back over at Dr McGrath who waves his hand at me to continue. I'm kind of relieved he's not asking probing questions, I'm not ready to answer any yet. Well, not voluntarily anyway.

"So," I continue unscrambling my thoughts. "He wasn't around all that much really. I would get up in the morning and he'd be gone by the time I left my room. Unless it was a weekend, then we'd all have breakfast together, as a family. I'm not sure why this became a ritual because no one would really speak. Breakfast was always blanketed by a heavy silence." I pause to think…and somehow elaborate so that he'll understand. Looking over at him, his face is open, urging me to continue.

"So yeah, it was never the comfortable kind of silence mind you, rather it was the silence that would make you feel irrationally guilty. I'd sit there and intensely think of something to talk about, something that was random enough and safe enough not to be turned into anything other than it was, if that makes any sense?" I smile sadly at him.

"What I think Izobel, is that there are so many types of silences that are left open to the interpretation of the individual." He stops talking and picks up the carafe of water pouring us both another glass, so I continue.

"Well it's hard to do you know, keeping silent that is. Especially when you're a child because as children we're known to speak our mind unaware of consequences that may happen because the subject is thought to be inappropriate, politically incorrect or just plain bad mannered. Well, that didn't apply my brother and me; we knew exactly what the effect of our words was. Just like we knew what the inevitable consequence would be for us. Well I did first, but then I was older than my brother." I look up at the ceiling, counting the cracks in the plaster while I think back.

"I knew my situation was not like any of my friends. I picked up on the danger signs. This was very important, it *became* important. I would end up wishing I was anywhere but where I was, and so many times I'd try and hold my breath for as long as I could." I look back at Dr McGrath as I take a sip of water. My hand is shaking and I spill a bit of water on my leg. I hope he didn't notice.

"Izobel, you became an observer of your Dad's behaviour in order to safe-guard yourself and your brother. It was instinctual. It served to protect you and to avoid situations that were out of your control." He hesitates before his next question, I can see his eyes working and I prepare myself by trying to fight my fear.

"Do you *feel* loved by your father now? And more importantly did you *feel* his love when this happened? Or was he a paradox?" He steeples his fingers in that classic way that lets me know he is paying the outmost attention to my every single word.

"Yeah, I never really doubted that he loved me, and I still don't. But I've never understood his kind of love. It's not the kind of love you'll find in the Good Parenting Guide or on the Father's Day cards in the shops," I answer, the best way I can. "To be honest, I think the way he loves is unique to himself; his personality his view on life I suppose. I can analyse why he's like this forever, but from what I heard about his childhood, I know he had it tough growing up. I know because he told me things…." I shake my head in frustration, my words falling out like disorganised ramblings.

"My poor Dad was apparently so unloved, he was adamant he was going to be different, show his kids the love he never received.

But to be honest with you Dr McGrath this is where I think he's wrong," I say looking down at my hands, picking at my fingernails.

"How so Izobel?" he asks leaning forward in his chair.

"Well, I think he *did* get the love that matters. The love that comes from being a part of a family. A bond that exists only from spending time together doing fun things. Time, that *yes*, maybe didn't involve much money, but it was time spent together. They stuck up for one another. Yes, they had their rough times, and a hand would strike once in a while. I know that's not right of course, I know, *believe me* I know. But the good times were far outweighed, his own admission not mine, by the togetherness which I know he did value."

I look up from my hands, which now have ten mangled finger nails; it's been a while since they last looked like this. I feel sorry for Dr McGrath. He got in, the door's opened. He unlocked it. But instead of looking rattled and hassled, he looks back at me with a kind smile on his face so I know its okay to keep going. I don't want to stop now, I don't think I could even if I tried or wanted to.

"How do you feel your Dad quantifies his love Izobel. You say it's different?" he asks me gently as if he senses how petrified I am of this conversation which was never meant to be.

"Well..." I say trying to rationalise it in my thoughts so they make sense. "I guess my Dad equates love with money and prestige. I think that became very clear to us early on. When he was happy we were happy, as a direct result. When things were not so great we felt it. We went through it with him. It swung in roundabouts."

"Sounds as if life became a vicious cycle and you were all pulled into a vortex of unpredictability and fear as a consequence," he replies with deep frown lines appearing.

"I guess so, he had a map of how to get where he wanted in *his* life and we were all meant to follow his journey. We had no choice, we had to stay quiet while he chased, for the want of a better word, his holy grail." I take a deep breath...my throat feels constricted and the tears silently make tracks down my cheeks. I'm starting to shake, I feel so tired and emotional. "And he wonders why he's so exhausted. He replaced actions of love with responsibilities of a lower priority, all the while thinking he was doing something from which everyone derived enjoyment. Putting off the important things like affection and time spent together. The signs became more and more transparent the older I got." I close my eyes and lean back in the chair wishing once again this wasn't my life.

"How did you react to these signs Izobel?" he asks me looking genuinely curious.

"I think I learnt very early on to categorize them. A beacon would go off when I knew to hide in my room. Well, that's until I realized that this meant someone else would be *'in the line of fire'*." I shudder at the memory. "So instead I'd go hide my brother in his room then go stand in the spotlight so he'd forget about Zack. I refused to ever run and hide, I'd do anything for my brother, but it wasn't easy, it didn't get any easier. In fact it got harder and harder to tell him to take my hand so I could lead him to safety; run and hide....be safe. He grew up though. No it definitely didn't get easier."

I'm starting to stumble over my words; I know I can't go on. Dr McGrath is still sitting in the same position, watching me, almost statuesque in his posture.

"I want to stop now...*please*," I whisper to him. The lump in my throat is growing and I feel so cold. The pounding in my head is getting louder and louder. I actually feel like I'm in pain and all I want to do is crawl under my duvet and make myself small and invisible.

I jump in my chair when my mobile suddenly beeps, alerting me that I've got a text message. I feel as if I'm coming out of a trance and realise where I am. It's obviously getting late, I can tell and I'm feeling very unnerved by the door I just opened. I let him in. Dr McGrath smiles over at me reassuringly, looking genuinely pleased with me. He nods and stands up, walking over to his desk shuffling his papers in search of something. He picks up his diary and turns back to face me.

"Well done Izobel. Very well done. We need to put our next tutor meeting in to go through your progress and any other issues you may have."

He gives me such a kind look I can actually feel how proud he is of me opening up, letting go. We settle on a date and time in two weeks and I immediately know what he's doing. He's letting me open the door to my past in the safety of his presence without judgement under the pretence umbrella of coursework struggles and tutoring. Maybe by the end he can take the pieces and build them up to become something tangible that I can set alight, letting it disintegrate so I can place the ashes in a jar and bury them somewhere. So I can go and reflect, but also leave it all behind. I've honestly forgotten how it feels to be truly alive, but I'm not sure our past ever really dies. I want nothing more. It sounds crazy I know, but I'm still struggling, I know this. Every day I pray no one else who means something to me will let go, let go of me, because I'll fall apart and I'm not sure anyone will be able to put me together again. I pack up my stuff and say an awkward goodbye to Dr McGrath who looks at me with a caring smile and a look of something like pride or admiration. What a clever man he is. I knew though, as soon as I met him, I knew.

It's dark outside, I look at my watch and realise that two hours has flown by. Aiden isn't outside so I check my phone and see a text from him saying he's been held up and is sorry he couldn't come get me. I text him back saying it's all good. I'm actually exhausted but strangely enough I feel like celebrating. Celebrating what, I'm not quite sure, but I feel as if now the door has been opened to let out my thoughts, fresh air has replaced them. It eradicated the stuffiness and I can take a breath of clean air. Never one to be afraid to walk into a pub alone, I decide stop at the local and walk in to get myself a pint.

I find a corner table in the darker end of the pub. It's not too busy yet for a Friday night. Just as I sit down I hear my phone and go hunting for it in my bag. Why is it that when you need something out of your bag it becomes bottomless? As I'm hunting down my mobile I hear her before I actually see her. I sit completely still, hoping she doesn't realise I'm in here.

It's Lina.

I refuse to look up. I don't want to see if Declan's with her. I finally find my phone and see I've got a missed call from Sofia. I listen to the voicemail but have a hard time hearing what she's saying, there's too much background noise wherever she is. It sounds like she's saying something about coming back next Friday, but I'm not sure, so I send her a text asking her to ring me again to explain. When I look up I can feel Lina's eyes on me, if looks could kill I'd be truly dead and buried in five seconds flat. She walks over full of some sort of intent and purpose, looking like she wants to throttle me. I'm pretty sure she's about to warn me off Declan.

"So, Izzy, yeah I know who you are," she says spitefully, my name sounding like a bad taste in her mouth as she leans over the table. I swear I can see everything underneath her top, that's how low-cut it is.

"I want you to leave Declan the hell alone, he's mine, always has been and for the last week you've been putting ideas into his head that makes him question that and has him feeling shit he shouldn't be, poor guy is confused." She looks me up and down, judging me with her eyes and I know she finds me lacking.

"We have a history that you have no place interfering in so get the fuck away from him you slapper."

With that she turns around and goes back to join her mates. I seriously wonder after that display how old she thinks we are and whether she still thinks we're in high school. I start humming the Rocky tune to myself and can't help laughing, what a stupid twat. I get back to checking my phone for any other missed calls and messages. I suddenly hear my name and see Aiden bouncing across the pub, this guy's got way too much energy, he's like the energizer bunny, well that's until he sees Lina at the bar. He quickly looks over at me with deep frown lines on his face.

"Hey Aiden, take that look off your face, madam over there's had her say, but it's like water off a ducks back okay, it's all good, promise," I say to him, trying to draw him back to me.

"Well Declan doesn't know what the hell he's doing, his head's all over the place mixed up in guilt and responsibility but Lina, she's a different story, you've got to watch out for her Izzy, she has venom coursing through her veins. She's a bloody snake at times."

With that he goes to get me a refill and himself a pint and settles in for the night next to me. We exchange more stories about ourselves. I skirt around my childhood as much as I can without giving too much away. I'm pretty sure I can trust Aiden but he doesn't need to be tainted by my memories. I know he realises that I'm giving him superficial stories, because he probes and searches. It's as if he tries to throw me a rope to pull me out once I bite, but I can't let the words outside again today without the panic and fear coming back. I'm stuck and the doors have closed again as of the minute I walked out of Dr McGrath's office. The walls are back up and yes there are chips in it, cracks even, but it's going to take a lot for a permanent rescue from the darkness. I know I need to be rescued but only I can do that. Ultimately I know this, but like my brother I need some helping hands. I just hope they'll be stronger than what mine where when he needed me most. I hope Dr McGrath is the one to do it.

I shake myself back to the moment and Aiden. It'll do no good thinking these thoughts because he'll see them written on my face.

"So…Aiden tell me more about how you grew up and your family," I ask him needing to hear and feel the love. Knowing that there are happy families out there is like crack to me. I want to soak up some of that love.

"Not much to say really Iz, you know most of it by now," he says smiling at me.

Yeah I guess he's right, I know he grew up in a home full of love. He clearly loves his parents and his younger brother. They never had much but what they undoubtedly had was love and respect. That much is clear. His Mum sounds like the ultimate definition of what a Mum should be, and his Dad, well, he's the polar opposite to mine yet surprisingly I feel no jealousy or resentment. Aiden is without doubt one of the most caring, level headed and intelligent men I know, he really does remind me of my brother in so many ways. He tells me how he was one of the lucky ones regarding his sexuality. His Mum knew before he did. When he finally realised and tried to speak to her about it she'd apparently hugged him and said she was glad he'd finally found himself and she's been there for *and* with him since that day. He has this reverent look on his face as he is telling me this and his eyes glaze over.

"Did you ever have anything bad happen to you because of it?" I ask him, dreading his answer.

"Yeah, there'll always be haters Izzy," he shrugs as he tells me of some of the nasty experiences he's had and I want to go on a one woman ninja crusade to avenge him against these ignorant shits for putting him through such hell. I know that doesn't solve anything but I still want to do it. We finish our drinks and start walking home when my phone rings, it's Sofia again.

"Sorry Aiden I've got to get this," I say as we walk into the house, he nods at me and goes to join the lads in the kitchen. "Hey Sofia," I answer. She sounds so far away, but then again apparently she is. She's in New York waiting to get a ticket to come back to London. Not only is she coming home early, she's in a country she shouldn't be in and she's all alone.

She thinks she may be able to get in next Friday but can't get a direct flight. Just before the connection breaks she manages to tell me that she's left Taylor and is coming home with nothing but her bag and no place to go. Dammit. I start walking upstairs to my room all worried and stare disbelievingly at my phone at her news, not looking where I'm going. I bump into Declan who's bounding down the stairs, I stumble but he catches me. As I sway backwards he draws me into his arms and sits down at the same time, which means I end up straddling him.

"Whoa Izzy, you okay sweetheart? You look like you have the world on your shoulders."

How can he sit and smile at me with that cheeky and addictive grin like the other day didn't happen, like we haven't been through the ringer since the day we met? I look at him in disbelief and am getting so angry I know I've got to get to my room before I literally explode. His mouth draws me though, I look at his lips and can't help wanting to lick his full pierced bottom lip, feel the hot and cold which makes me feel things I know, I shouldn't be feeling. I shift my eyes up to look at his. No better really, his eyes are mesmerising and right now they're looking at me with what can only be described as intense piercing want.

"Let me go Declan," I whisper to him, barely audible even to myself. This makes him hold on to me even tighter.

"I can't Izzy, I really can't," he sighs and rests his forehead against mine. I can feel his hot breath on my skin and I feel it all over my body making me very aware of my pounding heartbeat.

"You have to Declan, I can't do this, I don't have the fight in me to continue what we're doing. I mean, I don't even know what the hell we *are* doing." Even though I say that, I pray that he keeps holding on to me because I know that if he does I won't put up a fight, I lied, my heart is his, I know that. But he doesn't, instead he releases me and lifts me to my feet.

Just as he's about to walk off he puts his hand on my face and bends over, puts his lips to mine and whispers against them, "I'm so sorry Izzy."

As soon as I'm back in my room and close my door, I burst into tears. I'm angry at myself for getting into this situation with him. Just as thing's were looking up. Trying to start my life again, searching for a new beginning rescuing myself from the cluster-fuck that is my life, I put myself in a situation that only adds to the bloody pile of hurt. Fuck this. I'm not going to let him do this to me; I've come so far in just over a week, further than I thought I would. My thoughts wander to Connor. Sweet and funny Connor; who is, in reality, perfect for me really. I know he's quite a bit older than me. But maybe that'll work even better? Who knows? Yeah I don't need a man to help me forget or help me heal…I know this. But pathetic or not that's what I want right now. I need to feel wanted, loved, desired and protected. I need that little bit of help whilst I re-build myself from the inside out. Then I can stand on my own two feet. As long as I don't hurt anyone in the process, this is my plan. I get ready for bed and crawl under my duvet and roll myself into a protective ball. I'm so exhausted that I fall asleep immediately.

Chapter Ten

Five days pass in the blink of an eye as I get stuck into my studying. Declan and I dance around each other warily during those days, both of us polite and courteous, but both knowingly sneaking looks and somehow, making excuses to bump into or touching each other. Every time his fingers graze mine, I feel it everywhere and want more. But I know this'll never, should never, happen.

I'm sitting at the kitchen table with a pile of books trying to get my head round a new topic while having my breakfast. I'm shovelling Lucky Charms down my throat as quick as I can as they're Aiden's and he hates when anyone steals them. But they are just so good though, and being American import they cost a fucking fortune over here. So I can't really blame him.

"What the hell Izzy? Are you eating my charms?"

Shit, it's Aiden, I didn't hear him come in and now he's caught me.

"Ummm would you like me to eat your charms Aiden?" I wink at him, looking everywhere but his face. "By the way that was a stealth move, silent like a ninja." I do a quick judo chop. "You pesky ninja's get me every time."

"*Ha ha* very funny….gold dust Izzy," he growls, pointing at the charms in my bowl. "*Gold dust!*" He walks over to the cupboard and dramatically removes his cereal box, returning my judo chop as he takes the box back upstairs with him.

I know I should feel bad, but I don't. Instead I shovel the rest of the bowl down and get back to my studying.

I've forgotten all about my date with Connor until he phones to let me know what time he's picking me up. I feel so shitty about this, so guilty. He's got something planned for us and tells me he's picking me up at eight. I have to say, despite my feelings for Declan, I get that nervous anticipation and am actually looking forward to seeing Connor tonight. To treat myself I decide to go shopping for a new outfit. My rapidly depleting car savings bearing the brunt of it. I'm past caring though. I find the most gorgeous black dress in the autumn sale in the high street, as well as a pair of silver high heeled sandals that criss-cross half-way up my calves. The dress is quite tight but not uncomfortably so. It only has a thick strap over one shoulder, the other one bare, very Grecian. I love it and can't wait to get home to get ready. I wish Sofia was already here. She used to do my hair and make-up and we'd have a few glasses of wine before I went out on my dates. Her and Taylor got into the habit of staying in towards the end before they took off abroad. I can't help but wonder what's happened with them and their relationship. They've been together for six years so it had to be something bad, they've always been so tight. I think about all the things it could possibly be while I get ready for Connor. Singing along to *'Centrefold'* by The J. Geils Band, whilst drinking copious amounts of wine as I continue to get ready. I look at myself in the mirror and can't help but think Sofia would have done a better job. I've left my hair down but put a few small braids through one side. My make-up is smokey but subtle and I've covered myself in chunky silver jewellery. I pick up my purse and go downstairs to get a top up of wine and wait for Connor. While I'm filling up my glass I hear the doorbell, but as I move to go open the front door, I hear someone coming down the stairs to get to it before I do. Bollocks, it's Declan, this is not a situation I wanted to happen. I rush out into the hallway where both lads are staring at me with open mouths. I need to get out of here pretty damn quick to avoid an uncomfortable situation. Actually. Too late for that.

"Hey Connor, I'm ready to go," I smile at him nervous for more reasons than he's aware of. Connor stands there smiling at me, but it's not an entirely comfortable smile, his eyes are narrowed half on Declan.

Declan suddenly grabs my arm and looks over at Connor. "Sorry mate hang on a second," he says this as he turns to me, "Izzy can I have a word?" He pulls me into the kitchen and closes the door behind us. He pushes me up against the door putting a hand on either side of my face boxing me in before he leans his face down close to mine. "You can't go out with him Izzy, he's not right for you, this…thing right here, well it's not fucking right," he sneers more at himself than at me.

My blood begins to boil in my veins. "How do you know and frankly, why do you bloody care, huh… I'm single, Connor's single and he plays no sodding games Declan…none." I've lost it with him, shocking myself at what's coming out of my mouth and the spite with which it's said. "Oh and he's gorgeous so I think this one is a win-win situation for me really." Ha….I'm not quite sure what it is about Declan but he's starting to bring out the feisty in me, which has been supressed for so long. I give him a sarcastic smile, which doesn't last long as he looks at me completely crestfallen.

"Izzy baby, I can't watch you with him, it pisses me off and you're meant to be mine," he suddenly sounds fierce and any vulnerability that was there a second ago in his face has now completely gone.

"Too bad Declan, you could've had me but you chose Lina so this is over right here, right now," I retort.

"But I didn't Izzy, you don't understand…I need to explain…"

I manage to get away from under his arm and open the door before he says anything that'll make me want to stay. Connor's still standing in the hallway looking slightly pissed off with his hand on the door handle waiting for me. Waiting to escape this madness that's descended on us all.

"Everything okay Izzy?" he asks me, whilst looking in the direction of the kitchen, waiting for Declan to come after me I'm sure.

"Yeah of course it is Connor, let's get out of here shall we?" I literally push him through the door before Declan manages to completely ruin everything for me. Yet I can't help but feel a pang of sadness at his words and the look on his face in the kitchen.

Connor takes my hand as we walk together in silence down the road. My cold small hand dwarfed in his large warm one.

"So where are we going," I ask him trying to lighten the mood and change the subject.

"Do you and your housemate have something going on?" he asks, which is not at all what I was expecting.

I sigh and take a heavy breath. "No Connor, Declan and I are complicated, we met, we had a connection, one that didn't work. I don't know what else to tell you….that's all I've got for you."

"Am I wasting my time with you Izzy, I need to know because I feel a connection with you, but I'm not stupid, I can see something's happened and has been left unresolved back there."

I look up at him and I know this guy deserves the truth. He has a guarded look but at the same time, he looks concerned for me. How can this amazing man, who I barely know, treat me like I'm something important already? Does he give himself so freely and easily…does he trust his heart so much that the thought of it getting hurt doesn't cross his mind? I stop and turn to him, reaching up for his face with my hands.

"I want to give us a try Connor, but I would totally understand it if you want to stop here, we haven't really begun yet and I want to be honest with you from the start. This Declan thing, well I don't know what it is but he's very special to me and yes I have feelings for him. But I really like you and I'm attracted to you…very much so." I'm not sure if that made any sense to him, but saying it out loud, I realize that Declan came into my life at a time when I was at my most vulnerable and despite it being brief he made such an impression, had such an impact that when it didn't come to anything it left a void. I'm not entirely sure if Connor is the one to fill it, but I know I don't want to hurt him in the process of finding out.

"How about this Izzy, we just spend some time together, no pressure and take it from there, what do you say?" he smiles at me.

I smile back at him. "I'd say that I'm not sure I deserve you but yes I'd like that very much."

He leans down and gently places a kiss on my cheek, then he pulls away, keeping my hand in his and we continue our walk into town. He takes me to this tiny restaurant in the Crooked House; it's quite dark in here. There are no electric lights; it's lit up purely by candles. There are only ten tables, all scattered, making it feel very intimate. It's very romantic but homely at the same time. The shadows of small naked flames flickering, reflecting lights that play upon the faces of animated diners. As we eat Connor has me in stitches of laughter, he's got a great sense of humour, I have tears running down my cheeks and there's been snorting as he tells me one story after the other of random events that have happened to him over the years.

"So Connor, tell me, what's your biggest passion in life?" I ask him as I think this is one of the most telling questions you can ask someone to fully understand them.

"Football, no question. I've always loved the game and I've played it ever since I could stand upright on my own two feet," he laughs as he continues. "I was convinced I'd make it professionally but yeah, that didn't happen. So I became a coach instead; 'those who can't - teach'…isn't that what they say?" he winks at me and I laugh. "No, seriously, I love teaching kids the game and the discipline; getting them away from the telly and active again."

I beam at him for being so nonchalant about his brilliance. "I have so much respect for you Connor. You found something that makes you happy so you made it so. Those kids are pretty lucky to have someone like you. I bet you teach with passion and that's the best teacher you can possibly have," I say to him and he looks at me all embarrassed.

"Hey stop it or I won't get my head through the doorway when we're done here," he laughs reaching over gently stroking his knuckles across my cheek. "So Izzy, enough about me, tell me something about you that will shock me," he asks, as he tops up my wine.

So many things spring to mind but most of them would completely ruin the nice and relaxed mood of this date.

"Hmm well, I had three years of crazy at college. I can tell you that during one year my hair had every colour of the rainbow. Orange probably being the least appealing out of the lot of them," I laugh, as does he. "I will say though, that this particular shade of orange was not intentional and I had to cut it out in the end, it was pretty disgusting."

He reaches over to tuck a strand of my hair behind my ear and leaves his fingers on my jaw. "You have beautiful hair; it feels like silk, so soft." He tilts his head and gives me an intense look. Seriously this guy's got the perfect moves, I'm really enjoying myself and am so caught up in the mood and him that I can't help but rest my head into his hand.

Connor signals to the waitress to come over so he can settle the bill, he refuses to let me pay. Standing up he takes my hand pulling me up and guides me out of the restaurant, his hand on the small of my back. It's still quite mild so we go for a walk through the park before he takes me home. I lean into him and he guides us to a bench by the lake in the middle of the greenery. It's such a beautiful evening I can't help but feel that this is pretty damn close to perfect. Almost.

He sits down and puts me on his lap wrapping his arms around me, my back against his front. I lean my head back on his shoulder and we sit like this in silence for a long time.

I feel his warm breath on my neck followed by his lips. I close my eyes and revel in the warmth of Connor's embrace. If I don't think too much about it right now, I feel happy and content. His lips trail down my neck and across my bare shoulder. I'm not cold but the touch raises the small hairs on the back of my neck and I can feel the goose bumps following his trail of kisses. I moan involuntarily and try to turn so I can catch his lips. Just then my phone rings and I'm stunned to see it's Declan. I ignore his call and turn my phone on silent. I don't need to be distracted by him.

"Izzy…" Connor reluctantly starts to pull away from me. My hands are tied up in knots in his hair and I can't help but close the gap between us and lick his bottom lip.

"Stop Izzy," he groans. "Unless you're ready to take this back to yours, we have got to stop." He shakes his head at me so I grab his hand and pull him off the bench and we start walking back to my house. After all this is what I do best right? I think to myself cynically. Declan comes running out the front door as we walk up, he must've seen us coming.

"Izzy for fuck sake, I've been ringing you for the last half-hour, why aren't you answering your bloody phone?" He looks at me strangely.

"Because I'm on a date Declan, and I was having a pretty fucking perfect time until five seconds ago," I yell back at him. Connor squeezes my hand to calm me down. I'm fuming, I can actually feel my cheeks burning in embarrassment and I'm clenching my free hand into a fist at my side.

Declan's face suddenly gets all soft and concerned and he takes my clenched hand, straightens my fingers out and starts stroking my palm with his thumb.

"Izzy sweetheart, I'm so sorry, it's your Mum, she's been taken to the hospital. They wouldn't tell me any details because I'm not family," he says with a mix of pity and concern written all over his face. I feel as if all the oxygen leaves my body and I can't breathe.

"Izzy, let me take you to the hospital," Connor says as he pulls me into his arms away from Declan.

Declan pulls me right back out again like I'm some kind of incapable soft toy. "Nah man you've been drinking…I'll take her."

I can literally feel the tension, which snaps me out of my shocked trance. "Connor it's okay, I'll go with Declan, he's right, we've both been drinking. I'll ring you in the morning, okay. Thank you for a lovely evening," I say as I give him a quick kiss on the cheek and make to leave. Connor pulls me back and fiercely hugs me. I look into his eyes and burst into tears.

"He's here with the car Izzy, promise me you'll ring me, no matter what time it is okay, and if you need me to come to you I will, straight away, I promise." He tucks a lock of my hair behind my ear and smiles at me sadly. I nod at him afraid to speak past the lump in my throat and start walking over to where Declan is parked and get into his car.

"What did they say Declan?" I whisper as the car pulls away from the curb. I look over at his profile, all serious and grim with the flashing streaks of street lamps in the dark night as we shoot past them, bouncing off his face. He doesn't look back at me but moves his hand to rest on my thigh, gently squeezing it to reassure me.

"They rang and asked for you. Apparently, your Mum had a piece of paper in her back pocket that had 'Izobel's new number' written down on it. They said she was in an accident but they wouldn't say how it happened or how bad she is. I'm so sorry Izzy."

The patch of thigh that has his hand resting on it feels like it's on fire, whereas the rest of me feels, ice cold. I look out the window at the passing houses, some with their lights on and I'm guessing that in all of those homes, families are getting ready for bed or are already sleeping, curled around each other. As we get closer to the hospital I feel my pulse quicken with each mile and a cold sweat begins to break out all down my back. A familiar feeling of fear and panic sets in as I wonder what I'll find when we get there.

"Izzy, we're here sweetheart," Declan breaks into my thoughts. He's parked up in the multi storey car park which surprisingly is almost empty. What follows is like a dream sequence, I watch him get out of the car, I feel the cold where his hand left my thigh, he walks over to the ticket machine; sticks some coins in, gets his ticket and returns to me. I count; it took him twenty seconds, which is how long I've held my breath for.

"Izzy baby, come with me." I feel his hand grasping mine and look up at him. He's crouched at my side. "Come on sweetheart." He looks at me with such concern I let him pull me out the car. He takes my hand and we walk in to find the hospital reception. I look down at our hands. Quite shocked at how small mine looks in his, my eyes follow a path up his arm, from the manly veined and sinewy muscles, up to the beginning of his tattoo just visible under the edge of his shirt sleeve. I end up looking at his face, his strong handsome face and notice that he mustn't have shaved today, he has the signs of dark shadows along his jawline. I reach up with my other hand to feel whether they're soft or rough, but Declan's so bloody tall I can barely reach him. He looks down at me with a half-smile that makes me feel even weaker at the knees than I already do.

"Yeah...I couldn't be arsed to shave today."

"I think I like it," I say back to him with a small smile.

His eyes look at my mouth as I say it. Shit, I must stop this, my thoughts go back to Mum, the reason I'm here. We walk through the doors and suddenly the smell hits me like a freight train. The smell of hospital and death. I'm right back to eighteen months ago. The day my brother died. The smell is exactly the same, different hospital, identical smell. I have no idea what it is that makes this smell. I know it stays on your clothes and on your skin though. The stale and harsh air stays in your body until you've replaced it with enough clean breaths later. We walk up to the front desk, but I've lost my voice, I can't get to it, it refuses to come, the memories of that night assaulting me, brought on by the smell. I can't help but think the worst and my anxiety is taking over with black spots seeping into my vision. I look up at Declan pleading with my eyes for him to find my Mum. I vaguely hear him asking all the right questions and feel him pulling me in the direction of the A&E department.

"Izzy, I have no idea what we're going to find but they said she's still in A&E, they might not let me come into her cubicle with you." He's pulling me along following the signs in the long hallways.

"Don't leave me Declan…please don't leave me," I whisper, my voice barely audible, the noise in A&E is deafening as we approach the receptionist in her round glass office in the middle of the madness. As soon as she looks up at me I find my voice again from deep down. I can do this, I repeat over and over again in my head as I attempt to clear my throat of the growing lump of emotion.

"My name is Izobel…Izobel Jerome, my Mum Elizabeth Jerome is here as a patient somewhere. I don't know what's happened but my…umm…" I hesitate, what is he? "….house mate Declan here received a phone call earlier tonight." I'm suddenly waffling and when I look up at Declan, I see he's looking at me like he's desperate to say something. He looks angry and his grip on my hand is slowly crushing my fingers.

"Please can you go sit down in the family waiting room through the door on your left, I'll buzz you in and let the duty nurse know that you're here," she replies in a bored monotone voice.

I always did wonder where they find the receptionists in places like this. Were they always devoid of emotions or did the sickness and irate concerned family members desensitise them over time? As Declan and I go through the door we enter a huge room and find two available seats. I look around the sterile and drab room. It looks like a before picture in a house restoration programme, straight out of the eighties' with dirty pink walls, pastel paintings of flowers and non-descript brown wood furniture. There are water marks staining the walls in the corners where they meet the ceiling. A TV show is blasting in one corner and I look to see if I recognize it and find that I do. It's that weekly show that makes fun of people hurting themselves and doing stupid stuff. I'm guessing this is supposed to make family and friends feel better for a while, watching to forget the reason that brought them to this room in the first place. The TV rests on a tall carrier with wheels. A family has wheeled it over so they can watch it, their two young children giggling, captivated, whilst their parents send each other worried looks. There's a water station that slowly drips, continuously forming a chalky stain that runs down the side making it look dirty and unappetising. The door suddenly opens and everyone's attention follows. A nurse comes in with a clipboard, she looks hassled and tired. I wonder where she is in her shift.

"Izobel Jerome," she calls searching the room of anxious faces, looking for recognition.

"Yes Nurse," I reply, standing up and walking over to her apprehensively, my feet dragging wanting to prolong this if it's bad news.

"If you could please follow me," she says as she walks down the hallway, her rubber clogs squeaking with each step. She takes us to a cubicle, but doesn't open the cloth divider; instead she turns to me and Declan. I brace myself as Declan draws me into his arms.

"So Izobel, your mother has several contusions on the right hand side of her face, there is also some traumatic injury to the soft tissue on her left side, as well as ecchymosis in her mouth."

"Wha....what does that mean, in her mouth? I don't understand what that is?" I shakily interrupt her with every ounce of the fear I'm feeling marking my words.

"Well, in the most generic sense it means that she has haemorrhaging in her mouth from ruptured blood vessels," the nurse explains understanding my fear. "Now, these injuries are quite severe so I have to warn you, the police will be showing up shortly to take a statement from your mother, and most likely you too." She looks at me sympathetically and I feel my legs turn into jelly. Just as I think I might collapse I feel Declan's arms tightening around me.

"I've got you," Declan whispers in my ear. "Just breathe Iz, I'm here and I'm not leaving you."

The nurse slowly pulls the curtain back and I see Mum. I gasp at the state of her bruised face. She looks so tiny and fragile in that big bed. She looks like me. But an old beaten up version of me. A version of me from a few years ago, though this time he must've really lost it. This time I doubt even Mum can explain the bruises away with accident tales.

"She's sleeping at the moment. We've ruled out the possibility of damage to the brain and related tissues. As far as the tests showed there's no traumatic brain injury. However, we'll be keeping her in for observation for the next twenty-four hours and she'll be moved as soon as we have a bed ready upstairs."

"Can I sit with her until you do?" I ask the nurse. Edging closer to the bed, I can see Mum's foot peeking out from the bed sheet she has covering her. She's wearing her white trainer socks. For some reason they make her look even more fragile than she already does; makes her look innocent and young.

"Yes, you can stay with her, as you'll need to answer a few questions soon." As the nurse walks past me to leave, she squeezes my arm gently. I stand in silence just trying to get my head around what's before me.

"You don't have to stay with me Declan," I whisper, so I don't wake up Mum.

"I told you I wouldn't leave you Izzy, I'm staying as long as you want me to." His tone is firm, yet he doesn't move any closer. He's trying to keep a respectful distance. I move a chair over next to the bed and sit down looking for Mum's hand under the cover. When I find it, I gently put it in mine. Mum's hands have always been soft as silk. It's one of the things I've always admired. She has the softest youthful looking skin without a single blemish or dis-colouration. Well normally.

"Mum, it's Izobel, I'm here, you're not alone, and you're safe now," I whisper to her, as I feel the tears coming. I've always been the master of silent crying, the wet tracks being the only evidence. I was taught from an early age that crying and excessive display of feelings could have dire consequences. Zack and I quickly learnt the importance of hurting in silence.

"Izzy sweetheart, the police are going to be here soon. Do you have any idea who could have done this to your Mum?" Declan sounds so pissed off and out of the corner of my eye I can see his hands clenching at his sides as if he himself wants to hit something or someone.

"Oh Declan, it's such a long story, one I can't tell you right now, maybe someday…maybe never," I say as I nervously un-tuck the hair from behind my ears trying to hide my face, the guilt and the shame clearly showing. I have no idea what to say to the police when they get here.

"Ms. Jerome?" I nearly jump out of my seat when I hear and see two police officers enter Mum's cubicle. They introduce themselves as PC Moore and PC Stevens.

"Yes, yes that's me…can you please tell me what happened to Mum and how she came to be here…please?" I look at the two officers who have made themselves comfortable, one taking out a notebook and pen noting things down already.

"Well we were hoping you could shed some light on your Mum's situation. We got a call from a neighbour, a Mrs Gardner who reported a disturbance at your Mum's address. When an officer turned up, the front door was locked, so he walked round the back to check through the windows and saw your Mum lying on the floor in the living room. An ambulance was called and the rest I've been informed you're aware of." He stops talking and looks at me waiting for me to say something. What...well I'm not sure I can or even want to.

Mum stirs in her sleep and I stroke her hand, as I shudder. I feel so uncomfortable and I can feel Declan next to me, his hand resting on my chair as if he's ready to grab on to me any second now. Waiting for me to fall or go crazy...something.

The officer looks at me. He has such a kind face, he looks as if he's in his mid-thirties, short cropped black hair with scattered grey in it. His partner is texting something on her phone; she hasn't looked at me once. She seems very young, probably not far from my age I reckon. As if she feels me looking, her head snaps up, but looking at Declan not me. I shake my head at the obviousness of her actions as she starts flirting with him through her movements rather than words.

"Declan would you mind getting me a coffee?" I ask him. I need him out of here in case we get on to the subject of my Dad and no way do I want Declan in here for that. I still don't want anyone knowing the other me, my other life. My secrets and shame. The female police officer probably thinks I feel threatened by the way she suddenly blushes and starts to look really busy on her phone again.

"Sure thing Izzy, anyone else want a coffee?" Declan asks, as he stands up. The officers both mumble no thanks and I look and wait as Declan leaves.

"Now Izobel, we haven't been able to contact your Dad, we contacted his PA but the details were hazy as to his whereabouts.

She mentioned a business trip to the States?" He looks into his notes, his forehead getting that tense pattern of wanting to broach something in the best possible way.

Before anyone gets a chance to say anything else Mum wakes up. Her croaky voice calling for me. "Izobel darling…" I leap out of my chair and throw myself on her forgetting her bruises and her hurt until I hear her wince.

"Oh Mum…I'm sorry, I am so so sorry." I burst out crying yet again.

"It's okay Izobel, I'm okay," she whispers, stroking my hair like only a mother knows how to do to calm down her distraught child.

"Mrs Jerome, I'm PC Moore," the kind looking officer says. "Do you remember what happened to you, how you came to be in this condition?"

Mum shakes her head as much as she's able to with the pain. "Not really no, I was cleaning the floors and I must have slipped in the water, hit my head on the sideboard and fallen awkwardly." She's such an accomplished liar when it comes to Dad and the pain he inflicts on us; on her. I can't look at the officers; instead I focus on picking at the loose thread in Mum's blanket, repeating in my head the wish that she'll put an end to this once and for all. A wish I have internally repeated as far back in my childhood as I can remember. But it's a double edged sword, because at the same time I can't imagine the struggle and the heart ache of our life coming out in the open, if she does, which inevitably will happen.

PC Moore looks sceptical, he doesn't believe her, it's written all over his face. He looks over at me and I quickly look down at Mum's hand which is now firmly gripping mine, letting me know how she wants this to play out with just a squeeze.

"Well…." he sighs with a frazzled look on his face as if he sees this every day, an aftermath of domestic violence with a victim unwilling to tell the truth. "We'll have to leave it at that then Mrs. Jerome, but, I *will* leave you with some contact information and some leaflets."

"Thank you officer," Mum replies in a tired voice. "But that won't be necessary."

"Still…" he insists. "Do take care Mrs Jerome and remember that suffering in silence is an unnecessary exercise in this day and age." They make to leave just as Declan returns with my coffee. Either he went to grind the beans himself or he's been hovering on the other side of the curtain not wanting to come in. I'm not sure I want him in here at all now. I cross to where he stands looking completely unsure of himself and pull him back out into the hallway.

"So umm…Declan, I need to stay with Mum and sort a few things out. Thanks for taking me here and for staying…I'm so grateful." Declan looks at me with his dark eyes and I can see the conflicting emotions in them.

"You know what happened to her don't you Iz?" He runs his large warm hand down the side of my face.

"Just go Declan, please…I'll see you at home and we'll talk then," I say this knowing it's a barefaced lie. No way am I telling him anything. Not yet anyway.

"Okay Izzy, but please ring me when you need picking up, promise," he says, as he puts his arms around me.

I can't help myself so I cling to him, burying my face in his chest, holding on, wishing this was not happening, not again. My insides are shaking and all I want is to stay in the safety of his arms. Before he lets me go, he kisses the top of my head. Such a simple gesture, but I feel it in my heart as he lets me go. I watch him walk down the corridor with slow laboured steps and out through the sliding door. Why do I feel like my heart is breaking yet again? I feel overwhelmed. Right now all I want is to run out of here, away from everything and everyone I know. The pressure is too intense. My brain feels as if it's growing beyond the confines of the bones and skin surrounding it. I walk back into the cubicle to see Mum. She's still awake staring up at the ceiling. I look up to see what she is looking at, what she could possibly be seeing. What is it with hospital ceilings? I remember back to the times I've been where Mum is now, lying in a hospital bed when I was younger, every time the ceilings have fascinated me, trying to make shapes out of the brown and yellowed water stains. Making something ugly into something bearable, something beautiful. Something recognizable. When I was young, I saw animals, now I see them for what they are; ugly water stains.

I feel my Mum tugging my hand; it comes as such a surprise I tumble onto the side of her bed.

She's always been strong. Very strong in fact. If only she'd used this strength when she needed it the most over the years.

"Izobel, I really did fall honey, all this, this is mostly not him." Her eyes are clear and strong piercing into mine wanting me to believe every word.

I sigh in defeat and look at her face, clear green eyes in a beautiful face marked by bruises. "I don't believe you Mum, how many times have we used that excuse, it's getting old."

"No Izobel, he didn't mean this, for me to fall. He lashed out, but too hard, I slipped in the water on the floor...honestly I did. I must have passed out when I hit the floor." Her voice is so strong and convincing I understand why people who don't know better, would fall for it every time.

"Mum however you dress this up, he's the cause, what did you do this time? Actually let me guess, you were cleaning and hadn't finished by the time he got home. Is that it? Is that what warranted this?" I gesture at her damaged body in the hospital bed. She cringes before my eyes and if possible shrinks even more, looking child-like in this huge sterile white bed. "Where is he Mum? Where's he gone and when will he be back? Does he even know?" One question after the other rushes through my mouth on a single breath.

"He has a business trip to New York, it was a last minute meeting darling, I think he said he'd be back in a week as there is a conference scheduled at the same time."

I want to cry in frustration but she doesn't deserve that so I pick up the coffee Declan brought me and gulp it down, burning my throat raw as I swallow. *Declan.* My heart hurts. I feel like a traitor, like some evil person, here's Mum suffering and I want to cuddle into a ball in Declan's arms. I want to feel protected. But I can't, I can't do that, I need to protect Mum. I close my eyes and take a deep breath, "What do you want me to do?"

She finally looks at me and it's a completely broken look. She takes my hand and squeezes it ever so gently. I feel the tears again, she is so gentle, so small and sweet. She's the classic victim.

"Nothing Izobel, nothing but keep re-building your life, that's what I want the most. I want you to keep doing what you need to; become your own person again." She looks to the corridor where a child is being rushed past on a stretcher and I feel the tremor in her hand. I forgot to pull the curtain across. The scene before us is so familiar my heart aches and I know hers hurts too.

"I want you to let go of the past Izobel, let go of the bad and only remember the good." She blinks away tears and looks back at me with a trademark look of strength in her eyes that always comes just after an incident but will soon be forgotten. I realised this as well at an early age. "Once they release me I'm going back home and I'll sit down with Dad and we'll see how it goes."

I know she will, but I also know it'll make no difference; the day she leaves will never come. He'll leave first, but he always comes back. Very much like a vicious circle. Like a record player with its needle stuck in the same groove repeating over and over.

"Now Izobel, I'm ever so tired, I need to sleep. Please lovely girl; go back to your place and that handsome fellow of yours and I'll ring you when I get back home. We'll have a chat then, yes?"

"Mum there's no way you're taking yourself home in this state, I'll find out when they're releasing you and I'll come back and get us a taxi home," I say defiantly.

She suddenly looks ever so cross and that tiny independent streak that Dad has tried so many times to quash fires up in her eyes.

"No sweetheart, I'm the parent, not you. I'll do well to remember this, I've already let one child down, but I'm done, finished, I refuse to let you suffer anymore."

I can't talk to her when she's in this state, I've tried many times before, and she's as stubborn as me so I know it's a lost cause.

"Okay Mum," I sigh, rubbing my face tiredly with shaking hands. "But promise me you'll ring me when you get home….please." I lean over her trying my best not to hurt her anymore and give her a hug, kissing the one patch on her forehead that's not marked by purple bruising. "Bye Mum," I whisper with a huge lump growing in my throat.

"Bye Izobel darling, please look after yourself, make *your* recovery the priority…not mine." She lets me go but as she turns her head I see the tears escape her eyes. I run out of the hospital as fast as I can and continue till I'm outside where I can breathe fresh air again.

I collapse in a heap against the wall and hang my head between my knees. It's freezing out here and I'm shaking from the cold and the emotions raging through me. The craziness of A&E is all around me; manic shouts, screams and blaring sirens. I practice my breathing to calm myself as I remember the night my brother and I were brought in nearly two years ago. I was conscious; he wasn't. I flinch as I feel a warm hand on my arm and look up.

"Come on Iz, let me take you home."

"Declan…" I gasp, shocked to see him. "You're still here?"

"Do you honestly think I'd leave you here sweetheart after everything you've been through, what kind of man would that make me?" He pulls me up into his arms and walks us to his car. I laugh when I see how it's parked in the drop-off bay all haphazardly.

"Nice parking Declan, you're lucky not to get a ticket."

"Yeah well I didn't want to miss you leaving," he says as he pulls me into his side, rubbing his hands up and down my arm to warm me up.

"What time is it?" I ask him as I slide myself into his car.

"Just gone two am," he says as he starts the car to drive us home, turning the heating up high. I'm suddenly struggling to keep my eyes open and as we leave the hospital grounds I feel myself falling asleep. It's as if I'm floating, being swept away, scared of falling I hang on to something, I can't seem to speak but I get a frightened moan out. I feel some hard arms tighten around me and I feel safe again.

"Shhh baby we're home, you're safe," Declan's reassuring and comforting voice calms me.

I open my eyes and realise he's carrying me up the stairs into my room. He sets me down and starts to undress me. For reasons I can't even begin to explain, I let him. He glides his hands up my arms raising them like I'm a child pulling off my dress in one swift movement. I'm not even embarrassed about standing in front of him in nothing but my strapless bra and knickers. Everything seems like slow motion as Declan gives me that amazing smile as he lowers my arms.

Seriously when did I lose my ability to function? I close my eyes as I feel his fingertips trail slowly down my arms and I feel his hot breath by my ear. "Show me those perfect blues, open your eyes Izzy."

I take a deep breath and slowly open them, looking up into his warm dark eyes. I hear his sharp intake of breath as his hands once more glide up my arms, one continuing into my hair, one framing the side of my face. "Beautiful, my beautiful Izzy. Do you realise that you have my heart?" he asks, all the while his intense eyes haven't left mine. I stop breathing as I search his eyes for the truth of what he's just said. Declan is confusion personified.

He bends his head down and lightly moves his lips across mine, such a faint touch it almost feels as if I imagined it.

"Declan…" I whisper, he freezes and I suddenly stumble and feel cold as he jumps back running a hand furiously through his hair whilst pacing with a frustrated look on his face.

"Climb into bed Iz," his voice demanding and cold all of a sudden.

"Huh?" My mouth drops in confusion.

"I don't like having to repeat myself, get into bed sweetheart," he says, gently moving me towards the bed. I stumble in and quickly get under the covers pulling my duvet all the way up to my chin. Feeling rejected yet also relieved I watch stupefied as Declan removes his t-shirt in one swift move, seriously this guy has the most incredible body, so defined and strong, the kind of body Sofia and I used to drool over when we used to stalk hot guys on the internet. My mind wanders. His muscles flex when he removes his jeans to leave him only in his black fitted boxers, his tattoos ripple and I feel it between my legs, a slow burning need and want. *Seriously* not fair.

"Don't look at me like that Izzy, this is torture enough for me," he moans, moving closer to the bed.

"This?" I ask him as I honestly can't think what he means.

He sighs and climbs in beside me. "Yes *this*....lying beside you, knowing what we briefly had Iz, what we could have, knowing I can't do a bloody thing about how I feel. Knowing I fucked up and it's too damn late," he yells in frustration.

I turn onto my side to face him, looking up at his angry face. Declan's lying on his back with his hands folded behind his head. I secretly wish he was underneath the duvet with me. He looks angry and kind of lost. Staring up at the ceiling his hair a dark mess. I scoot over a bit and rest my head on his naked chest. I can't help nuzzling into his dark patch of chest hair with my nose smelling him, he's *that* addictive.

"Did you just sniff me Iz?" he chuckles and looks down at me, my head bouncing off his hard chest.

"Mmmm..." Great I have lost the ability to speak and I can feel my face heat up so I snuggle closer and put my arm over his middle and bury myself in all that is Declan.

"Go to sleep Izzy girl, I'll stay with you, you haven't got to worry okay," he sighs, wrapping me up in his arms.

"Okay Declan," I whisper, not because I'm worried but because I'm so tired and confused.

Declan

She really makes my heart stop. I'd give anything for more than just these moments with her, but I've got no one to blame other than my stupid self. This separation isn't getting any easier, if anything it's getting more and more fucking difficult to stay away from her and pretend like I don't care. She's found a way in and there's no bloody way she's ever leaving, I know that.

Looking at her sleeping, making those fucking cute noises when she sleeps is enough to make me want to crush her in my arms and never let go.

Fuck!!!

When did I turn into a sodding woman…all feelings and shit. I swear I'm going to beat the crap out of that wanker Connor if he touches her again. Well, I want to but I haven't got the right. I lost that when I stepped back and let someone else take her from underneath my nose. I had to though, she deserves more than I can ever give her, someone better than me…I'll screw up, it's what I do best.

I look down at her clinging on to me like she's scared to let go. Izzy, I confess it to myself 'cause I'll sure as fuck never tell her, I'm falling in love with you.

Chapter Eleven

I wake up to the sound of my phone persistently ringing. My head hurts and my chest feels heavy. I try to remember why I feel like this and as the fog slowly lifts. I flinch and open my eyes. Declan's gone. I can't help but feel relieved, but also kind of sad. My phone's still ringing so I reach over to pick it up and see who it is. Bloody hell its two o'clock in the afternoon. How the hell did that happen? The number comes up as unlisted and straight away I feel my stomach drop, I pick it up thinking it's the hospital.

"Izobel, I'm ringing to see how your Mother's doing, I've been trying to ring the house and no one's picking up the phone." Holy shit. It's my Dad. His authorative and cold voice immediately gets my back up and the feeling of pins and needles spreads across my body making me feel numb.

"She's in hospital Dad," I reply suddenly feeling anger seeping into my blood as I think of how Mum looked in that bed. Gathering every bit of that anger, I try to stand up to him albeit over the phone. Yeah I'm not that brave yet. "You should've probably guessed this though knowing what happened. Why would you leave her, really Dad, how could you?" I almost shout this as my voice fails me and I start sobbing. The realization hits me all at once that he actually left her there on the floor…on her own. Helpless.

"Why is she in hospital? She was fine when I left her yesterday, what's wrong with her?"

Is he for fucking real? I can't believe he thinks he can play this game with me. Granted, Zack and I never saw him lay a finger on her but we saw the bruises she tried to hide; her cringes and her flinching. Sometimes he didn't even need to raise his voice; we still knew it happened.

"Dad, you went too far, she hit her head as she fell, she was unconscious," my voice sounds strong and accusing yet I feel anything but right now.

"Is she okay?" he asks after a telling silence in which I think he actually realises.

"She will be, but Dad it's got to stop." There I said it, but then I feel braver on the phone and out of the house.

"Izobel, I will not have you speak to me in this manner young lady. You may be an adult now but you're still my daughter, I suggest you think about your tone and show some respect," he barks down the phone, giving me chills. I begin to shake, this is hopeless. Dad stole my life a long time ago and yes I'm slowly taking it back, but it's not easy to retrieve something that hasn't been yours for so long you've almost forgotten what it was like.

"Yes Dad," I say giving up. I'm too tired to put up a fight right now. I need time to think, to plan and to act. It needs to be perfect as I know I'll only have one chance to get Mum out and away from him. Aggravating him now and standing up to him over the phone will achieve nothing.

"Right then Izobel, I shall be away for another week. I expect an update on this situation. Give your Mother my love and wish her a speedy recovery. Goodbye." God, this man is cold…so cold, I actually shiver as he hangs up on me. I lay here just staring up at the ceiling as my phone rings, again. I look at the display thinking I'll leave it if it's unlisted. It's not. I smile as I pick it up.

"Hi Connor."

"Izzy, am I glad to hear your voice. I've been so worried about you, how's your Mum, what happened?" He fires one question after the other at me, his voice full of worry.

"She had a nasty fall, but she's okay, thank you for caring Connor."

"Can I come over later to see you? I want to check for myself that you're okay." I can hear the hesitation in his voice and can't help but wonder what's brought that on.

"Yeah I'd like that, come on over after you've finished work, just send me a text when you're on your way."

We say our goodbye's and I decide to get up. I can still smell hospital on myself so I'm itching to take a shower. I have a quick sniff of my bedding and sure enough, even on there I can smell the tell-tale signs of where I was last night.

After my shower I put on my joggers and a tank top. I don't bother with make-up or drying my hair, I just braid it loosely. I strip my bed and go downstairs to make myself a much needed coffee and put the washing machine on. The house is eerily quiet; all the guys must be at their lectures or work. I should be in a lecture right now, but I can't pretend that I care, seems insignificant to me at this moment in time. There's a note resting on the side of the coffee machine, which is happily brewing away already. I inhale the addictive smell and close my eyes. Pure heaven.

The note's from Declan. He's apparently rung my tutor and explained what happened yesterday. Dr McGrath got him to pass a message on to me saying I had the rest of the week off and not to come back in until Monday. This is on the order that I go and see him when I've finished my lectures in the afternoon. Great. He knows and wants me to talk about it. I shake my head as I start pouring the fresh coffee into my favourite Winnie the Pooh mug. Oh the lads still ridicule me for this mug, but I don't care. Mum bought it for me many years ago and it reminds me of a better time. A quieter time. A time before the shit really hit the fan and Zack left us for good. I take my coffee upstairs and go sit in the chair by the window.

It's definitely turning into autumn now, the leaves on the trees have that beautiful orange glow and I feel like getting my camera out or even my art supplies. I decide that seeing as though I have a few days of nothing planned, I might go to the park and take some photos. I get my sketch book out from the box it's been in since moving. This is the longest I've ever gone without it in my hand. I open it to the first page and see Zack. I run my fingers across his pencil drawn face with a smile. His gorgeous face in profile, laughing. He was always laughing at something, more often than not he was laughing at me. But lovingly. Despite me being older he always said he should have been born years ahead of me. He said I had the silly streak and not only did I make him laugh, as soon as he became a teenager he felt protective of me. His height being part of that reason I'm sure. I find a blank page, and with no specific thought in mind I start to idly sketch. A heavy knock on the front door scares the shit out of me and I jump out the chair, my sketch pad falling to the floor face down. As I go downstairs I realise it's nearly five o'clock which means it's probably Connor as he works school hours, lucky sod. I realize too late what I must look like, a true slob. Bollocks, oh well too late, he should have remembered to text me like I asked him to.

I open the door and when I see his handsome smiling face I surprisingly throw myself into his arms. Lucky for me he's huge and strong, so he catches me without falling backwards down the steps.

"Hey Izzy," he laughs at me. "I missed you, are you okay?"

I nod and pull him by the hand inside the house without speaking. Once the door's closed he folds me back into his arms. I have no idea how long we stand here when he finally draws back and looks down into my face. "You sure you're okay? Because you don't look it to me."

"No, I really am, well as much as what's normal," I add stupidly. I suddenly decide that Connor's not the person to confide my life in. I don't want to inflict my story on him. He's too caring and happy. He doesn't need my crap.

"Hey, do you fancy going out for a drink and something to eat? I'm starving; I haven't had anything since our meal out last night, which feels like weeks ago." I hope he says yes and that my eager smile convinces him that I'm okay.

He smiles at me. "Yeah I could eat." He leans down and gives me a kiss on one cheek then on the other. I stand on my toes so I can wrap my arms around his neck. This man is amazing and he makes me feel like there is nothing else to worry about. He pulls away reluctantly.

"If we don't go and get you something to eat now I won't take responsibility for how long you'll go without food," he says with a cheeky smile. My stomach immediately protests and I embarrassingly blush and look down at my feet. Good timing though, as something feels not quite right here. Connor starts laughing. "Come on Izzy, let's go get you some food."

"Hang on let me just go get my bag and get ready," I say, as I run upstairs and quickly change into my favourite pair of jeans. I put on my fitted hoodie and pull on my boots. I quickly put a bit of black eyeliner and mascara on. I never leave the house without it. Connor is patiently waiting by the front door looking at something on his mobile. He looks so relaxed and gorgeous in his dark jeans and light blue button up shirt. The blue looks amazing with his olive toned skin and his dark brown hair. It's not tucked in but I reckon it must be fitted because I can see his defined build through it; it's that snug on him. He looks up at me as I come down the stairs.

"Right what do you fancy?" he asks me opening the door.

"You," I badly joke back, but it earns me a head shake and a laugh from him. He looks kind of sad too which makes me wonder what he's thinking.

"Right, well I'll decide then shall I?"

"Sure, as long as it's hot and stodgy I don't care." My stomach voices its approval at that thought.

Connor takes my hand and we walk through the park into town. He stops outside Pizza Express. "Stodgy enough for you?"

I smile satisfied with his choice. "Yeah, this is perfect."

I literally devour a huge red onion, spinach and goats' cheese pizza in record time and wash it down with a Peroni. Connor looks at me amused as he eats much more restrained and leisurely. Total boy-girl role reversal.

"Bloody hell, I was starving," I say as I lick my lips in utter food satisfaction rubbing my food baby belly.

"Yeah I can kind of tell," he laughs back at me.

We pay up and I realize I've put my camera in my bag. The early evening light is beautiful so I'm itching to bring it out.

"Fancy coming to the park with me, I want to go take some photos?" I ask Connor and realise I'm already half dragging him there by his hand.

"Sure Izzy, I didn't realise you enjoyed photography."

"It's more of a hobby really. I'm not particularly great at it, but I just love it so much."

As we walk around the park Connor sticks with me in the background, a comfortable silence surrounding us. I get so lost in what I'm doing I don't realise when he's no longer next to me. I stop what I'm doing and look around for him. I find him sitting under a weeping willow with his elbows resting on his knees, head in hands looking up at the sky. I quickly snap a load of photos of him from different angles, before he realises what I'm doing. When I've finished I walk over and sit down next to him. We sit in silence for a while when he suddenly looks over at me.

"Izzy...I have something I need to tell you," he says, his voice taking on a deep and serious tone.

My stomach drops when I see his worried and torn expression as he rubs his head with his hand. He takes my hand in his and starts rubbing my palm with his thumb, it kind of tickles but I'm scared to break the moment, of what he's going to say next.

"What is it Connor?" I whisper apprehensively.

"I really like you Izzy, but I should really never have started anything....this situation is entirely my fault," he sighs and pulls me into his arms, kissing the top of my head. l freeze completely in his arms; I knew something felt off today.

"I know you like me too Izzy, but I just don't think you like me enough. I saw it in your face last night and in Declan's, you two have a bond, a bond that runs deeper than you think and a bond that I don't think I could ever have with you."

I sit up abruptly and try to interrupt him but before I get the chance he silences me with a closed mouth kiss.

"Please don't argue this, I know what I see and feel, and I have to stop this now Izzy. For you *and* for me, because I know in no uncertain terms, that the day will come when you leave me, for Declan."

I feel my eyes welling up, the tears starting to fall, all I can see is a sad blurry looking Connor. I fall into him and break down in uncontrollable crying. This is too much. Too bloody much.

"I'll always be here for you Izzy, always. It doesn't mean the end of you and me, just the end of *this*." He gestures manically between us with his hand. "I still want you in my life, but I know I can't have all of you, I can't have the part I really like right now, so I'm letting you go. I have a sports camp coming up next week so I'll be gone for a short while."

"Connor..I…" I really don't know what to say. I didn't see this coming. "I hate it, but I think you're right Connor, no matter how much this sucks, I know you are." I also know I don't deserve him, but I don't tell him that. He deserves a woman who gives him everything she is, everything she has to give. And yeah I'm not her. I know this, deep down. "I'll miss you." It's not the only thing I want to tell him but it's all I've got right now.

"Yeah I know Izzy, and I know what you're thinking too, but you're wrong, so very wrong."

We sit in each other's arms and I can't help but slowly realize, he's completely right. He makes me feel safe, secure and yes I fancy him. But I don't know if that's enough and I would hate to break his heart because I think I will, eventually, because Declan has mine…still. I feel like a bitch and the guilt starts to eat at me. As I try to rationalise my feelings for Connor it comes down to feeling safe and protected, friendship and yes attraction. But that essential feeling is missing, the extreme want and unbearable pain and need for another person. Exactly how I feel when I'm not near Declan, for reasons I'm still not sure of.

It suddenly gets very chilly and I know we can't sit here forever so I stand up and Connor does the same. I wrap myself in his arms and rest my head against his chest.

"I really do care about you Connor, I really do, and I'm going to miss you like crazy even though you haven't been in my life very long," my voice breaks as I tell him this.

"I know you do Izzy and I'm going to miss you too, we'll still be mates though okay; 'cause I couldn't fucking stand to lose you completely." I nod my head but stay silent. Willing that to be true; to be real.

Connor walks me home and I'm surprised by how much this actually hurts, I can't help but think whether this is the right thing to do. I look up at him and he smiles down at me.

"You've got to ring me Izzy, if you ever need me, you promise yeah?" he demands, looking all serious at me. I nod my head and I see him clearly swallow as he briefly closes his eyes.

"You've become very important to me in such a short time and you always will be," he laughs, it sounds kind of cynical as I hear him say, "Mates?"

Before I answer I launch myself at him and attack him with kisses. I know this'll be my last chance and he gets as carried away as I do. We can't keep our hands off each other. I slow down and just cling to him as I reply, "Yes….mates. Always."

"Goodbye Izzy," he says shrugging his shoulders.

"Bye Connor." I watch him walk away and stay rooted to the spot until I can no longer see him.

Feeling like shit on a shoe I decide to go to the Off Licence to get a bottle of something alcoholic. I feel like getting blind arsed drunk. Yeah not very mature I know. But who the fuck cares? When a little piece of your heart breaks it's the only thing that'll do. Connor is the kind of bloke anyone would be lucky to have and I just threw away that possibility because knowingly hurting him is unforgivable. It's Declan I want.

I buy a litre bottle of Cranberry Vodka from the *'Offie'* and thank the stars the day they started selling these, saves me having to mix it myself. Taking my bottle up to my room with no glass, I think to myself that I might as well go the full hog, I plug my iPod in and select Black Stone Cherry. I take off most of my clothes to get comfortable, leaving me just in my vest top and knickers. Sitting in the dark; in my favourite spot by the window, I watch the world go by. Fuck, I'm wallowing in my own self-pity here. Such a bloody cliché, such self-indulgence I think to myself as I down another huge gulp of vodka.

I'm starting to feel dizzy and the room is spinning, but I'm not stopping this pity party for one until I've finished this bottle. Once I'm done I'll move on and let go of Connor and feel lucky that I've got him as a friend. Because truly, I will be lucky.

Who knows how much time has passed when I hear voices downstairs…many voices…I place my finger over my lips and chuckle to myself ssshhhhh. I don't want anyone to know I'm home. Shit, the bottle's empty. Why's the bottle empty? How? Who drank it all?

I try to turn the music down but end up falling onto the floor with a loud thump making the bottle roll across the floor, where it ends up resting against the door. Ssshhhhh must be quiet. This makes me laugh. It's not even funny, but I can't stop laughing.

"Izzy?" Someone's calling me.

"What?" I shout back. Shit why am I shouting? I meant to be quiet, bollocks.

My door opens slightly, rolling the empty bottle back to me.

"Can I come in Iz?"

"Fuck it's Declan."

I hear him laugh, "Yeah...*fuck* it's me."

"Shit did I say that out loud?" I slur and start laughing like a maniac.

"Are you smashed Iz?" Declan joins in the laughter.

"Nah," I shake my head. Oh, not a good idea, I'm concentrating really hard and now I feel a bit sick.

"Izzy sweetheart, why the hell are you sprawled on the floor?" He starts to walk over.

"I like it....s'good place to think 'bout stuff," I say.

He crouches down next to me and looks at me, he's so close I can't help reach up and flick his nose. His face is classic, he looks shocked. This makes me laugh a proper belly laugh.

"Did you just flick my nose?" he laughs, as he pulls me off the floor and somehow manages to sit me down on my bed. I try and sit straight...man it's hard to do when the world spins.

"Hey...are you wearing guy-liner?" I ask and accidentally prod Declan in the eye, when all I meant to do was point at it.

"Fuck Izzy, that hurt and no I'm not wearing bloody eyeliner." He's frantically rubbing his sore eye.

"Guy-liner my gorgeous man, not eyeliner, you know...like eyeliner but for guys so..." I stop talking because suddenly Declan looks all serious and weird. "What's up with you? Why are you suddenly looking so bloody weird?"

"You called me yours; you've never called me yours before." His eyes are staring down at me so intensely. I stare right back at him, I'm so sure he's wearing guy-liner.

"Oh well whatever Declan, so as I was saying eye-liner is for us girlies and guy-liner is for you boys...makes it more masculine when you wear it. So, like umm, before a gig when you spruce yourself up it would totally make you sound a bit wimpy asking...say, Max for an eye-liner but if you asked him for his guy-liner, well completely different story." I give him a smug smile all pleased with myself. I make total sense.

"Shut up Izzy," he replies.

"Shut up Izzy? What the hell Declan, that's just rude." That's all I get out, because next minute I'm on my back and Declan's on top of me both hands framing my face, nose to nose, his hot breath mixing with mine.

"If you weren't so out of your fucking tree right now, I'd show you exactly what you calling me yours, all sexy like that, means in barely any clothes and fucked up hair that looks as if I've already had my wicked way with you."

Oh…

My breathing speeds up along with my heart as what he's saying, sinks in.

"I'm not that guy though Izzy, I'm not going to take advantage of you in this state, and especially not when you're taken." He closes his eyes and it looks as if he's counting.

"Declan…" I say on a breath. "I'm not that drunk, and yeah I'm already taken but not by who you think." Well I'm not, but right now I don't want to announce that. Why, I'm not sure, I've forgotten.

Declan rests his head against mine and gently presses his lips to my mouth whispering, "Still not going to."

I feel sick…shit I'm going to be sick. "Sick…I….sick!" I shout so loud it hurts my head. I clamp my hands over my mouth. Declan picks me up and quickly carries me to the bathroom where I immediately start puking my guts up into the toilet bowl. I can feel his hand on my back stroking it, trying to comfort me, whilst holding my hair back with his other hand.

In between my spasms of sickness I plead for him to leave me, but he refuses the stubborn git. I'm so tired and my whole body hurts and yes something just died in my mouth. I have no idea how long we sit in the bathroom, but I know I must've fallen asleep because I wake up with my head in his lap feeling completely sober and so bloody embarrassed I want to crawl into a hole and never come out. I refuse to look at him but I need to say something.

"Thank you Declan, please, you don't need to stay, just leave me, I'm okay now." I sit back up and lean against the bath. Eeew gross, I have sick on my vest top. I groan and attempt to stand up.

"Come here Izzy, let me help you." He puts his arm around me, lifting me up to stand. I sway slightly as I reach over to try turn the shower on but Declan stops me.

"You're having a shower? Are you steady enough for that Izzy, I don't want you falling over in there beautiful girl."

He called me beautiful, I'm anything but. "Yeah I'm okay and I really smell and I have sick in my hair Declan," I whine childishly back at him.

He starts to chuckle. "I'm not leaving you sweetheart, I'm staying right here. I've seen you naked and besides, the screen will cover you," he smirks.

"Yeah I don't think so Declan, you need to leave right now." He's right though we've been naked together before, but it was dark, he hasn't *really* seen me, seen my scars.

"Yeah not gonna leave Izzy." He stands here, arms crossed all defiant, daring me to make him leave.

"Fine, well turn around then if you insist on staying in here."

I look everywhere but his face, suddenly feeling very shy. Declan turns the shower on and immediately turns around resting his hands on the sink, his head hanging down. I can't help but admire his arse in those jeans, he really does have a…

"Stop staring at my arse Izzy unless you're prepared to do something to it," he laughs.

Shamefaced my head snaps up and I see Declan's winking reflection in the mirror over the sink. I hurriedly step into the shower, close the screen and realise I'm still wearing my knickers and vest top. I take them off and throw them over the top of the screen and laugh as I hear them hit Declan. Serves him right I chuckle to myself. As I'm shampooing the sick out of my hair Declan starts to ask me about tonight.

"So what happened then, why the drunken stupor?"

I'm not sure how honest I should be with him, because he's obviously keeping his distance because of Connor. I'm not sure what's best for us, whether I should be selfish and tell him. "Pass me my toothbrush with some paste on it will you." Yeah that's right I think to myself, I'm such a wimp. Declan hands it over the screen and I brush my teeth vigorously as I stand under the spray. I actually start to feel human again.

"Connor left me tonight," I say. Bollocks, why the hell did I just confess to that, I wasn't going to say anything?

"He left you…what do you mean he left you?" Declan asks sounding shocked.

"As in, we split up and he's going up North for a month," I reply squirting a huge glob of coconut shower gel into my hands and rubbing it all over my body. I hate the smell of vomit, it's disgusting.

"How do you feel about that Iz?" he asks me and I can hear the tension and maybe even some hope in his voice.

"Umm it's for the best I guess, he would never have my whole heart Declan, it's not mine to give away anymore." Oh bloody hell, have I been drinking fucking truth serum? What's wrong with me? I hear rustling and I wonder what he's doing.

"Declan!" I scream, as I try to cover myself up with my hands. A very naked Declan is right now stepping into the shower. "Shit…Declan get out," I shout at him.

"No way baby. No. Fucking. Way," he exhales loudly, and the next minute he has me plastered up against the shower wall boxed in by his arms, a palm on either side of my face, his tongue trying to gain access to my mouth.

My head's all over the place, but I automatically sink into him, I can't stop myself. My body is literally buzzing and I feel myself wanting this more than anything. The only thing holding me up is one of his legs between mine. I let him in and his tongue immediately starts exploring my mouth. I frantically kiss him back, my tongue wrestling with his. I can't get enough of him. I want to crawl inside him and never come out. Actually no, I want him to get inside me. Like right now.

One of his hands grabs my face whilst his other hand slides down my front, slippery in the water. Sliding across and palming my breast as he trails kisses across my jaw, moving down my neck, slightly licking and sucking on my collarbone.

"Fuck Izzy…." he growls at me.

"Yes please Declan," I moan back, feeling his smile against my breast. A throbbing ache starts to build between my legs and I press down on his hard thigh, moving involuntarily to try and satisfy it.

"That's it babe, just let go," he groans, as his teeth gently bite my nipple, before his tongue soothes the bite away. His other hand trails down to help me fall over that aching edge. His thumb pressing down while he sinks first one finger, then a second into me. I clench around them feeling myself letting go, as the pressure quickly builds. Just as I get there I launch myself at him wrapping my arms around his neck as I bite down on his shoulder, still I hear myself screaming his name out.

"Fuck Izzy," Declan pants in a low and husky voice. "Hold on to me beautiful." He lets go, but is still supporting me with his leg. Reaching to the side of the bath he picks up a condom and rolls it on;

immediately surging into me. "Bloody hell, you feel so fucking good Izzy," he shouts.

For about one second I wonder where the hell he got that condom from, but then all coherent thoughts disappears. He has me up against the wall and I can't get enough of him. I'm biting, licking and kissing while Declan's impaling me hard and fast; as if he can't get deep enough. "So…fucking….hot Izzy," he breathes as he pounds into me making my head knock back onto the tiles. Strangely though, it doesn't hurt, if anything this raw lust and complete loss of control gets me even more excitable. His mouth closes around my breast and he sucks my nipple into his mouth biting me hard as his other hand squeezes my arse while his thrusts get harder and deeper.

"Declan…" I yell out, as I come more violently than ever before. Declan follows closely, groaning my name as he tucks his face into my neck latching on with another bite. My guy's a biter, and I love it. I feel like jelly and I swear, if Declan lets go of me, I'll melt into a puddle and slide down the drain.

The water suddenly feels icy cold. "Eeek Declan the water," I scream like a girl.

"Fuck that's cold," he yells and helps me out of the shower, wrapping us each in a bath towel. He takes my hand and quickly drags me into my room and literally pushes me under the covers where he joins me, wrapping me up in his arms. As I snuggle into his warm broad chest I'm so content but kind of freaked out at the same time. Actually, as I realise what just happened I start to feel like a bit of a slag too. Thinking about it; who goes and sleeps with someone else less than a day after calling it quits on another possible relationship? That would be me I guess. Circumstances aside though, I think this was probably still going to happen. At least I'm not a cheater in the official sense of the word. Although that doesn't make me feel any better, I know it's Declan for me, it has been since day one, whether he feels the same…who knows. But I'm going to guess he feels *something* because what we just did, well it was pure raw emotion.

Declan's stroking my hair, running his fingers through it, combing the knots out with his fingers. My breathing relaxes and I start drawing circles in his light sprinkling of chest hair.

"I love this," I say as I gently tug at the hairs.

I feel the rumble of his words and laugh. "Good to know sweetheart."

I follow it down his hard chest then run my fingers across that luscious six pack that makes me want to lick it every time I see it. Instead, I lick the swirly end of his tattoo and feel his heart rate pick up. My fingers decide on a path of their own and follow the happy trail down where I can already feel the effect of what I'm doing to him. I slowly slide my head down to join my fingers as I wrap my hand around him and let my tongue join in. There's nothing more empowering in bed, than feeling and hearing what this does to him. I can actually feel him growing impossibly larger and harder in my hand and it's making me want him like crazy.

"Izzy, you don't have to…" I can hear the desire in his voice so I know I absolutely do have to, but I know I also want to. I take him deep into my mouth and think I might just come myself because the groans he's making spur me on and I too, feel pretty bloody amazing right now.

"Izzy you've got to stop," he groans, trying to pull me up. I don't want to stop, I keep going, teasing him and I know any minute now he will drop off that edge.

"Izzy…Fuck…." he growls as he releases into my mouth. I pull away from him, kissing my way up and slowly snuggle back in his arms. His wraps them around me all protectively as he kisses the top of my head.

"Sweetheart that was fucking fantastic," he grins as he lifts me up and spins me onto my back so we're face to face and he ends up lying on top of me. "Perfect Izzy, you're bloody perfect." He kisses my nose and I smile. I'm really not but he doesn't need to know this yet, this moment is way too precious to ruin or spoil with the truth. Declan looks deep into my eyes as his tongue parts my lips in a deep kiss. I squirm under him still wound tight from before.

"Yeah I know what you want babe and I'm going to give it to you, hang on." He starts kissing and licking a trail down, paying attention to every inch of me, teasing me and leaving me completely ready for him as he nudges my legs apart with his broad shoulders. He picks up my legs and moves them over each shoulder, grabbing my arse with his hands.

"So ready for me aren't you Izzy," he groans as he runs the flat of his tongue up and over me. I already want to scream, the way he shows me how much he wants me, how much he enjoys me and how I taste. My whole body is wound tight and I'm going crazy, wanting that moment of pure free falling dizziness.

"My perfect Izzy," he smiles up at me as I feel his tongue lick me with a hunger I don't really understand. It doesn't take long for me, between his tongue and his fingers he soon makes me scream his name in passion as I feel myself falling. I'm light-headed and start to shake. He moves back up and kisses me deeply, cradling my head in his large hands which are way too sexy; because the things these hands can do is beyond amazing. When I open my eyes I see him smiling at me.

"Do you know how crazy you've been driving me since the day we met Izzy?" he whispers to me, stroking my hair. "I've wanted to do this to you since pretty much day one, since we first met." His voice holds so much passion and sounds deeply emotional. He almost sounds relieved. And I hear the words and I feel them too but how the hell do I process them. It's what I've wanted to hear, to confirm it's not just me, feeling this intense connection. Every word he just said repeats over and over in my head and I feel them touching me in all the right places, leaving a trail of heat in their wake. I know he really must think this but I also know as soon as we leave this room, everything on the other side will be too big, too complicated. What we have right here, right now, in my room will be overshadowed by everything. I wish we could stay here forever.

"I feel it too Declan," is all I say, feeling overwhelmed, my emotion so intense I know he hears it in my voice. He shifts us onto our sides so we lie facing each other. Raining kisses all over my face, his hand starts to slowly stroke my back, covering every bit of my skin. I realize the minute he feels it and I freeze as my insides tie up in knots. My stomach drops; I can't believe I forgot. This moment made me drop my guard and forget. He looks at me questioningly and tries to turn me onto my front.

"Don't Declan, just don't," I whisper, scared of his reaction and having to face an explanation.

"What *is* that Izzy, let me have a look," he demands angrily as he tries to turn me over again.

"No please don't, just don't....it's nothing," I cry out in shame, closing my eyes from having to face him. I'm amazed it took him so long to come across them, but then *that* first time it was dark and I was pretty much on my back. But then I realize that there may be no way of Declan not seeing it now and understanding what it is.

"Izzy turn over for me sweetheart, this is important. Please," he whispers soothingly against my hair. I shake my head, closing my eyes chewing on my lip because I'm not ready for him to know. I want to go asleep dreaming of what Declan and I just had rather than dreaming of the day I had to show Declan my scars. He kisses me gently making me release my lip, licking where I've bitten through, before languidly kissing me until I forget. We roll over but Declan's too quick for me and as he rolls, he somehow ends up sitting half off, half on me; with me laying on my front. I bury my head into the pillow and clench my hands underneath me. I know what's coming. I'm shaking and the silent tears start to fall. I feel his finger trace the shape of one scar after the other, until he's felt all three. The silence is deafening. I'm waiting for him to say something, anything because I can't. The rushing white noise in my ears is getting overwhelming.

"Izzy, tell me sweetheart, are they what I think they are?" I hear his voice break as he continues to trace them. "Please tell me they're not, that it's my fucking crazy imagination, because, if they are, I'm gonna kill the motherfucker who did this to you." He's enraged, fuming even. The tone of his voice makes the hairs on the back of my neck stand up. I can literally feel his eyes and fingers scanning me till he gets to my lower back. That's it, the last scar I ever got from my past…he's found it.

"Jesus Izzy. What the fuck?" I've never heard Declan like this before and it scares me, the tension could be cut with a knife and my shaking starts to get out of control.

"Get off me Declan…GET OF ME NOW," I scream trying to buck him off me.

"Sshh sweetheart. Shit I'm sorry; I didn't mean to scare you," he says, as he rolls on to his side again, pulling me over so he can see my face. He cups the side of my face in his big hand stroking his thumb across my cheekbone.

"Is it Izzy?" he asks me gently.

"Is it what Declan?" I ask defiantly, getting pissed off, which is kind of odd as a minute ago I was scared.

"Did someone do that to you?"

"Well I'm hardly likely to do it to myself am I?" I shout back at him, immediately regretting my words.

"Izzy for fucks sake calm down. I've just discovered that the girl I'm falling in love with has three dodgy scars on her shoulder blade that can only have come from something that should be smoked and not be anywhere near there. But not only *that*, she's got a fucking burn scar on her lower back too." His eyes are intensely burning into mine as my shaking stops. He's falling in love with me, that's all I hear…he's falling in love with me. The butterflies, the tingles and every single hair on my neck stands to attention. My heart overflows with emotion. I know I'm already pretty much there, falling in love with him that is, but I had no idea that he was getting there too.

"What?" he smiles at me. "You didn't realise how much you've come to mean to me? I am Izzy, falling in love with you," he smiles at me. "Which is why I tried to stay away, because I don't do love, never have, but you make me want to try."

I'm pretty sure I have a massive stupid look on my face because I can't believe that this gorgeous amazing man is falling in love with me. I want to laugh, cry, shout, maybe even do a tap dance. Actually no, but the way I'm feeling now; nothing would surprise me. I reach my hand over to touch him; I want to make sure this moment is real, that something amazing actually just came out of something ugly.

"No, Declan, I didn't. I really didn't. I…I feel the same Declan. You wanting to try this with me, I have no words." My smile is plastered all over my face. It's involuntary, it comes straight from my heart.

His cocky half smile melts me until it suddenly falls from his face, replaced by a serious frown. "But you need to tell me Izzy. You need to tell me why you have three perfectly round fucking burn marks on your shoulder."

"Not now Declan, please not now, later…I'm not ready to tell you yet," I plead for him to drop it and it looks as if it's working as he goes silent studying my face with those warm dark eyes of his.

"Okay sweetheart. Okay…I'll drop it for now but we're going there soon, because I need to fucking know okay."

Kissing my lips so gently I can't help but nod my head, "Okay."

"Okay," he breathes so close to my mouth I get chills even though his warm breath is hot as he kisses me again.

"Now let's try and get some sleep shall we, I think we've got about three hours left before the fucking birds start," he says as he covers us over with my duvet and turns me so my back is up against his front. He places a lingering kiss on each scar as he presses against me with a protective arm around me, leaving one hand against my heart. As I fall asleep, I feel safe yet the tears still quietly fall as soon as I hear his gentle sleeping breath.

Chapter Twelve

Something's ringing...it's my phone...where's my phone? I fumble around and my eyes spring open when I feel a hard body in my bed. As I see Declan next to me fast asleep, everything from last night comes flooding back and I can feel the silly grin on my face. The phone starts ringing again and I quickly scoot off the bottom of the bed to grab it. Realizing I'm naked I quickly slide on some knickers and put on Declan's t-shirt which has his own brand of that manly smell that I love. Declan mixed with that fresh water scent.

I hit the pick up on my mobile. "Hello?"

"Open your sodding door you lazy cow."

"Oh my God...Sofia."

How could I forget she'd be arriving today? "Coming my love," I reply as I bound down the stairs and fling myself at the door. I've barely opened it before Sofia throws herself at me. I stumble back feeling slightly awkward as I'm wearing barely any clothes.

"Oh wow Izzy I'm so bloody happy to see you." Sofia grabs my face and gives me a sloppy kiss. "Umm what are you wearing...or should I say who are you wearing?" She grins at me with a wink. I have a stupid grin on my face because my gorgeous friend is back and she looks happy. I was not expecting that.

"Oh I've been so worried about you Sofia, never mind who's in my bed right now," I wink back at her.

"Where's your room, I need to sneak a peek." She bounces up the stairs with me following close behind. I point into my room where Declan's still asleep. He's lying on his back his arms splayed at his sides with the duvet tangled between his long muscular legs. He looks amazingly hot with his olive skin against the white sheets. I feel my insides tighten and all I want to do is pounce on him.

"Bloody hell Izzy, he's fucking gorgeous," she stutters in surprise. I look at her and see her mouth is hanging open as she blatantly stares at Declan.

"Close your mouth girlie or you'll catch flies," I laugh at her reaction, because mine is the same every time I see him, so who can really blame her. I close the door so we don't wake him up as we walk back downstairs.

"So…umm what happened with Taylor?" Yeah, I had to bring up the pink elephant in the room, otherwise it'll hang around and it'll get awkward. I put on the kettle for some much needed coffee.

"Is it too early for a drink?" Sofia sighs as she snoops around the kitchen opening cupboards and looking into the containers on the kitchen counter.

"One more hour and we can go down the pub, you'll just have to put up with coffee for now," I say sitting down at the kitchen table with my coffee. Sofia sits down opposite me laying her head down with a thud on the table.

"Six years Izzy. I gave him six bloody years of my life. Urgh, I'm still so pissed off," she sighs heavily. Yeah she looks it, I'm surprised though that she doesn't seem sad but then maybe she's moved past the sadness onto the angry stage.

"I'm sorry I wasn't there for you my lovely, I really am. But you haven't told me what happened and why you're back so early."

Sofia looks at me as her eyes well up. "I caught Taylor with someone else Izzy, some skanky bitch was on her fucking knees blowing him off and I walked in on *that*." She throws her hands up in the air dramatically.

I know I shouldn't smile but I can't help it, I love Sofia, truly she's like my sister, and I love her foul mouth even more, she says it as it is and I love her for it. "I'm so sorry Sof, but I just don't get it. Why would he do that to you?" I ask, still very confused.

"We grew apart Izzy, that's what happened. The travelling, we wanted to see different things. Once I started the exchange placement, I met a fun group of people who I'd go out with at night to shows and clubs. Taylor stayed home more times than not or he'd go to the bar across the road from our apartment. I guess this is where he met the slapper who later blew him."

"Oh Sofia love, where is he now?" I ask her.

"He stayed, he couldn't get out of his teaching contract so he's finishing his year abroad, then coming back to London to find a job here." She runs her fingers through her long hair. Her curls bouncing right back.

"Are you in trouble for coming back?" I ask, feeling so sorry for her that her dream was cut short. She starts to pick at the lino cloth covering the table making the already small hole in it even bigger.

"Yeah, I kind of am. I lost my position at the school I was going to work in, so I need to get my applications out soon before I run out of money. And before all the vacancies are gone." She face plants on the table again.

Her muffled words break my heart. "What am I going to do Izzy? I have nowhere to stay, we gave up the lease on our apartment before we left, thinking we would find something together when we came back next year. Such a bloody mess." Her shoulders rise and I know she's trying not to cry. Trying to stay strong.

I put my arms around her and she hugs me back fiercely. Poor Sofia. She survived one a hell of a year before Taylor got her out of the black hole she was in. She was fifteen when her year of hell started and if it wasn't for Taylor, I think I would have lost my best friend. This is why I can't believe that he would've done this to her. Well obviously I believe her, but there has to be more to this story. As we sit here, I can hear Declan move around upstairs and I suddenly worry whether he's upset I wasn't there when he woke up. I can hear him coming down the stairs and then I see him in the hallway walking into the kitchen, in just his boxers. My body immediately reacts and I feel my face heat up.

"Hey I was wondering where you went. Oh shit, let me go stick some clothes on," he laughs, as he spots Sofia.

I laugh as he runs upstairs; Sofia joins in shouting up to him, "Don't get dressed on my account." She turns to me, "Didn't we used to Google blokes like him?"

"Yeah we did," I smile at her and stand to go make Declan a coffee. Sofia catches me up on everything I've missed from her time away and it feels as if she never left me. I missed her so much and even though she's been through hell, selfishly, I'm so glad she's back. I offer her the couch in the living room until she finds somewhere of her own. I don't think the lads will mind too much. Sofia is hilarious and oh so gorgeous they'll love having her here I'm sure.

"I'm just going to have a quick word with Declan, why don't you go sort yourself out and I'll be right back."

"Sure thing Izzy. Man, I'm so glad to be back and here with you again."

She gives me another hug and I run up the stairs to find Declan. I stop and stare…he's sitting on my bed with my note pad looking through the visual diary of my past. He looks up at me with an expression that tells me nothing, as if he's trying not to show me how he's feeling. I'm counting up the years in that book as I stand rooted to the spot. I have no idea if he'll make the connections on the pages. I wonder if he can see what I see in there. He doesn't know the truth so maybe he won't. I hope that's true.

"Come here sweetheart," he finally says holding his hand out for me to take.

I hear him but I can't move. He puts the book on the bed, stands up and walks over to me. I'm caught like a deer in headlights. I flinch at his touch when his hand cradles my face. His eyes like melted dark chocolate with gold flecks in them, look at me with such affection? Or is it compassion? Pity even? But not love…at least I don't think that look is love.

"Izzy we need to talk about this. But before we do I want, no I need you to know that I'm serious about us. About trying to…*fuck*…" he sighs, and runs his hand through his hair while looking up at the ceiling, closing his eyes. He looks like he's in pain so I say nothing. He looks back down at me and holds my head in both his hands, his thumbs stroking my cheeks.

"Please don't let me run," I whisper in fear. "I always do the running…and you…please don't you run anywhere either, please stay. Please *make* me stay." I'm not even sure that makes any sense, but before I can even try to explain myself, I feel Declan's lips crush down on mine as he pushes me up against the door. Slowing down our passionate kiss, he starts to speak, his lips never leaving mine.

"I'm not running anywhere Izzy and I promise you I will *not* let you run either, *never*. Not now I've got you."

A fire builds in me and I can't get enough of him, my hands, my mouth eagerly, furiously seeking contact with him everywhere and I'm not the only one. I feel Declan everywhere as he moves me to the bed and literally throws me on it following me down. I relax my legs and he fits in between them as if he was made to be there. He pulls off his shirt that I'm wearing and immediately my breast is in his mouth as his hand slides into my knickers, his amazing fingers making me feel dizzy and lost in the overwhelming sensation. It doesn't take long for me to reach the pure bliss I've only ever experienced with him and I cry out his name.

"That's it Izzy, let me make you feel good, feel wanted. I've never wanted anyone more than you sweetheart." He sounds desperate, his voice laced with pure want. I push off his boxers with my foot as he flips me over pulling me onto my knees. For about a second I feel vulnerable and exposed because I know what he'll see. But that feeling doesn't last long when his hands move across my back, gently over my scars. He bends over and places open mouthed kisses all over my back.

"Declan…" I moan needing him inside me so badly, the moment overpowering my voice.

"Right here Izzy…right here."

I hear the rip of a foil packet and he enters me in one fluid hard thrust. Leaning over me, I hear him whisper words of love but I can barely make him out, I'm so lost in the hazy passion. It's frantic and rough and there's no mistaking what this is. This is desperation. I can't have him hard or deep enough. I need him to take me in a way that'll keep me at his side, marking me. I'm pretty sure he feels the same because this feels like he's marking me as *his*. Making sure I know that I'm his and he's mine.

"You are *mine* Izzy," he growls as he comes with me, one last push for declaration of who we are, where I belong. Where he belongs. I'm not sure I can explain how I feel right now. But I know I feel safe. The one thing I haven't felt in a long time and it makes me shiver.

"I didn't hurt you did I Izzy?" His eyes suddenly searching my face are worried, thinking he has.

"No, no you really didn't Declan, it was perfect," I smile up at him and reach up to find his lips with mine. We are interrupted by an impatient Sofia.

"Izzy stop fucking about and get your arse down here right now," Sofia yells from downstairs.

"Oh no I forgot, how could I forget Sofia's downstairs?" Mortified I try to push Declan off me. He starts to laugh and pulls me up by my hand and smacks my bum.

"You look thoroughly fucked so you might want to go freshen up babe. Actually don't, I want to see you like this knowing I did that to you," he winks at me as he swaggers into the bathroom. I shout down to Sofia that I'll be back down in five minutes and follow Declan in.

"Don't even think about it buddy," I tell him as I step under the hot shower he started. He laughs as he leans against the wall with his arms crossed watching me shampoo my hair and wash the remnants of our morning off me. As I step out the shower he hands me a towel, gives me a quick peck on the cheek and steps into the shower.

I quickly put on my knickers, jeans and a Black Stone Cherry concert t-shirt, my lucky t-shirt that I got at their last gig in London and I rush down the stairs.

"Seriously Izzy, I come back and you leave me after like an hour for a quick shag?" Sofia pouts at me, then she grins and sticks her hand out for a fist bump. Yes very mature, I know, but Sofia and I will never grow up, not in true sense of the word.

The front door opens and I hear Aiden shout from the front door, "Honey I'm home."

I look over at Sofia and smile at her, "That's Aiden, remember I told you about him?"

"Hey Izzy, I haven't seen you to tell you how sorry I am about your Mum. Declan told me she was in hospital. Are you okay?" he asks me coming into the room. Sofia's eyes immediately dart to mine with that God-awful knowing look. She's pissed off I'm sure for not telling her earlier. I quickly go for a diversion.

"Aiden this is my best mate Sofia…Sofia this is the lovely Aiden," I say, avoiding her eyes.

Aiden squeezes past me on the couch and gives her a hug, which she returns; Sofia is a hugger just like him. He then turns around and gives me a quick hug too and whispers, "You and I need to talk about what happened." I nod at him and plaster a fake smile on my face.

"So aren't you guys playing in the pub tonight?" I ask him.

"Yeah we are; will you girls be popping over?"

"Sure we will, oh and I said to Sofia she can stay on the couch till she finds a place to stay, I hope that's okay…long story but she's homeless so..."

Sofia interrupts me and shrugs looking over at Aiden. "Yeah a skanky whore tripped and fell on my man's cock," she explains and I have to cover my mouth or I'll burst out laughing, which would be totally inappropriate right now.

"Right," Aiden's trying not to laugh too, his lips looking pinched as he looks over at me. "Yeah that's no problem Sofia. But I'm sure we can sort something out so you don't have to sleep on the couch. Let me have a think on that," he says to a smiling Sofia.

"Izzy can sleep with me in my room," Declan says, as he comes walking into the room. "Then Sofia can go into Izzy's room….and there you have it, problem solved." I look over at Declan who's looking rather chuffed with himself, and I can't help feeling cornered and shocked at how fast he's moving us along. He still kind of gives me whiplash.

Aiden looks at Declan and I with a surprised look on his face but quickly composes himself. "Right Dec, whatever you decide is fine with me. Are you ready to go get our stuff together for tonight?"

"Sure man, just let me have a quick word with Izzy, then I'm good to go." Declan takes my hand and we walk into the kitchen away from Sofia and Aiden. "Too fast Izzy?" he asks looking at me questioningly whilst rubbing his hand up and down my arms in a comforting gesture.

"No...I just…you want me to stay with you?" I mumble looking up at him.

"Yeah. If we're going to try and do this I want you in my bed, where you belong. You're mine Izzy. I have a second chance with you here so I'm not going to waste it following rules that are nothing but bollocks."

"Okay," I whisper, stunned by this turn of events but there's no escaping that warm feeling spreading in my stomach.

"Okay," he replies, kissing me gently. "Now, I've got to go get our stuff together for tonight. I'll see you at the pub later okay?"

I nod but don't get a chance to respond as he gives me a deep lingering slow kiss, winks at me and then he's gone.

As Aiden and Declan drive off Sofia pins me to the spot with her eyes. She has the most expressive eyes I've ever known. She leaves you in no doubt as to what she's feeling. And right now she's feeling pissed off and worried.

"Right missus, no escaping, just give it to me…*all of it*, uncensored." Her face is full of concern. I sigh with a deep breath as we sit down on the bed in my room, actually her room now.

"Sof, I don't even know where to start."

"Does Declan know about what happened?"

"No, he's seen my scars and he saw Mum in the hospital, but he doesn't know the *'what'* and the *'why'*."

"Is your Mum okay?" she asks taking my hand in hers.

"Yeah, she will be…well as okay as she ever is." I close my eyes; this defeated emotional feeling so familiar now.

"Oh Izzy, I'm so sorry that it's started up again. And I'm sorry that when trying to escape, you still end up being dragged back into it," she shakes her head in frustration.

"It was always going to happen Sofia, I just know I'm not ready to tell anyone yet. Especially not about Zack," I shudder.

"I know hun," she says. "Listen, why don't you go downstairs and get a bottle of wine, catch me up on everything else and we'll get dolled up and ready to go get bladdered down the pub?" She smiles at me wanting to do what she does best. Make me forget.

"I can't think of anything I'd rather do Sof, I'm so glad you're back, I missed you so much, I'm just sorry for the reasons why I got you back."

I hug her within an inch of her life as I hear her whisper, "Me too girlie."

Over a bottle, I fill Sofia in on everything that's happened since she left and I started Uni. I tell her about Connor which is hard because re-telling our brief story makes me tear up as I feel like a right bitch.

"Izzy, he must've known all along, he pretty much admitted to it. But he sounds like a keeper, so if you can stay friends, he's one for life, I'm pretty sure of that. Oh and he sounds hot so maybe I'll have a crack at him," she laughs, re-filling our wine glasses.

I look at her mortified. "Umm not there yet Sof." Though saying that, I can totally see them together and the thought actually makes me smile.

"Fine, just saying though that it sounds like you're with who you were meant to be with. And yeah it doesn't sound like it'll be easy, but from what you're saying you and Declan are like two peas in a pod. So go for it hun, it sure sounds like you both need each other." She smiles at me and heads off to take a shower. I begin to clear a space for her clothes in my wardrobe and help her sort all her stuff out, thinking about what she said.

While she's still in the shower, I decide to try and ring Mum. The phone rings for ages until the answering machine kicks in, so I leave a message for her to ring me back. She should be home by now and I'm regretting not going to make sure she got home okay. But she was adamant…fiercely so, that she wanted some space. Sofia comes back into the bedroom in just her towel.

"Bloody hell Sof you finally got yourself a tattoo," I excitedly get up close to inspect it. It's a beautifully scripted 'Semper Fidelis' on her right shoulder blade.

"Yeah, well at least I didn't get arsehole's name on there huh," she frowns over her shoulder.

"How bad did it hurt Sofia? You know I've always wanted to get one to cover my scars, I need to make something ugly into something beautiful." I can't stop looking at the beautiful script on her shoulder.

"Yeah I know Iz, now that I'm back why don't I come with you and we can go have a look. But you need to be sure. Make it mean something."

I know exactly what I want, I've had it planned for ages but I've been too much of a wimp so far to go get them done. I sigh as I look through my clothes wondering what to wear. Sofia hands me my glass of wine and cranks the music up high and starts dancing round the room. God I've missed her. Sofia and I are the same size and she's as short as me so she lends me a pair of her gorgeous new black skinny jeans and an awesome halter neck top made up of roughly sewn together patches of different coloured and brightly patterned material. It's absolutely gorgeous. People always say we could've been sisters. We're both tiny, have blue eyes and blond hair. Only difference is where my hair is long and straight, Sofia has the most beautiful long white blond curls and her eyes are a lighter shade of blue than mine.

We are almost half-way to being pissed and we look like we're off clubbing rather than just down the pub, but who cares. This is what we used to do, this is what I've missed.

We get to the pub late and as we open the door we can hear the sound of *'The Standards'*, the pounding beat reverberating in my chest, the sound of Declan's voice surrounding me, giving me chills every-bloody-where.

"Wow, they're alright aren't they Iz," Sofia says as she looks at the stage gobsmacked.

"Yeah," I sigh lost in the sight of Declan up on the stage.

"Shit girl you've got it bad," she laughs at me and takes my hand promptly dragging me up to the bar. We get our drinks and walk towards the stage in the corner of the pub. We can't get too close as it's really busy already. Sofia sees two bar stools free by the side, next to the bar. We go sit down and luckily we have an unobstructed view.

"So tell me Izzy, how come they just play in pubs, did they ever try and take it further?" she asks me. Downing half her drink and clearly eyeing up the talent.

"Apparently back when they were eighteen they went to some dive in Camden and cut a demo but it never really came to anything. So they decided, rather than giving up completely, they'd stick to doing gigs round London pubs and clubs whilst going to Uni at the same time."

"So I can see Aiden and Declan, who's the stunning hottie on the drums?"

I burst out laughing. "That's Max he's a couple of years older than them at twenty-six. He's Declan's older brother's friend. He's beautiful isn't he?" I smile at her.

"Yeah he really is, though I doubt it's something he wants to hear when he is in the throes of passion," she laughs back at me.

Sofia pops off to the ladies and I sit here, unable to stop smiling as I look up at the stage and lock eyes with Declan. The intensity in his eyes as he looks at me gives me chills and it's as if I can feel his hands all over me. If I could, I'd jump up on that stage and rip his clothes off. I seriously would, because right now I need him between my legs. My naughty thoughts are interrupted by a warm hand on my shoulder.

"Hey Izzy." Bloody hell it's Connor, where did he come from?

"Hey yourself, I thought you went up North for that footie camp?" I ask him confused.

"I'm off first thing tomorrow morning so thought I'd have one last night out with the lads tonight," he nods his head in the direction of a group of lads propping up the bar. Sofia comes back with another round of woo woo's, she must've taken a detour from the ladies. Perfect distraction I think as I take my drink from her.

"Connor, this is my best mate Sofia, Sofia this is Connor."

I immediately see Sofia's eyes light up as she steps up on her tip toes in an attempt to kiss him on his cheeks. Connor starts to laugh and bends down slightly for her.

"You're a tall lad aren't you," she laughs.

"Nice to meet you too Sofia, Izzy's told me a lot about you."

"All bad stuff I hope?" Sofia winks at him.

"Umm yeah sure," he laughs as he seems to take all of her in with his eyes.

I clear my throat without wanting to sound too obvious but Sofia gets the hint because she looks away and picks up her woo woo. An awkward silence follows.

"Right well, I best be going back to the lads as it's my last night. Just wanted to say hello and make sure we're good Izzy." He looks down at me with a genuine smile, his eyes warm and tender. I actually melt a little at those words because truly, I care very deeply for him.

"Connor, we *are* good and I hope we can be mates because I couldn't bear to lose you," I say as I give him a fierce cuddle, resting my head on his chest.

"Always Izzy, *always*," he whispers in my ear as he hugs me back.

I look at him, and sitting on this stool I am nearly at eye level so I place a gentle kiss on his cheek. "Take care Connor and let me know how you get on won't you. Oh and ring me when you're back so we can go for a drink."

"Sure thing Izzy, see you later," he winks at me. "And Sofia, it was nice to meet you." He smiles at us both as he walks off to re-join his mates.

"Bloody hell Izzy, he's gorgeous, I can see your dilemma now, though I have to say the way Declan looks at you and you at him, I'd say there is no doubt who you should be with. But damn Connor is one fine specimen of a man." Sofia looks over at the group of lads where Connor is being slapped on his back as they all belly laugh at something he said.

I shift my attention back to the stage and drink in all that is Declan. Yeah for sure Connor is amazing but Declan has my heart. He's given a part of himself to me and has seen and knows more than any other man I've ever been with. Saying that though, it's not a lot.

A man suddenly walks past where Sofia and I are sitting and I freeze immediately. I look at him and I swear his profile is almost like seeing Zack and his scent is unmistakably the same cologne as what Zack always used. Even though I'm sober enough to realize this man isn't Zack, I still leap off my chair and grip the man's arm trying to get a good look at his face. I feel like I'm in a trance, forced to feel as everything stops around me. I don't know what possesses me.

The tears start to fall and I know this guy is not Zack…of course I know, I'm not crazy. But it's as if my sane self has been gagged and bound and the wishful me wants this to be Zack, to wish the last eighteen months have been only a nightmare.

"Hey what the hell?" the bloke yells as he pushes me off him. Unfortunately I'm already unsteady on my feet so I fall backwards and feel my temple hit the side of the bar before my hand gets hold of it. I stumble but manage to grab hold of it before I face plant on the floor. Shit, I feel all dizzy and my head starts to throb immediately. The silence is deafening as the music suddenly stops. Then the commotion starts and I see Declan flying off the corner stage with his arm already drawn back in readiness to land a punch on the guy who pushed me.

"What the fuck man," I hear him say as his punch lands bang on target followed by a quick jab to the guy's stomach. They both end up on the floor with Declan straddling this poor bloke who's desperately trying to claw one back.

"Declan stop," I shout at him trying to pull him off. But yeah I have no chance, I'm still feeling a bit woozy and Declan seems lost in blind rage. I've never seen him like this. I can't stand it, I feel sick to my stomach, confused and scared so I decide to make a run for it.

I run till I get to the park where I collapse on the ground, my head swimming and throbbing. I feel sick but as my breath slows down to normal, the nausea passes. I can hear Declan and Aiden calling for me but I can't see them. The look on Declan's face scared the shit out of me and I'm still shaking. I quickly crawl behind a large blackberry hedge cutting my arm in the process while I try and hide before they make it past me.

I can suddenly see them through a gap in the hedge. They're standing on the path looking around, Declan holding one fist against his chest, wrapped in his other hand as if in agony. I can see Aiden roughly run his hands through his hair looking around frantically.

"Fucking hell Dec…why the fuck did you go on a punching rampage right in front of her? What's wrong with you? Surely you've realized by now that she comes from an abusive home, come on mate that much is bloody obvious." Aiden's right up in Declan's face all pissed off. Declan pushes him back with his good hand but not like how he went for the guy in the pub. This is gentle in comparison.

"Shit Aiden….I saw him push her and she hit her fucking head….I lost it man and you fucking know why, so don't think for one minute I haven't realised by now who she really is. I should know better than anyone. I knew the minute I met her."

I can see Aiden put his arm around Declan, "Yeah sorry Dec, come on, let's check if she's run off home, her head has to be fucking killing her." They start walking off in the direction of our town house.

I have no idea where to go or what to do. I left my bag in the pub so I haven't even got my mobile to ring Sofia. My head hurts, I feel like shit and I'm so confused over my feelings of what happened. I stand up and start walking towards the bus stop. I'm not really thinking of where I'm going but I'm surprised when I find myself walking the path back home. Home as in back to Mum. I wish I had money for the bus because my feet are killing me and I'm freezing cold. I decide to take my spiked heels off and walk in bare feet.

By the time I make it home my feet are bleeding and I can't feel my body; I feel numb. I stumble up to the front door and ring the bell not even knowing what time it is. When Mum opens the door, I all but collapse into her arms.

"Oh my goodness Izobel, what's happened darling girl? You're freezing and oh my…are your feet bleeding?" The horror in her voice freaks me out and I start to shake. Mum puts her arm around me and takes me into my old room. I feel like I'm in a daze. I can hear the sea in my ears and my head feels like a giant throbbing cotton ball. I lie down on my bed and can't help but sigh in relief because I'm so bloody tired. Mum comes into the room with a tray in her hands. She puts it on the floor and sits down next to my feet at the end of the bed. I look over at her as she starts washing my feet with a cloth that smells of lavender. Such a strong smell that takes me back to my childhood. She still has her bruises and is favouring her right side, I can see her flinch when she tries to get the grime and stones out of the soles of my feet. I can't feel a thing, I figure my feet are still frozen.

"What happened to you Izobel?" she asks me as she gently dries my feet in a lavender scented towel before beginning to rub an ointment into them. She looks so concerned which is wrong. She's broken and bruised yet here she is looking after me.

"I'm sorry Mum…I didn't know where else to go, but please, I'm okay," I wince at the cream stinging my feet. Mum's looking at me as I'm talking and suddenly, she moves my hair off my forehead in a gentle stroke. She freezes.

"Who hit you Izobel?" she whispers, a scared expression on her face. "Please no Izobel, please tell me you're not with a violent man." She's clutching at her chest as I try to take her hand.

"Mum no, it was an accident. I got pushed at the pub and stumbled in my new heels. No one hit me. I promise." I grab her hand to convince her I'm telling the truth.

"If you say so Izobel but the state you're in, turning up here of all places I'm finding it hard to believe this is the full story. I hope you feel you can tell me though so I can help you. Heaven knows I can't help myself, and I couldn't help Zack, but you my lovely girl I *can* help."

Hearing her mention Zack, I close my eyes in pain. The memory of Zack is what started it all tonight and I'm struggling to breathe. I can feel my Mum touching my temple; I'm guessing I have a bit of a bruised egg there because her gentle touch still hurts.

"Take these tablets Izobel and try to rest, have you been sick?" she asks.

"No Mum, I just have a headache…no more dizziness either."

"Well I don't think you have a concussion then, so you should be safe to have a sleep." She rolls out two tablets from a jar. I take the tablets from her hand and close my eyes and feel myself drifting off straight away from pure exhaustion.

I'm not sure how long I sleep for, but it feels as if I'm drifting in and out of consciousness when I suddenly smell fire. Something is burning and I feel it envelop me and pull me under. The smell of a burning will always be a trigger for me. It's very hard to explain. Depending on what's been set on fire the smell will be different. I love the smell of a log fire; it smells safe and warm. Like an embrace. The smell of a fire lit by a discarded cigarette on the other hand will haunt me forever. The smell so acrid and suffocating when teamed with the smell of burning flesh it'll literally bring me to my knees. I know this because of that night when we lost Zack, the smell was brutal….so pungent, so heart breaking and it's imprinted on my brain; my heart…forever. I will never forget. Only people who've been in the same room as a burning body will understand when I say it's reminiscent of burnt pork. A loved one whose personal smell you treasure, reduced to smelling like an overcooked piece of meat. Morbid and disgusting but so true.

I remember screaming at the fire officer who dragged me out of our burning house. Screaming; questioning why it smelt like that, what did it mean for Zack that it smelt like that. My hands bleeding, my nails half pulled off from where I tried to pull Zack out from underneath the beam. The burning beam that had fallen and landed across our backs when the fire reached the ceiling, poor Zack taking the full weight of it before it grazed me.

I try to shout but no words come out. It's so dark and I can't see anything. I can feel the gagging smoke in my throat and struggle to breathe. I scream for Zack. I know he's here somewhere in the darkness, I know it, but I can't see him or feel him. I can feel hands on me holding me down. I struggle against them screaming for Zack.

"Shhh…wake up Izzy, you're dreaming honey, wake up please." I hear the desperation in Sofia's voice, but all I see is darkness and smoke. Why do I hear Sofia? She wasn't there that night. Something isn't right here. I feel a strong set of arms around me pulling me up, much like that night. I struggle to get them off me I need to get back to Zack.

"I need to get Zack," I scream… "Let me go, he's hurt, he can't move…he's stuck…burning…"

"Izzy…I need you to wake up right now...wake up baby." Is that Declan? What's Declan doing here? I don't want him here, he shouldn't be here I try and push away from him but he's so much stronger than I am, I feel his lips by my ear whispering loving words that I can barely make out as the sounds in my head remind me of being in a wind tunnel. I realise now I'm stuck in a nightmare but I can't remember how to get myself out of it. I suddenly feel desperate to wake up from this trance which the smell of fire put me in.

"Come back to me baby…breathe Izzy….come back to me." I feel Declan's hand; his flat palm right on my chest. As if measuring my heart beat, stilling it with his will and touch. My breathing starts to calm down, it's not as frantic and I slowly open my eyes, blinking away the darkness until I see Declan's worried eyes.

"Oh Izzy I'm so sorry, this is all my fault….I started this. I'm so fucking sorry," he whispers as he leans his head down resting his cheek on the top of my hair. I move my head away and look up at him and Sofia, the looks on their faces worried and slightly horrified.

Sofia looks at Declan. "Let's get her in the car and take her back, being here isn't going to help her right now."

"I agree with Sofia," I hear Mum say. "She needs to be where she feels safe, and that isn't here, I know that even though it breaks my heart to say it."

I clear my throat as if to say something but I don't even know what I want or need to say. Mum leans over stroking my hair and whispers to me how sorry she is, she accidentally dropped a piece of paper on the gas flame on the cooker. The burning smell. The memories, they all came back just because of a piece of paper caught fire. An accident. Declan stands up and easily lifts me in his arms.

"I can walk Declan, you really don't need to carry me, I'm not a child," I almost shout at him. Seriously I have no idea why I feel pissed off but I do. Now I'm going to be the one to give this guy whiplash.

"I know you can Iz but let me do this, let me look after you, I need to after what happened."

Mum comes over placing a sweet kiss on my cheek. "Ring me tomorrow okay darling girl. We need to talk about what happened tonight."

Declan carries me out to his car and slides me into the front passenger seat. I shiver with cold again but Sofia's immediately there with a blanket she took from my bed.

"Seriously guys I'm fine, just stop," I plead with them, feeling ashamed about this situation I've put them in.

They both ignore me as they get into the car. On the drive home I see Declan's hand hover, wanting to touch me but scared of my reaction. I ignore both him and Sofia, knowing full well I'm acting like a petulant child, but it's the only way I know to hide my shame. Sofia knows everything but I haven't told her about my recurring nightmare. I wanted her to stop worrying about me. Not much chance of that happening now. Declan parks the car and rushes to my side to lift me out the car.

"I know you don't want this Izzy but you have no shoes sweetheart and your feet look sore. Did you walk all the way home?" he asks picking me up.

"Thanks…Yeah I did, I forgot my bag in the pub," I whisper feeling really embarrassed.

"I have your stuff Izzy, don't worry," Sofia says as she walks ahead and opens the door for us. Declan carries me up the two sets of stairs to his room in the attic, laying me down on his bed. Sofia's hovering in the doorway itching to talk to me I'm sure.

"Hey Declan can you get me a bottle of water from the fridge?" I ask him so that Sofia and I can have a minute. As he runs down the stairs Sofia comes into the room and lies down next to me, our faces so close our noses are almost touching. Just like when we were kids and used to hatch plans for world domination.

"What happened Izzy…you scared the shit out of me; you scared the shit out of everyone." She reaches up and gently pushes the hair out of my eyes. I close them and try to explain something I'm not even sure of myself.

"That guy in the pub…he wore Zack's aftershave Sof…I haven't smelt that since our Zack was with us and it's like something made me grab him. Probably the drink," I say searching her face to see if she thinks I'm crazy. Her face is passive though waiting to hear more.

"So yeah, he obviously freaked out. No surprise really, what with some crazy chick grabbing him like that. Then next minute Declan being on top of him, hitting him…the look on his face. Sofia, I freaked out," I whisper. "I thought of the last time I saw Zack and Dad…I don't know…I couldn't breathe and had to get out of there. I felt scared, confused and just needed out."

Sofia puts her arm around me. "But why did you go back Izzy? What if he'd been home?"

"I knew he wasn't, he's in the States." I look over at the door and see Declan standing there and I immediately know, he's heard every word, he looks ready to blow.

Sofia must have realised he's there too because she gives me a quick kiss and stands up. "I'll see you in the morning hun…sleep well and please don't even think about having one of those freaky nightmares again."

I nod at her as she leaves the room. I hear her go downstairs and Declan closes the door behind her. He stands there leaning his head against the door, his back to me his hands clenched into a fist. "I let you down Izzy….I'm so fucking sorry, more than you'll ever realize."

"Declan come here please," I whisper.

He turns his head and the expression on his face floors me. He feels responsible. His violent outburst was the cause of what happened. But it wasn't, not really. It was me freaking out over the bloody after shave. The rest was just a domino effect.

"Declan...please." I sit up in bed and motion for him to come over to me. He slowly walks over on a sigh and kneels on the floor by the bed in front of me, putting his head in my lap and his arms around my waist. I start stroking his hair.

"I let you down Izzy, I told you I would, and at least it was sooner rather than later. I should've tried harder to stay away but I'd do anything for you, absolutely anything. When that guy pushed you I saw red...I didn't bloody think...there was no other option right in that moment Iz."

"Declan it's okay, I get it. I really do, not to say I agree, but I get it. Please just come to bed." I pat the space next to me on the bed as I scoot over to the side. Declan gets up on the bed and moves over to the side of me sitting on his knees.

"Sit up Izzy," he demands, his voice strong and a determined look on his face. I sit up on my knees in front of him, mirroring him in posture. He slowly unties the knot in my halter neck, pulls it over my head and removes my bra. He doesn't touch me anywhere else. Then he gently pushes me back straightening my legs out in front of me and unbuttons my jeans pulling them off me, minding my feet. He's so gentle I feel a tear escape my eye. He runs his hands up my legs then pulls the duvet over me covering me to the top of my chest. He moves off the bed and removes his own clothes stripping down to his boxer shorts and climbs into bed next to me. He lifts me into his arms so that my head is resting on his chest, my leg entangled in his.

"My Dad was a violent man too Izzy." The words tumble out so quickly, it's as if he's regretting the second the first word left his mouth. I freeze and hold my breath apprehensive of what's coming next.

"He never touched me or Finn, but my Mum used to get it, every time he came home from the pub. Friday nights were the worst. Friday's were pay day. He used to finish work at half past four and him and his mates would go down the pub straight after, rolling home in a fucking state after closing time." Declan's absently stroking down my arm as he's telling me his story. Which I now realize is so closely connected to his reaction in the pub tonight.

"He did it for years Izzy. Mum was never sure what started it, just that it did. One random day he just turned." He looks down at me and smiles, but it doesn't reach his eyes, it's an uncomfortable and apologetic smile.

"I'm so sorry Declan." I reach up and hold his face as I lift myself up and place a tender kiss on his soft lips. He catches my face with his free hand before I get to pull back again. His lips working mine with an intense need, his tongue begging to be let in. A fevered kiss later he whispers against my lips.

"I love you Izzy. I told myself that you were meant for me. I just knew it. I knew *you* the minute I saw you at the bus stop. Your eyes. I recognised what I saw in them, they told the same story, I saw you. I knew you. Fuck…I'm not making any sense, I sound like a dick." His voice is frustrated but genuinely sincere as he pulls his hand through his hair on a curse. I can feel the tears running down my cheeks. Declan suddenly trying to catch each and every one with his lips.

"Declan I need you…please," I whisper, as I look up at him.

He smiles and nods at me, "I need you too sweetheart."

He rolls me onto my back and stands up to go turn the light off. The street lights leave the room lit up enough through the open window in the attic for me to see him as he walks back to the bed. I look at his naked chest so tight with muscles, the defined abs so beautifully decorated down one side with black script and swirls leading to the most sexy v-cut that is begging to be licked. He stands next to the bed, his tall and lean body looming over me before he finally comes back to bed pressing his body flush against mine, making me feel how much he wants me as I feel the hard solid length of him on my stomach. Declan puts his hands on either side of my face, holding me to him as he looks into my eyes, so intense I can't bear to keep my eyes open any longer. I feel his lips on my forehead, kissing me on my nose moving down to gently suck on my neck, moving up to my ear where he whispers, "I love you Izzy."

Every word laced with so much emotion I choke on a sob, "I love you too Declan."

His hands begin to follow his lips, moving from my face as he kisses a trail, starting behind my ear, down my neck till he reaches my breasts where his tongue swirls over my hardened nipples followed by short sharp bites; alternating between mouth and hands. Overcome by total desire I frantically run my hands down what I can reach of his back, his tight muscles flexing under my touch. I can't get enough of him; his skin is so hot to touch. One of his hands reaches for mine and he pins both my wrists to the bed as his other hand moves down between my legs. As he strokes me with his thumb he plunges two fingers hard inside, no warning.

"Declan…" I cry out his name from the sudden explosion of lust surging through me.

"Beautiful baby…so beautiful," he moans as I arch and push into him wanting him to know I need him deep inside me. He slowly moves up my body again until he is poised above me then he stills.

"Open your eyes Izzy, open them and look at me," he demands, his breathing erratic. I open my eyes, find his and just as I do, he fills me in one fast deep thrust to the hilt. I cry out his name as he begins to pound into me, deep hard and fast making me lose control immediately. It doesn't take long for us, the emotion overwhelming, and I miss a breath as he takes my mouth, swallowing my cries of passion.

"Izzy," Declan shouts as he pulls out and comes on my stomach, falling down on his elbow, trying to keep his weight off me as he buries his face in my neck. "Fuck Izzy….always so incredible."

I feel his hot breath against my skin and it gives me goose bumps. I smile in the darkness and move my arms so I can hold him to my chest where he will know I feel the same. My pounding heart letting him know what he does to me.

"I love you Declan," I whisper to him, hoping that he can hear me over our hammering hearts. I truly love this man with all my beating heart.

"I love you too Izzy. It scares the shit out of me. But I bloody love you." His arms tighten around me. We lie there for a moment before Declan moves off me. He puts on his jeans and just does a couple of buttons up making them hang on his hips. The sight of him makes me almost sigh in pure bliss. I do a complete body stretch and actually feel more relaxed than I have in ages as Declan returns. He sits down and starts to clean me off with a warm wash cloth. Oh yeah….I forgot.

"I'm so sorry Izzy, I didn't use a condom. I got so lost in you and suddenly I needed to feel all of you. But I promise, that's never happened before. You're the first girl I've slept with without protection and fuck, it felt good Izzy, you felt good. No strike that. You felt bloody amazing." He gives me a cocky smile and kisses my now very clean stomach, resting his chin on it.

I look down at him with a shy smile. "It was perfect Declan," I blush and look away. "And you're my first in that way too, but I'm on the pill so you don't need to worry next time, you know, about *that*." I pull a pillow across to hide my blushing face. I suddenly think of his words and I have to admit they make me jealous of everyone that came before me, but I can't be hypocritical.

"Izzy sweetheart, look at me," he laughs, pulling at the pillow, climbing up my body till we're face to face. "Only you," he laughs. "Can be an absolute sex kitten one minute with a virginal blush the next. So fucking sexy," he groans and attacks my mouth with his before sitting up, and tossing the wash cloth into the pile of dirty clothes in the corner of the room.

I can't help but cringe, "Eeew…seriously Declan, that's so gross." I fake gagging noises.

"What?" he chuckles, looking all boy-ish with his rumpled hair and big brown eyes.

I shake my head at him and pull him onto the bed by his arm, snuggling into him under the covers, my back to his front. I feel him kissing my scars almost reverently.

"Will you tell me about these soon Izzy?" he asks in between kisses.

"Maybe one day but not right now, not today, I just can't. I'm not ready yet."

"Okay sweetheart, no rush, you tell me when you're ready, don't worry. Just go to sleep, I'm not going anywhere, I promise you're safe now." He holds me tight, running his knuckles down the side of my face softly. I feel safe, safer than I've ever felt and I can feel myself drifting off wrapped in Declan's strong arms.

Sometime in the night I wake up to the low sounds of Declan playing his guitar and singing softly into the room. I keep my eyes closed and steady my breathing as his voice and words penetrate my mind.

"Rising above/the words unspoken/denying ourselves/thoughts are all broken...

Falling below/surfaces bleeding/hiding ourselves the lions are feeding/

Marking our ground/commonly drawn/taking a hold/the pages are torn

Open up a thousand arms and hear the waves roll in/United in divided states/let this time begin...Release

Talking out loud/silently screaming/cornered inside/where thoughts have no meaning...

Open up a thousand arms/hear the waves roll in/united in divided states/let this time begin...Release

Pray to the night/wishing for sunlight/deciding a fate/preparing to fight...

The thousand arms are open and the waves have all rolled in/divided in united states...Release....This time begin..."

Chapter Thirteen

I wake up very early on Monday morning feeling great. The lads, Sofia and I actually managed to have a fun, relaxing weekend. My breakdown was pushed firmly into the background. Sofia and I had quality girlie time Saturday night when the lads were out playing a gig. We had a complete pampering session that left every inch of us smooth, shiny and smelling sweet. Declan returned to me a hot sexy sweaty mess in the early hours of Sunday morning reducing me to a puddle with his talented tongue when he saw what I'd done. Spending what felt like an hour down there saying all his dreams had come true. Who knew? On Sunday all of us stayed in our PJ's and watched eighties movie classics all day only pausing to go get more beer from the Off Licence and to pick up a Chinese take-away. So yeah, we had a great weekend.

I reluctantly get out of bed noting that Declan's already up. Since I've been in his bed, I've been sleeping in just my knickers so I go to his dresser and get a t-shirt out. It's a very old Foo Fighters one and I put it to my face, inhaling all that is Declan before sliding it over my head. I look around the room for my messenger bag to make sure I have everything I need for Uni today. I know I have to go see Dr McGrath and I have to say, I'm not looking forward to it one bit. I know he'll not ask me a single question. He'll sit there all warm and encouraging and I'll feel like I have to share. He's so different to anyone I've seen before, I'm scared to see him but at the same time I want to give him *me* because deep down, I know he's helping me. His presence is like a warm embrace that makes me feel so strong, and even though my past is a nightmare that'll never really die, he will help me wake up from it. I go downstairs to make myself a coffee before my shower and the house is eerily quiet. Everyone must have early lectures today. I know Max must still be in bed because he doesn't start his shift at the record store till mid-day, so I make him a coffee too.

I carry the two steaming hot cups upstairs and set mine down on the sink in the bathroom before I go and softly knock on Max's door. There's no answer, so I gently nudge the door open, cover my eyes and look down as I softly pad into his room, but not before I see him asleep, naked on his front all tangled in white sheets. Seriously this guy has one of the most built bodies I've ever seen. His skin looks darker than it really is, set off by the white sheet.

I hear a gruff sleepy laughter, "Like what you see? Not sure how Declan would feel about that."

I can feel my face burning as I quickly set his coffee down on his night stand. "Umm I made you coffee Max."

I blush and quickly run out of his room, my exit followed by his laughter as he shouts after me, "Thanks Izzy, I'm only messing with you pretty girl."

I lock myself in the bathroom, so embarrassed, but Max is a nice guy, so I know he won't take the piss too much. I run a bath and take my kindle in with me as well as my coffee. Pure quiet bliss with no need to worry. I thank whatever lucky stars landed me in this house with Declan, Aiden and Max. In a strange way it's such a relief to only hurt on the inside. Now, at least I don't have to worry about hurting on the outside from one of Dad's tempers. Having to worry about both makes me unable to breathe and forget. I relax and get lost in a story about romance and a hot guy, my favourite.

Later that day, I'm sitting in my last lecture daydreaming about Declan and our weekend together. How easy it felt and wishing we could lock ourselves away and not have to face any obstacles that could make things difficult for us. My past, my present and…I'm abruptly startled out of my thoughts when I feel something bump my table. Lina. She would *have* been the next obstacle in mind, no doubt.

"Oh sorry Izzy, did I wake you up?" she sneers at me scrunching her face up in disgust. If it hadn't have been sneered with venom I would've smiled and said no worries. But it was and the expression on her face says it all.

"Are you five years old Lina?" I ask looking at her with a bored expression as I try to look as though her action and the threat she brings, doesn't hurt and unnerve me.

She sends me one last look of disgust before she takes a seat as close as she can to me. I find it hard to concentrate on the lecture, feeling her eyes drilling a hole in me throughout the hour. I know she's not going to go away and I make a mental note to question Aiden and Declan about her as soon as I can. After my lecture I walk to Dr McGrath's office wondering why I'm starting to shake. It's not like I have to say anything or divulge my secrets. But as my heart hesitates, the beats increase as if it knows the barriers will be beaten down further. That's just what this kind gentle man does to me. As I knock and walk in after a hurried *'come in'*, it's as though the world stops, only for me. It's the darkness inside that terrifies me, but in this room, the reasons for me being here, the light is what terrifies me the most. Shining a spotlight on me.

"So Izobel how have you been?" he asks as he motions for me to sit down whilst pushing his glasses further up his nose before sitting down in that worn and patched up chair of his. I note the green velvet fraying on the arm-rest, which is probably where he rubs his hands and fingers as he listens whilst thinking. The chair looks as unkempt and tired as its owner, yet just as warm and wise. I look into the kind, aged eyes and from out of nowhere I blurt it out.

"I can't breathe when I smell fire," I feel the first tear run down my cheek as I swallow the huge lump that is forming in my throat. "I can't breathe and I fall down a long black tunnel that takes me back to the night my brother died."

I can't break the eye contact I have with Dr McGrath as he steeples his fingers and takes a deep breath as though he's relieved and thankful for my words, yet shocked at the same time. We sit in silence for what is surely only seconds but feels like an hour.

"Izobel, I need to ask you a question before we begin, can I turn the tape recorder on? I will leave it running and it'll never be used without your permission," he hesitates while picking the recorder up. "I do think it may help you further down the road. But this is entirely your decision and I will respect your answer either way," he solemnly says as he nods his head at me reassuring me that I do have a choice and to take my time.

I nod my head as I see him press a button and a red light coming on. I look away not wanting to acknowledge that my voice will be captured. I look everywhere but at him. "Since the night Zack my brother died, every time I smell fire, I remember," I whisper, as if saying it too loud will make it all become real again.

"Do you feel ready to tell me about that night Izobel?" He leans back in his chair as if to show me that I don't have to fear him and my space is in no way invaded by any outside forces, only from my own.

"I don't know, I want to, I have to because I'm scared I'm losing control. I lost control and I'm embarrassed. I'm scared of being left….of being alone…my heart feels empty," I hesitate, realising that I stand to lose so much more than what I've already lost by living in the moment of loss, which still pulsates inside my heart, making it scared to heal and love again. The air in the room suddenly feels very thick and heavy and I can see the air molecules, carried by dust motes through the low streaking sun, coming through the windows and signalling the end of the autumn day.

"Just take your time Izobel," he says reassuringly, his tone making me feel stronger, braver I suppose.

"My brother died eighteen months ago in a fire," I say in a broken voice, as I look back into those kind eyes. "I couldn't save him, I tried, but he ended up saving me. I couldn't reach him. I tried but I wasn't strong enough." My breath hitches as I look down at my hands, hands that are always referred to as a child's hands, so small and in my eyes, so weak. I keep looking at my hands spreading my fingers as I try to confirm or justify the reason for my failure.

"Izobel; can you tell me what happened that day but from the beginning? Tell me how your day started," he asks, as his eyes look encouragingly at me, one of his hands resting on the frayed part of the velvet arm rest smoothing down the loose strands.

"You need a new chair," I say and he smiles at me.

"This chair and I can't be separated; we're both old and worn and have history. They'll be carrying me out in it," he laughs, a deep but gentle laugh that warms me from the inside. So without thinking and hesitating I begin.

"I got up in the morning, it was a Saturday. I remember being excited because I got my place at Uni. Zack was coming home for the weekend and I couldn't wait to tell him. Tell him that I was getting out…away." I look up, desperately wanting him to understand, but knowing that he won't yet understand the importance of why.

"Zack and I were safer together. Always have been. I know no one would understand why it was like that, I mean it's not like we were kids anymore. But when you're living it, pain and control doesn't care about age. And age means nothing when you can be reduced to nothing with just one look or a single word. To fully understand you have to have experienced it." I look at him pleadingly, willing him to understand because if he does, then I won't feel so bad for not understanding it myself, for feeling ashamed and weak. He looks at me and I know he understands, his eyes tell me, so I continue feeling safe that I can.

"I woke up early but stayed in bed reading when I heard Zack come home. I knew he'd be straight into the kitchen to make a cup of tea for himself, so I waited knowing he'd bring a coffee in for me like he always does…" I stumble with my words, "…did when he came home."

"Did he not live at home with you and your parents?" he asks me with a frown as if he knows what's coming.

"No, Zack moved out as soon as he could. He got a scholarship to a private college with the opportunity to board at sixteen. So he took it. He didn't want to, because of me, but I convinced him he had to, that it would make me happy. He knew I'd get out as soon as I could." I look down at my hands in my lap and start to pick at some loose threads in the worn patch of my jeans near my knee.

"As I knew he would, Zack came into my room with a mug of coffee and sat down on the end of my bed. We caught up on life in general, staying clear of anything to do with our parents, though they were, as per usual, the proverbial pink elephant in the room."

By now I've picked an actual hole in my jeans and I catch Dr McGrath looking at my hand, taking note of what he sees before looking back up at my face. He reaches for his glass of water on the coffee table and before I realise, I do the same. The offending hand leaves my knee, reaching for my glass, which I had no idea he'd put there for me. I clutch the cold glass with both hands and marvel at the fact that it's still so cold when the room feels so hot and that it feels as if I've already been sitting here for hours. I note that time has barely passed, before I continue.

"We sat there for hours, or what seemed like hours, before we heard Mum moving about in the house. Zack gave me a cuddle and went to catch up with her as I got ready for the day." I flinch at that memory thinking if only I'd known what I was getting ready for.

"Were you doing something special that day?" he asks me in a curious voice.

"Well, we're a family of traditions. Dad made it so. Always the family lunch at a restaurant, which despite being an hour away in the car, was a must. We'd sit in silence except when Zack or I was asked a question. No one wanting to say anything that could be misinterpreted into being something it wasn't and offence being taken." I look away from my glass of water that strangely has ripples in it. I realise my hands are shaking. I look up at Dr McGrath whose eyes have turned sharp as if he is getting ready for me to freak out, pass out or something. I take a deep breath.

"When we got back to the house after a long lunch during which my Dad had too much to drink making Mum, who's a nervous driver, take us home. Everything was still routine as it always is. I was in my room reading until dinner. Time lost in my book world where I feel safe and at home."

I look up at Dr McGrath waiting to see if he has a reaction to me living in a fictional world as an escape. His face reveals nothing but concern and encouragement, remaining as it was from the start. I take a big gulp of water as my throat feels too dry and restricted by the words I've said and the one's I know will be leaving my mouth soon.

"During dinner…that's when it began…" I falter and know I need to move, I feel like I can't breathe and the rushing in my ears gets louder as my heart feels like it's starting to beat its own path out of my chest. I stand up and walk over to the window placing my shaking hands against the glass, resting my hot forehead against the coolness of the window pane.

"Go on Izobel, it's okay, you're safe. Nothing can hurt you in here and I'm with you, you're not on your own, take deep even breaths…count with me."

He starts to take deep even breaths and I mimic them, like a child learning to breathe properly for the first time. My head clears but I remain in position looking out over the busy campus square where students are running around like head-less chickens, either rushing to classes or rushing home.

"You were having dinner Izobel," he starts, guiding me back as the memories flood my vision tinged in red and playing out like a dream sequence to a soundtrack of haunted, broken melodies.

"We were having dinner and Zack asked me about my Uni applications, he was still at college you see and was considering where to go after his finals. I'd taken longer than most people to decide where to apply to and what to study, knowing I wanted to be completely sure, not wanting to waste my time and effort. Also, in my heart, what I really wanted to study was a sore topic of conversation, as my Dad thought it was a waste of time and every chance he got, he would ridicule it." I smile a bitter smile and look back over my shoulders at him. "I got here though didn't I? In the end I won *that* battle." Involuntarily, a shudder runs through me as I look back out the window, not really seeing anything but the look etched on everyone's faces when it all began.

"Isn't it strange how you can push a bad memory to the back of your mind, lock the door and seal it shut, yet when you need to recall it, only a smell, a feeling or a sensation can spring that door open as if it's a magic key." I get lost in the past again, the chills running down my spine like ice cold fingers. I wonder why I can talk about it now, so freely, even though the pain's immeasurable. I turn around and look at him all confused. "But here with you, I see it all, as if it's playing out right in front of me. Why is that?"

"I'm in the belief that you're ready to confront your memories and resolve your emotions and the guilt that's eating you up from the inside," he says with such frankness. He's right.

I walk over to the wall opposite the window, which is made up purely of shelves, full of books. I run my fingers across the spines as I walk the length of it. I continue and walk back to the couch, where I sit down and pick up my glass again, taking another sip before I delve into the memory of that night. I feel really strange. Oddly apprehensive, scared yet relieved that I'm finally going to tackle that night. Say the words out loud in front of someone.

"As we were sitting eating our dinner Zack suddenly jerks and turns to me and excitedly tells me he brought a present home for me from his trip to the south coast."

I look at Dr McGrath and whisper, "He forgot...he forgot the rule, he got caught up in his excitement. You see when we were very young, my grandmother bought me a snow globe. It had a fairy in it. The fairy had a sparkling turquoise dress and glittery wings. I think she was attached to a hill with green sparkles for grass. Surrounding this hill were bright coloured flowers floating in water. I am not sure how it was made but when you shook it the water didn't move but sparkling flakes would fall all around the fairy. Despite her being somehow attached, it would seem as though she was floating in the globe. It was called 'Fairy tale'," my voice breaks and I feel the tears threatening so I stop talking as I picture the snow globe Zack bought me.

I shiver and take some deep breaths as I continue to pick at the hole in my jeans pulling at the threads, exposing my knee, the hole getting bigger. My vision is getting hazy and my pulse is roaring in my ears.

"Are you okay to continue Izobel?" he asks as he places a no frills tissue box on the table in front of me.

"Yes...yes, I think so…" I shake my head unsteadily, I can't stop now, the words are there, waiting to come out.

"So, Zack suddenly left the table and went to his room. I remember Mum's expression before she quickly looked down at her plate. She knew…she was scared. Dad straightened his spine looking in angry surprise at Zack's retreating back. Such a small indiscretion really. A moment of impulse which started a nightmare like a domino effect. When Zack came back with a white plastic bag and sat down he didn't realise what he'd done but excitedly took out a box and gave it to me. Inside the box was an exact replica of the snow globe my Grandmother had given me." I look over at Dr McGrath with blurred vision, feeling tears as they begin their trail down my cheek. My emotions overwhelm me.

"My first one broke you see….the one my grandmother bought me. In a fit of rage Dad picked it up and flung it at the wall to punish me. I can't to this day remember what I'd done or said, but I remember the terror I felt as Zack and I crouched behind the couch. I'm not sure whether Dad knew what he was throwing, but it was the closest at hand when his temper blew. I think he took his anger out on that instead of me; perhaps a second of clarity that he could really hurt me this time. One minute earlier I had been sitting with it in my hand, only to put it down to have a drink of milk before bed. When he started shouting I ran over to Zack to drag him behind the couch but left my snow globe on the coffee table. The broken pieces were everywhere and he made me clean it up even though he was the one who threw it. I remember cutting my fingers on the glass but the pain in my heart was worse."

I lose focus and the room fades, I feel lightheaded and my heart starts to skip beats, I feel them and it's making my chest hurt. I'm openly crying now, grabbing at the tissues on the table.

I hear Dr McGrath's voice from far away as I try to re-gain control of my breathing, beating away the black tunnel that is trying to swallow me up. I know he's exaggerating his breathing trying to get me back.

"Izobel, do you want to stop for the day?" he asks me again, concern in his voice.

"I don't know….no I don't think I do. I need to tell you….tell someone, I'm scared of going crazy," I whisper as my throat dries up. Dr McGrath stands up and walks over to the cooler on the floor by his paper strewn desk. He picks up a bottle of water and walks back to me handing me the bottle.

"Thank you," I say gratefully as I unscrew the cap and pour it into my empty glass. He sits back down and immediately resumes his position, as if we haven't had this interruption.

I start telling my story again. "So, when I saw what Zack had bought me I started crying. I couldn't help it. My heart burst with both pain and love and we sat there hugging at the table as if it was just us two in the room, lost in a memory. He looked so happy yet scared, I think he wasn't completely sure how I'd feel about this gift. But he did good, I loved it," I smile through my tears up at Dr McGrath. I move my arm to pick up the glass of water but my charm bracelet gets caught in the threads I've been pulling at and I begin to untangle them. I continue focusing on the trapped charm. Of all my charms to get caught it's the letter Z, which gives me chills.

"My Dad left the table abruptly and walked to his office slamming the door behind him. I think we all knew he'd be drinking and stewing in there until he was ready to face us again. It's what he did. It's what he still does," I shrug, defeated, because I realise the pattern of behaviour hasn't changed since and we still live with it.

"Mum, Zack and I sat there in silence for a few minutes before she rose and started clearing up the table. We stood too and did the same. I remember gripping my snow globe in one hand not wanting to let it go. But when we'd finished, I had to put my snow globe down on the kitchen table as Mum did something so surprising. I remember it gave me goose bumps at the time. She got hold of both our hands and pulled us into a hug and told us she loved us with tears in her eyes. I think at the time it shocked me because normally when she got scared and apprehensive of Dad's temper she would retreat to her bedroom."

I take a deep breath knowing that we've almost reached the nightmare moment I lost the person I loved the most in the world. I search but I can't reach the words that take me to it. These are the words I long to be able to say, but it petrifies me. What will happen if I say them out loud? I look over at Dr McGrath and ask him as I have to know and I'm not sure I'm ready to tell my final words yet. I need to calm my emotions down. But it's so bloody hard and I'm scared that I'll break down and get pulled under.

"How do you know my Mum?" I ask him. He looks surprised at my sudden question and quickly looks away as if to gain a few seconds to think of an appropriate story as to how.

"It's okay, you can tell me you know, I wish she could talk to you too," I say hopeful because I know she needs to see someone again and I can't think of anyone safer to see than him.

He clears his throat as if in discomfort. "Your Mum made an emergency appointment a while back with my practice and I was the only one available to speak to her at the time," he says with a sigh, looking really uncomfortable, as if he's already said too much. I feel bad for him because I know it is none of my business, well it is, but that was Mum's time not mine. I take another sip of water knowing if I don't stop drinking I'll have to make a quick exit soon which I surprisingly don't want as I'm without doubt here until I've given him my memory. All of this memory.

We sit in silence but it's not an uncomfortable one. I gather my thoughts making sure I have them in the right order, as at one point that night, I lost a whole hour. Hazy images are floating through my mind trying to slot into the right order.

"It was really late, Zack and I were sitting on the couch, he was watching some police action show and I was reading on my kindle. Mum was sitting knitting in the chair in the corner of the lounge. Dad hadn't come out of his office since he left dinner so suddenly. We'd heard the clinking of a glass and bottles so we knew he was drinking. Dad usually holds his alcohol well, but when he's drunk in anger, we know to leave the room," I pause, as we've reached the beginning of the end. I feel so cold I start to shiver and I can't feel the tips of my fingers, I start to rub them together before placing them underneath my bum to warm them up.

"It was quite dark in the lounge; the only light was coming from the TV. I always wondered how Mum could knit in such low light, but I suppose her knitting was automatic, she knitted on autopilot as a de-stressor, I'm sure it still has a calming effect on her now, as she sorts out problems in her head. We were just about turn in for the night when Dad came in. He looked so angry, no … furious more like," my voice is losing its strength and all I can see now is how the TV's blue flickering played across his face, the shadows of the TV light playing on the walls behind him. I pick up another tissue and sort myself out before taking a deep breath.

"Dad had a burning cigarette in one hand and my snow globe in the other. He must've picked it up from the kitchen and I remember I was cursing myself for leaving it in there. Dad was swaying as he walked over to us. He roughly threw the globe on the table and pinned me with his menacing blood shot eyes. Zack just flew at him. I think he finally lost control of his emotions. He jumped off the couch and pushed Dad away, shouting at him, asking him what the fuck he was doing." I immediately blush and look at Dr McGrath apologetically when I realise I've just sworn in front of him.

"I'm sorry for swearing....I'll try not to do that again," I apologise, feeling awful.

"Please Izobel, I'm an old man, I've heard much worse, just tell me your story as you remember it and use whatever words you need to, please don't apologise again," he smiles at me, encouragingly. It suddenly feels really hot in here and my palms begin to sweat so I rub them up and down my jeans as I feel a bead of moisture run down my hair line.

"My Dad punched Zack....he actually punched him," I shudder from the memory and the shock I felt...still feel. "He's never punched any of us before...ever. He would clumsily hit us or slap us, even push us but never punch. Sometimes he would hit us with something or hurt us in other ways but never with a clenched fist. Zack stumbled backwards pulling my Dad with him and they landed on the coffee table knocking off my snow globe. I haven't seen my snow globe since that night." I stop talking as I think of why that punch made such an impression on me. When you think of the scars on my back, a punch actually seems rather tame and a more normal form of aggression. Again the tears start and I wipe my face with clammy hands.

"In the commotion no one noticed Dad's cigarette until a huge patch of carpet started burning. Our house was a listed property, one of those old houses with the original beams, shag carpet, heavy curtains and visible wooden posts. It didn't take long…..the flames started licking up the walls as Dad and Zack fought each other, shouting….I remember Mum screaming in the corner of the room, divided by a wall of flames. I sat motionless…I couldn't move….why didn't I move?" I look up confused at Dr McGrath, fast streaming tears blurring my vision, my hands shaking as I clench them into fists, unable to stop them. I sit on them again, but this time it's to keep them still.

"Izobel, shock of sudden actions which frighten us, affects us all differently, the mechanisms reacting to unforeseen circumstance, is not predictable nor can it always be rationally questioned, or judged by hindsight," he explains so I understand. I can't pretend that I do though.

"But I sat there frozen until I realised that either of them could kill the other or the fire would get us. I yelled….no…I screamed at them to stop, the heat intensifying….and the smell…I'll never forget the smell once the fire touched Zack. His sleeve….his sleeve caught fire," I brokenly stutter as I stand up and once again walk over to the window. The sun's left the sky and the heavy grey clouds are making it seem darker and later than it really is. The rain's started and a sea of umbrellas are hurrying in different directions. My palms are cold as ice. They're violently shaking so I place them on the radiator under the window sill. Only in England will you find radiators underneath drafty windows I think to myself.

"Mum ran out of the room, I'm pretty sure she went to call the fire brigade as there was no doubt the fire was out of control. My Dad and brother seemingly unaware until the fire touched Zack. Zack screamed in agony…I can still hear it, I hear it every time I smell fire…I hear it in my dreams….I can hear it now." I'm openly crying now unable to stop, completely lost in the memory. I can smell the burning and my breaths are ragged as I try to continue.

"My Dad pushed Zack off him really hard, it was a shove out of the fire. Zack stumbled into me pushing me backwards so I lost my footing as we fell to the floor. Zack landed on top of me." I look back over my shoulder at Dr McGrath, but I can't see him for my tears.

"Why is it I remember every detail as if it happened in slow motion. Why am I remembering all of it in this room with you…remembering it so clearly?" I ask him, crying the words out.

"You're ready to remember Izobel. You're ready to come to terms with what happened, you know you need to, in order to move on with your life." I'm not sure if it's my imagination or whether his eyes look as if they're tinged with sadness and regret.

"Dad disappeared from the room, I didn't see him leave but I know when Zack and I sat back up he was gone. The fire had completely taken over now and I remember Zack pulling me up by my hand, frantically shouting for us to get out of there. Suddenly there was a loud noice. I can't even describe it, almost like a crunching sound. Like the sound the crack of a log in a fire can make. That sudden glowing spark; the noise of flints rubbing together to create it." I close my eyes and sink to the floor, resting my back against the heater, next to his desk. I bring my knees up to my chest as I hide my face in my hands, making myself as small as I can, as my body tries to suck the heat from the radiator. My memory is full of fire and scorching heat, yet I feel so cold and clammy, like I've been caught in the rain currently lashing at the window.

"It was the wooden beam," I whisper, not able to open my eyes as I see it breaking off the ceiling in my head. "The whole wooden beam dropped like a fireball…Zack pushed me out of the way, so when it made contact…it was with him…it landed on him and took him to the floor. I lost all sense…I don't even remember all the things I did to try and get him out from under that burning beam…I remember the smell, that God awful smell of burning flesh...the roaring in my ears so loud but I heard him...I heard him whisper his love for me and to get out, before he went silent, silent forever."

My words tumble out on a hitched breath as if the quicker they're said, the sooner this will all be over. "I tried to pull him, I tried to beat the beam with pillows, I tried with my pathetic glass of milk. I tried......I tried everything I could. I promise you Zack...I swear I tried....I was weak...I couldn't breathe...I had no air...then it all went black and I remember nothing...Zack left me....I failed him...I finally failed him after all those years of trying to protect him." I'm shaking with violent crying and I really can't breathe, I can't stop the noise in my head...The roaring sound of flames in my ears, the acrid smell of burning flesh in my nose.

"I woke up as they stretchered me out of the house with an oxygen mask on. I turned my head and saw a stretcher and even though I knew it was Zack, I was praying he wasn't the one completely covered by a white sheet." I feel so exhausted and my body starts to convulse. I feel dizzy and before I know it I begin to retch. Grabbing the wastebasket by his desk I throw up, until I have nothing left in me. I suddenly feel two gentle arms around me trying to still my shaking and I turn my face into a warm chest. I feel so tired and weak. Always so bloody weak. Time passes but I'm not sure how long or what time it is when I eventually feel all cried out. I retreat from the arms and look up into the concerned, kind face of Dr McGrath. I immediately feel bad that this gentle man has had to join me on the cold hard floor.

"I'm sorry," I whisper motioning to us sitting on the floor together.

"I'm so proud of you Izobel, so very proud, I'm rather proud of my knees too, I hope they make me just as proud by getting me up again," he smiles at me and I imagine it's the kind of smile a granddaughter or a much loved daughter would receive. In that moment I realise that this smile has reached into my heart, making the warmth creep back into my bones, my heart. I throw my arms around him.

"Thank you….thank you so much." I close my eyes and the exhaustion wraps me up tight.

"You still have quite a way to go Izobel, but you just took the most important and hardest step on the journey to healing. We'll take the next step another day." He stands up gingerly and holds his hand out to me. I place my small cold hand in his as I make a meal of standing up. I have absolutely no strength left in my body. I want to curl up and just go asleep. He guides me to the couch and walks over to his cool box where he pulls out a fizzy drink.

"Here, drink this and take your time getting yourself together. I don't have anywhere to be and you've just re-lived a very traumatic episode." He picks up my bag from the floor and places it next to me. "I think you need to call someone to come pick you up, I don't think you should try and get home on your own Izobel." I nod as if in a trance and riffle through my bag for my mobile to call Declan.

"I'll call my boyfriend," I tell him as I scroll through the contact list on my phone.

Chapter Fourteen

Declan

I've just finished my last lecture and start walking to the far end of the student car park, the only place safe enough to park my baby, my restored Ford Capri when I hear my mobile ringing in my backpack. I let it ring out as I'm gagging to get home to Izzy. Shit, I've missed her today and I can't help but think back to the weekend we've just had. I think it's the most relaxed and happy I've seen her since I met her. The smiles and laughter, actually reaching her eyes for once. I know blokes aren't supposed think about shit like this but I have no idea why the connection with her is so strong and why it happened so quickly. But I do know that I have this strong fucking urge to protect her, as well as an intense need to put a smile on her beautiful face.

The fact that she's a walking wet dream doesn't even come first, like it usually does, which is unusual for me. Izzy has no fucking clue at all. Yeah I need to get home and be in her, I think to myself, as my jeans get tighter. Just as I unlock the car my mobile starts off again. I slide into the seat and dig through my backpack for it. One missed call from Izzy and three from Aiden. I hit redial as I slide on my seatbelt and start the car up.

"Hey man about bloody time."

"What the hell Aiden?"

"You need to go pick Izzy up from Dr McGrath's office, she rang me to come get her but I'm stuck at work for another hour. Man…she sounded knackered; I think she's had one hell of a session mate."

"Thank fuck I'm still here…thanks Aid…see you later."

I hang up and quickly get out of my car, almost running to the admin offices as my worry for Izzy only grows. I see her sitting on a bench outside the building, her knees drawn up to her chest with her head resting on them. Her long blonde hair is covering her like a curtain so I can't see her face.

"Hey sweetheart, you okay?" I ask her as I sit down and draw her into my arms. She leans into me resting her head on my chest. I brush the long fine hair out of her face, away from her eyes so I can get a better read on her from her eyes.

"Yeah I think so. I will be, just really tired Declan it's been a long day. Would you mind taking me back?" she asks in a quiet voice.

"Not at all baby, come on." I pull her up off the bench and put my arm around her shoulders, drawing her into my side as her head rests against my chest. She's such a short arse but it only pulls more at my protective side. We walk to my car in silence and seeing as I suck at small talk I don't even bother, because I'm pretty sure something major happened this afternoon. Izzy is wound tighter than a coiled spring. I open the door for her and I'm sure as soon as her hot arse hits the seat, she falls asleep because by the time I get in and turn the car on she's making those cute sleepy noises.

Once we get back to the house she's still dead to the world, so I carry her upstairs to our bed. I put her down and take off her shoes and jeans. She curls into a ball immediately, almost as if she's trying to get as small as she can. I cover her up with the duvet and draw the curtains. Once I'm sure she's okay and fast asleep, I go back downstairs to get a drink. Aiden's in the kitchen with his head in the fridge.

"Any beer left in there mate?" I ask him as I jump up and sit on the kitchen counter.

"Yeah…want a Carlsberg or Heineken?"

"Carlsberg please," I answer, cracking the can open when he passes it to me. I take a huge guzzle.

"So, what the hell happened?" Aiden asks as he sits down at the kitchen table putting his feet up.

"Don't really know mate, she was done in though so I've left her sleeping upstairs. Once she wakes up I'll try and find out. Have you seen Sofia today?"

"Nope, I sent her a text after I spoke to Izzy, but I haven't got a response yet," Aiden shakes his head.

I finish of my can and jump off the counter to go stick it in the bin. "Right mate I'm going back upstairs, give me a shout when Sofia comes back because I have a feeling Izzy will need her when she wakes up."

Aiden nods his head and taking the stairs two at a time, I rush back upstairs. Izzy's still asleep so I pick up my guitar and sit down in the corner of the attic bedroom under the window and softly start playing Snow Patrol. I'm in the middle of *'This Isn't Everything You Are'* when Izzy starts to stir. I stop playing, worried that I've woken her up.

"Don't stop please, I love that song," she whispers, her voice raspy and full of sleep.

I pick up where I left off and stand up, singing to her as I walk over, before sitting myself down next to her and looking into her big blue eyes. She smiles at me, her eyes half closed with sleep. She's fucking gorgeous, I think to myself as I'm playing for her. When I finish, I put my guitar back on its stand and get into bed, pulling her into my arms. We're lying on our sides with her head resting in the crook of my arm, looking up at me. Her hand reaches up and a finger traces my lip ring giving it a gentle tug. I stroke the hair away from her face, tracing my fingers down her cheek and across her lips. Then cradling her face in my hand, I lean down to kiss her.

"Stop," she suddenly shouts and jumps out of bed. "Hold that kiss."

"What the hell Izzy?" I ask confused, as she disappears down the stairs.

Three minutes later, she's back in my arms smelling minty fresh.

"Did you just go brush your teeth?" I ask her.

"Yeah...long story," she blushes, reaching up to pull my head down for *that* kiss. The kiss was intended to be perfectly gentle but with Izzy, as soon as I taste her lips that's me done for. Her moan in my mouth, immediately stirs something inside me and I roll her over onto her back and brace myself on my elbows, taking the kiss deeper, tasting her mouth with my tongue.

"Declan..." she says on an exhaled breath. Hearing her say my name in such a reverent way, makes me lose all control. I kiss a trail down her neck, sucking gently on that soft skin of hers, as I gently tug her top up. I'm trying fucking hard to slow down and make this all about her as I want to take away whatever hurt she's gone through today. It's not easy though as we separate so she can pull her top off. I get back to kissing, sucking and licking a trail down her neck, feeling her pulse on my lips. Unfastening the front opening on her bra I slide it off her arms. I can feel her heart beating out of her chest, her rapid breaths, as I run my tongue over her hard nipple, taking her breast in my mouth. Her arched back is telling me she's wanting me to hurry up, but I want to take my sweet time with her as I kiss my way to her other breast. Her moans and fast breaths are telling me everything I need to know.

"Declan," she pants, as her hands grab the back of my head, her fingers tangling into my hair, pulling at it.

"I'm right here sweetheart," I say, as my tongue moves from her breasts down to her belly button tasting, every bit of her as I do. "You taste so fucking good Izzy." I bloody love the taste of her, like sugared strawberries and vanilla in a fucking perfect wrapping. Pulling off her knickers, I find she's already completely soaked for me as I lick, kiss and taste her until she screams my name in pure fucking pleasure. Pulling off my boxers, I enter her in one hard thrust. I hook her leg over my arm and grab her sweet arse for leverage, letting me go deeper, touching the part of her that I know will make her scream my name. And fuck do I want her screaming my name, I don't want there to be any question as to who she belongs to. I lean down over her and grab the back of her neck with my other hand, assaulting her mouth, sucking at her tongue, swallowing her moans. I let her mouth go and suck at that soft skin behind her ear and bite her earlobe gently.

"Let go for me sweetheart. Just fucking let go, I want to hear you scream my name," I growl like some mental cave man. But this is what she does to me.

"Declan...Declan," she chants, and the second I hear her cry out my name again, I let myself go, my body losing all control.

"Beautiful Izzy. Beautiful."

Hot and out of breath I collapse but roll us onto our sides, so I don't crush her. I rain kisses all over her face, ending by kissing her deeply as she clings onto me for dear life. We lie here for a while in complete silence. Izzy is hiding her face in my chest as one of her fingers trails the tattoo across my chest and onto my shoulder.

"That was amazing," she says, as I feel her warm breath on my chest.

"You're amazing sweetheart," I reply, meaning every single world. It's true, she is so fucking amazing. We lie in silence and I can feel myself dozing off when she suddenly stills, alerting me to the fact that something's changed, the mood feels *off* all of a sudden.

"I told Dr McGrath today about the night Zack died," she suddenly says and automatically I tighten my arms around her. "It was actually easier than I thought it'd be…but it really hurt Declan, reliving it all again. I can't explain it, but all the smells and sounds were there, how I felt. It was gut wrenching. But I did it." She sounds so bloody sad but kind of proud too. I reach down and kiss her forehead to show her I'm listening but I stay silent for her, knowing she's not done.

"I'm still a bit messed up and I'm worried you'll get tired of me because I have a way to go yet and I know I'm not easy to be with at times, but I can't lose you Declan because…I love you." She stops abruptly on a hitched breath as if she's said something she didn't intend to and is scared of my reaction.

I grab her chin with my fingers and move her face up so I can look her in the eyes, because I'm about to tell her just how I feel.

"Listen sweetheart, because I'm only going to say this once," I say making sure I've got her full attention as I run my knuckles over her cheek. She's looking up at me with her big beautiful blues, so I continue. "No matter what you throw at me from your past, that's exactly what it is, the past. Now, I fucking love you, you know I do, because I told you so and that's not going to change just because your messed up childhood is still playing out in the present." I search her face for a reaction. She closes her eyes and a tear runs down her cheek. I pick it up with my thumb and kiss her softly.

"You know Izzy, if anything, hell, it actually makes me love you and want to shield you from shit even more, because I lived part of that childhood too. You know I did and the fact that you're living with scars, tells me that yours was pretty fucked up. So no, you don't need to tell me, sure I want to know so I can help you deal, but you do that when you're ready, I will never pressure you to do or say anything."

As I'm talking, the tears are running down her cheeks in steady streams now, making me feel like a right bastard for causing her to cry. *Shit. Wank. Bollocks.* I try and capture each one with a kiss, tasting the saltiness as she sobs in my arms. She looks quizzically at my face as I tuck her hair behind her ear. She reaches her hand up tracing her fingers through the stubble that's started growing along my chin.

"I worry Declan. I worry that you may have fallen in love with a shadow of me," she whispers grabbing my hand and bringing it to her lips. "I worry that whenever my back is exposed my scars will shine like bright beacons showing the remnants of my childhood for what it was; completely broken." She places my hand over her pounding heart. "I worry that this will make you regret us and regret those beautiful words." Her words cut me to my bones, the feeling so fucking strong and infuriating, I roll away from her, raking my fingers through my hair.

"Jesus Izzy...no. No that's not fair," I shake my head in frustration. "And I'm not gonna let you push me away with bollocks like that," I say as I turn my face to her. She's looking up at me with scared eyes, so I know I need to show her; get my words right.

"Violence doesn't discriminate against who people are or where they're from," I tell her with a firm voice. "It happens, everywhere, the people who like to inflict it can be found in any place; have any social standing. They control it, not you. It doesn't choose you and it doesn't make you who you are. Not deep down," I explain, wanting her to see some fucking sense, not put herself down when this isn't her fault. I gently turn her over so her back is facing me and I can see her childhood, bared to me on the pale naked canvas of her back. "You did *not* deserve these sweetheart." I start tracing the first of three perfectly round scars on her upper back.

"I'm not going to lie Izzy, seeing these make me fucking pissed off and I want to beat the shit out of him. But they're part of you; body and soul, whether it's right or wrong, it's part of why I love you, so don't ever hide from me or hide behind these scars." I lean down and kiss each one reverently as I hear her breath catch. Her shoulders start to shake and I know she's crying again.

"I don't want it to define who I am, for it to be what people see Declan," she whispers.

I don't answer her; instead I push the duvet down further until her lower back is exposed, until I can see the small patch of scarred skin. I slowly run my fingers across it. I want to show her that scars are a map of a person's life, a piece of their history which tells their story. In no way does it make this beautiful girl ugly. It shows that this beautiful girl is strong and a survivor.

"This is you, all of you and I love *all* that is you, Izzy," I say, as I move down her body and kiss the last scar, leaving my lips on her long enough in the hope that she'll understand.

"Oh Declan…I love you," she cries on an exhale.

We both must've fallen asleep because I wake with a start in the darkness. Izzy's tangled in the duvet. I've never been with a girl who hogs the duvet as much as she does. I run my hand across my face and gently leave the bed so I don't wake her up. Pulling up the duvet, I tuck it in around her. She sighs loudly in her sleep but doesn't wake up. I put on a t-shirt, my grey joggers and pad to the bathroom to freshen up. There's noise coming from the kitchen so I go downstairs. Sofia and Aiden are sitting at the kitchen table with a large Pizza Hut box open between them. My stomach growls at the sight and I quickly grab a slice and sit down. As I polish it off I pinch another one as Sofia slaps at my hand with a fake frown.

"So what's up guys, what are we talking about?" I ask them as I take another bite.

"Your girlfriend," Aiden replies looking over at Sofia. I look over at Sofia as well, waiting on what she's got to say.

"Has she told you what happened to her Declan?" she asks, her expression full of concern.

"No, not really, I know bits and pieces, but apparently she opened up to Dr McGrath who's one of the Uni Professors," I say, taking another bite of the pizza, realising I'm bloody starving. "She told him everything that happened the night her brother died. I think it really shook her up but she said she felt better for it and that talking to him is sorting out the thoughts in her head." I stand up and walk over to the sink to get a glass of water, running the tap till the water is ice cold.

"Good, that's really good; I've been so worried about her keeping it inside, waiting for it all to come out at the wrong time. The fact that she's talking about it without being forced to like her parents tried, I have to say, I'm so relieved," she says as she picks up another slice of pizza.

"Bloody hell Sofia, that's like your fifth slice," Aiden laughs at her, pretending to look disgusted.

"So what? I'm hungry, I love pizza and yeah did I mention I'm hungry?" she replies as she flips him the finger with a proper *'fuck off'* face, taking another exaggerated bite out of her slice. Both Aiden and I burst out laughing and start talking about upcoming gigs, avoiding any further talk of Izzy. I figure she needs Sofia right now more than me. She is after all, the link to Izzy's past, having gone through it with her from the start.

Chapter Fifteen

I wake up feeling lighter than I remember feeling in a long time. It's almost as if a huge weight has been lifted off my shoulders. This is all because I shared with the right person, and probably because the timing felt just right. I feel alive and I think I forgot how that felt, as though I've been killing time for so long now, the breaths simply automatic for survival. I'm lying in bed looking up at the ceiling, warm and happy as I think this beautiful life, right here, right now, away from the hurt and pain, could be forever. It's possible. I wish, I wish for it so hard, making a mental note in my head. I turn my head to the side and look straight into a pair of loving warm chocolate eyes.

"Morning beautiful," he says smiling at me as he runs his long fingers down my face.

"Morning handsome," I reply blushing.

He smiles at me, knowing I'm embarrassed. "Want to pull a sickie today and go do something fun?" he asks on a yawn.

"Yeah, yeah I really do," I respond stretching lazily and content as I close my eyes in pure bliss. Before I know it Declan has scooped me up and I'm now lying on top of him.

"What do you fancy doing? Something outrageously crazy or something romantic and soppy?" he asks tucking my long hair behind my ears as he pulls my face down for a gentle kiss.

"Something outrageously daring and crazy and I know just what that something is," I wink as I jump off him and get out of bed, not realising I'm as naked as the day I was born. Declan's mood changes in a second, lunging for me and with an arm around my waist he hauls me back into bed. Our plans for today get delayed as he makes me even happier than I was when I woke up.

Later that morning Declan and I are standing outside what I chose to be my crazy outrageous adventure.

"You sure about this Iz?" he asks me, looking between me and the tattoo parlour.

"Sure, I'm sure, I've been wanting to do this for a few months but I don't know, something kept stopping me. But today…*today* I feel ready," I say, as I take his hand and drag him inside with a smile on my face.

He looks at me with a worried frown on his face. "It's going to hurt baby, you know that right?"

"Yeah, but this pain, this pain, I *choose* and it'll make something ugly into something really beautiful," I whisper with tears in my eyes, hoping he'll understand.

"I love you Iz," he says just before he kisses me with such passion, I feel an ache in my heart because right now, in this moment, I *know* that he does. If I had any doubts before, I realize right now that this amazing guy, who could have anyone he wants, loves me. Despite my scars, he loves *me*.

We walk up to the front desk, which is being manned by this freakishly tall guy who's covered in tats. Every bit of his face that is possible to pierce, is pretty much pierced. I feel Declan pulling me into his side and kissing the top of my head. Not sure why, but I get the feeling he's having a pissing contest with -'tattoo'- guy, who looks at me up and down intensely before he speaks, "You here for a tattoo or piercing?" he grunts looking over at Declan.

"Umm…I wanted to make an appointment for today, if you have one that is, I've brought my own designs." I sound like a five year old with a stutter and I feel the blush heat my face. Declan gives me a reassuring squeeze but doesn't say anything as I think he knows this is something I need to say out loud and do on my own. He stays quiet at my side whilst giving me strength and reassurance just by being here with me. I pull out the sheet of paper from my bag that has just what I want covering my scars. I've carried it round with me every day, just waiting for this moment.

"Lucky for you little lady we've had a cancellation this morning for quite a big job, so pass it over and let me have a gander." He studies what's on there. "Name's Steve by the way," he tells us rather cave man-ish, as he motions for me to come round the back with him.

"Now, you want the song lyrics in a continuous circle on your upper back and the angel wings on your lower back?"

"Yes please, all in black," I nod, as I sit down, back to front in the chair he's pulled out for me.

"Hey man, can you turn around while my girlfriend takes her top off at least," Declan snipes at Steve as he moves to stand in between us, his face right up in his. I whip off my top really fast and sit there shivering in just my strapless bra. At least the back of the red padded chair covers everything.

"Fuck girl," Steve exclaims as he sits down behind me touching the three perfectly round scars on my back.

"Just do what you can," I whisper as Declan squeezes my hand.

"Don't you worry girl," he says with a completely different tone of voice; now he starts to understand why I'm here. Declan was right, it does bloody hurt, but as Steve begins giving me beauty through a needle of pain, he's also removing the pain of the ugly, so *this* pain, well it feels pretty bloody amazing. All through my time in the hot seat, Declan holds my hand, stroking my palm with his thumb, kissing my fingers one by one. An odd sense of feeling washes all over me. One I've never experienced before and I love every minute of it. This is really happening I think to myself. I'm saying goodbye to the pain and scars that from now on will feel like an ache. An ache I know will always be there, but an ache I can live with. The angel wings are for Zack. They cover the burn that took him away from me. He'll always be here though and he's the reason I'm still alive and breathing, able to start my life afresh in his memory.

"Right hun, you're all done," Steve says a while later, as he tissues my back off and fixes a wrapping to each tattoo, handing me an aftercare sheet.

Declan quickly, but carefully slips my top back on and wraps me in his arms. "Beautiful Izzy," he says as he leans down to kiss me. I pay up refusing Declan's offer when he tries to pay for me. This is my ending and I need to do this all by myself. We walk out hand in hand and I feel as if a huge bag of bricks has left my shoulders. Instead, I feel the sweet sting of a new beginning.

We walk back through the park to the house, my hand, small and cold in his large and warm one. We're both walking in silence and I wish I knew what Declan was thinking. I'm hoping he's not regretting what he's gotten into with me, especially not now, when I think things can only get better.

A mum is playing footie with what must be her young son, who's no more than five years old. He's standing in between two Birch trees which I presume is the goal and she's taking shots, trying not to score, letting her son save them with a big grin on his face. His excited smile makes me automatically smile in return and I get all warm and fuzzy looking at them.

Declan suddenly breaks the silence as he pulls me over to an empty park bench where we sit down. I draw my knees up to my chest and rest my cheek on them looking at Declan's strong and gorgeous profile. Pulling his grey beanie back a bit as if he forgot he had it on, meaning instead to rake his long fingers through his dark hair, he looks over at me.

"Do you ever wish you could go back to when it all started Izzy? Do anything different, retrace your steps to when they mattered?" he asks with such a vulnerable look on his face, I take his hand lacing my fingers with his.

"I used to Declan, all the bloody time. But I think in all honesty, all you can change is your own behaviour and isn't hindsight a wonderful thing," I say cynically. "I've realised that you have no power over someone else's actions. They repeatedly take their own steps and all you can do is watch the inevitable happen, again and again." I look at him as he turns his face away from me; his eyes unfocused, as if a memory is being played behind them.

I continue, "Can you warn someone, yeah sure, but what will make them listen and change something which they have no apprehension of? We all think; if I'd done this or said that, would it have changed something? It drove me crazy Declan. I didn't sleep or eat. I retreated from everything, became a ghost hiding in the shadows of life. I slowly understood with help that we can't, we just can't, no matter how much we'd like to change things. We can't retrace our steps, we can't go back, we can't change anything," I say the last words on a sob and Declan grabs me and crushes me in his arms.

"Yeah, wishful thinking Izzy, but at least my Mum got out. Yours is still living it."

That reminds me; I must speak to Mum, see how she is, tell her that I finally did it and get her to seek help, so she can leave the edge she's living on too.

"I think I'm going to go over and see my Mum soon Declan, I need to speak to her face to face, hold her hand and show her the horror she lives in, needs to be stopped. She can't go on living this life, living in regret and fear." I stand up and shove my hands into the pockets of my jeans. Biting my lip in anticipation, I suddenly have the urge to run all the way to Mum's house, the impulsivity running through my veins in a hot and fast current.

"I want to come with you Izzy in case you need me," he says, standing up and putting his arm round my shoulder as we walk back to our house.

"I don't think that's a good idea Declan, I don't know what I'm going to say yet or how long I'll be. I need her undivided attention but I'll need you…after…I'll need you."

"Well, let me drive you there at least, and then you can ring me when you need picking up, deal?" He squeezes me tight into his side.

I smile up at my protective guy who makes me feel safe and as if I can do anything. "Deal."

"I'm going to kiss that smile okay?" He smiles back, leaning towards me.

"Okay," I say on an exhale. Standing outside our house, he kisses my smile and gives me something I've never had. Hope.

Chapter Sixteen

Later that evening all the lads decide on sharing yet another takeaway as no one can be bothered to cook. I've just finished a shower and am standing in my underwear in Sofia's room staring at my back in the full length mirror when she bounds in and throws herself on her bed with a big sigh.

"Shit, Izzy you went and did it," she suddenly squeals in excitement, clapping her hands as she comes up close to inspect my new tattoos. "They're beautiful hun, just beautiful," she says, and gives me a big hug.

"Yeah, I love them Sof, I can't believe I finally did it. The tide's changed, I feel it. I'm ready to let go now. No re-inventing, I'm just me Sofia, just me. Not defined by what happened." I look back in the mirror, feeling so overwhelmed by this moment that tears run down my cheeks.

She comes to stand next to me and we look at each other in the mirror. "Aah, I can hear the fierceness coming back in your voice, so why are you crying Izzy?" she asks, taking my hand.

"Happy tears Sof; I'm happy, I promise," I smile at her.

"Right that's it, we're going down the pub and we're getting pissed girl," she exclaims, as she starts pulling out clothes from the dresser. I smile at her and wrap myself in my towel before I go back upstairs to get ready. Declan's sitting on the bed strumming on his guitar when I walk in. He looks up at me as I close the bedroom door and puts his guitar back in its stand. Without a word he walks over to where I'm frozen to the spot by the intense look in his eyes, eyes that are roaming the length of my body. He slowly un-wraps the towel, his eyes never wavering as he lets it fall onto the floor.

I'm not sure why I suddenly feel so exposed standing here in my lacy knickers and bra set but my body starts to heat up. I don't know where to look so I just stare at him as my pulse speeds up in anticipation. Still not saying a word he unravels my hair from the lose bun that ties it and runs his fingers through it, tilting my face up so I have no choice but to look at him. He reaches behind me and unhooks my bra, slowly pushing the straps down over my arms with his fingers. Every touch leaves a hot imprint on my skin. My breathing is becoming erratic as he bends down, kissing a trail where his fingers have just been. He kneels down in front of me while his hands run down my arms and back up, then down my front, pausing at my breasts before he leaves them to rest on my hips.

"So perfect Izzy, all of you is so bloody perfect. You drive me crazy and I'll never have enough of you," he groans as he kisses my stomach, leaving his tongue to linger in my belly button before tracing a hot path up to my chest. I close my eyes on a sigh as he reverently worships me with his mouth and tongue. I feel so dizzy with lust and need, I think I might just pass out. He moves his scorching mouth and tongue back down my body steadying me with his hands making me lost for words. The intensity taking away any rational thought as he runs his tongue along the edge of my knickers, wrapping one hand around the edge of them, pulling them down in one swift motion. Lifting one foot out after the other; I'm now completely naked, standing in front of him.

"You are so fucking gorgeous," he whispers, his own voice full of lust as he parts my legs whilst looking up at me with burning eyes. I throw my head back on a moan when I feel his hot breath on the *one* part of my body that's desperate for his touch. I nearly come apart in his arms as he worships me with his mouth, his tongue and his fingers. I stumble from the sheer intensity and catch myself on his shoulders.

"Now Declan, I want you…*now*," I manage to whisper. He lets go of me to quickly pull his t-shirt over his head, baring that hard upper body of his which makes my mouth water, desperate to taste it.

"You've got me sweetheart," he grunts, as I move closer and start to unbutton his jeans pulling them and his boxers down. His arms wrap around me and he leans back on the bed pulling me on top of him as we fall. I end up straddling him as he curls a hand around the back of my head bringing my face down to his, crushing my mouth as he parts my lips with his tongue, before claiming it as though he needs it to breathe. Feeling overwhelmed I sit up, impaling myself on him in one quick motion and begin to move so he can ease the ache that's literally bringing me to my knees. I move as though my life depends on it, taking from him what I need, spurred on by the lust I see in his eyes and the feel of his hands roaming all over my body. Collapsing on top of him and as if from far away, I hear myself shouting his name as he grabs me on a final thrust and yells mine.

We lie still and I can hear and feel his heart pounding in unison with mine as I snuggle as close as I can, crawling up his body until my mouth is at his ear, "I love you Declan."

"I love you right back Izzy," he says with a smile, hugging me closer to his body.

We're interrupted from our satisfied daze by a loud pounding on the door. "Get your arse dressed and ready for the pub you slag," Sofia shouts.

"Be right there you slapper," I yell back at her laughing, deafening Declan in the process I'm sure.

"I guess we're going to the pub," he grins, as he shifts from underneath me and in one swift move I'm up and standing, still in his arms.

"Yeah and you're coming with," I say, as I put on his t-shirt and rush to the bathroom to get cleaned up. When I return to the bedroom Declan's already dressed and I look at him in complete wonder. No matter what he wears he looks completely awesome. Even now, just dressed in his faded jeans and long sleeved t-shirt with his trusted beanie on.

"Izzy get dressed and stop looking at me like that or we'll never leave this room," he laughs with a wink. I quickly put my jeans on and team it with a nice black halter-neck. I nearly fall over stepping into my black high-heeled boots, but just as I'm, about to face plant on the floor Declan grabs me around my middle. And as if he can't resist, he adds a gentle bite to the side of my neck before he releases me. God I love this man. We join the rest of the guys downstairs and all head on over to the pub.

Chapter Seventeen

A few hours later, I'm well on my way as is Sofia who's gone to the bar for another round. It's just like old times and my jaw and stomach muscles hurt from laughing. Declan, Aiden and Max are playing darts in the opposite corner of the pub leaving us to girlie chat. Sofia comes back from the bar with another couple of pints and picks hers up dramatically.

"So Izzy, cheers to new beginnings and the resurrection of the old us, pre all the bollocks like the stupid bitch whore and cheating arsehole I left behind. Shit, resurrection that was a big word huh?" She smiles at me looking so proud of herself, I can't help laughing.

"Cheers, my pretty, brave and foulmouthed bestie," I yell as we clink glasses and drink to just that.

"Oh I forgot to tell you my news Izzy. Guess who got a temp job teaching. Oh and guess who I bumped into when I went in for my interview…oh….oh and I'll be starting after half-term, yay me," she squeals.

I burst out laughing again. "Ah, that's fab Sof, I'm so happy for you. Oh and who did you bump into?" I ask as I take another sip of my beer. She gets all shifty and has a drink which seems to last forever before she looks at me in apprehension.

"Yeah, so I bumped into Connor. Apparently he runs footie classes at the same school and after half-term he'll be taking over from the P.E teacher who's going on a charity climb of Mount Everest or some mountain like that. Anyway, we had a long chat. He's not only gorgeous Izzy; he's a really nice man." She looks at me and I know instantly that she fancies him, which is okay but does make me feel slightly strange.

"Well that's cool, a friendly face is just what you need when starting somewhere new right?" I say giving her my most convincing smile to show that it's okay. She doesn't need to worry.

Her face immediately relaxes and she beams right back at me. Suddenly her smile falls and her eyes narrow as she looks over my shoulders at something. I wonder what's up just as '*Mr Brightside*' by The Killers starts playing over the speakers. I love this song and start singing along. Sofia still looks pissed off at something and isn't joining in, which is strange.

"What is it?" I ask her, as I turn to see what she is looking at. "Oh." It's Lina. Lina who's currently hanging off Declan's arm, pressing herself up against him.

"Who the fuck is that Izzy? And what the hell does she think she's doing?" she asks, not taking her eyes off Lina.

I shrug, transfixed at the sight. "Long story Sofia," I say as I'm in two minds on what I should do next. I know what I want to do and that's march on over there and pull her off him. However, another very small and perverse part of me wants to see what Declan's going to do about it. It's perfectly blatant to me that Lina wants Declan; especially now she hasn't got him anymore. I look to see what everyone else's reaction to this scene is, my eyes catching Aiden's, who gives a slight shake of his head. He obviously wants me to stay where I am. I know it. Max is busy chatting some slip of a girl up so no doubt has no idea what's going on. I make a move to walk over there, alcohol fuelled disgust at Lina's obvious behaviour tearing through me when I feel a hand grabbing my arm holding me back.

"Not without me you don't missus," Sofia says, and we start walking over to see what the hell Lina thinks she's doing. Aiden intercepts us and drags us right back to the table as I see Declan pull Lina outside the pub by her arm.

"Where the bloody hell are they going?" I ask him looking incredulously at the pub door slamming behind them.

"Sit down Izzy and let me explain," he sighs rubbing his face with his hands. "Fucks sake, Declan should really be the one doing this."

"What do I need to know Aiden, other than what you've already told me?" I say starring at the door wishing I had x-ray vision right now.

"Lina and Declan have been close since they were young kids, they grew up on the same council estate and both didn't have it easy, so they bonded I guess, *because* of that. Well you know some of the story, but how much has Declan told you about his parents Izzy?" he asks, trying to get my attention away from the door.

"Enough to know he understands what mine are like," I answer, dread weighing me down.

"Well not only would Declan understand some, but Lina would too, though for different reasons. Her circumstances were something no kid should ever have to endure," he says, looking so devastated I can kind of guess what he's talking about without him having to tell me the details.

"It fucked her up emotionally, and Declan being the one constant and good thing in her life through it all…well she clings to him when times get bad. She needs him to remind her that her life isn't like that anymore, that no one can hurt her." He shakes his head as if caught in a memory. I feel myself completely deflate, yet despite her bitchy behaviour, I feel for her.

"And how does he do that Aiden? How does he remind her?" I whisper, scared to hear the words.

"Before you, well they'd….you know, get together. He's tried to protect her since they were children, but since you, he tries to talk her down from the clinging bitch mode she goes into. It's been like this for years Izzy. Anyone can see though, that he loves you and would never ever jeopardize that. So *please*, don't fly off at him. Let him work this one out. He'll always have this connection with Lina, but they need to sort it out, sort themselves out, once and for all." He looks at me with sympathy in his eyes. Max walks over minus 'slip of a girl', joining us at the table.

"What's up guys?" He looks at all of us and obviously realises he's the only one smiling when a frown replaces his smile.

"Lina," Aiden sighs.

"Aah fuck mate not again," he says, standing up while shaking his head with a fierce look in his eyes. "Let me go and take over."

"Take over?" I ask, as I look at Max leaving the same way Declan and Lina did.

"Yeah, Max is one of the only people who can talk her down, give her back as good as she gives without repercussions. Being best mates with Finn growing up, he saw a lot of this over the years."

"Okay, well I don't know about you lot, but I need another drink, anyone else?" I ask, as I stand up and head on over to the bar after everyone gives me their order.

As I stand and wait for the bartender to acknowledge me, I hear a familiar voice next to me. "So shortie, what do you want me to order for you this time?"

"Connor," I exclaim, giving him a hug. "How are you?" I ask, genuinely happy to see him again.

"All good Izzy. Back to work now with more to come after half term," he smiles at me.

"Yeah Sofia mentioned she bumped into you at the school," I say.

He looks over at the table where she's sitting and I think I see something in his eyes before he turns back to me with a half-smile. "Yeah, she's something else that's for sure," he laughs, as if he's answering an unspoken question. It's our turn to order so I reel off the list of drinks. Connor helps me carry them back to the table, then sits down to join us entertaining us with hilarious footie stories from his camp. I notice Sofia keeps sneaking looks at him when he's not looking and I recognise those signs. They are ones I must've given Declan before we got together. Thinking of Declan, I wonder where he is and what he's doing out there with Lina. A part of me feels better though, knowing Max is out there too, but the jealousy claws at me, I just can't help it. I tune back to join in the conversation, when I suddenly feel a hand on the back of my neck giving me a gentle squeeze.

"You okay Iz?" Declan asks, as he crouches down next to my chair, searching my face with a worried frown.

"Yeah you?" I ask him hesitantly, not wanting to be the one that brings up the gigantic elephant in the room. He stands up suddenly realising that Connor's sitting next to me at the table.

"Connor," he acknowledges with a nod whilst pulling me from my chair and into his side.

"Declan," he responds with a smirk.

"Bloody hell guys, stand down," Sofia laughs, but when my eyes connect with hers I see a shred of hurt in them as she looks away and over at Connor.

"Want to head on out of here?" Declan asks, as he puts his other arm around me so I'm completely engulfed in them, in him. I can't really blame him for being suspicious about Connor suddenly being here, but then, he's the one who's just been missing in action for the last hour with his ex. Someone who seems to have one hell of a long shared emotional past with him.

I pick up my bag and take his outstretched hand as we walk out the pub. "Yeah sure."

"It's not what it looked like Iz, there's nothing you need to be worried about between Lina and me, not anymore anyway."

"Yeah I know that Declan, I really do. It's just hard to watch, you know?" I say looking up at him.

"You never have to doubt for one minute what I feel for you Izzy. But Lina," he sighs as he stops walking when we reach our house. "Well her story's not mine to tell really and I know she comes across as a fucking crazy person. She can be a right bitch, I know that," he stalls and suddenly lifts me up to sit on the low wall next to the steps that lead up to our front door. He moves in between my legs and grabs my face with his hands.

"You Izzy, you were dealt a fucking shit hand but you retained what made you. Your goodness never left, you still shine and you'd never walk over anyone to find the good, because it's still inside you." He gently kisses me and rests his head against mine.

"Now Lina, she was hurt so bad by her step dad for a long time babe. And Finn and me, hell even Max and Aiden, had to step in so many times." He leans back and rubs the back of his neck with his hand.

"It's okay Declan, you don't have to say any more, I think I understand. But I have to know one thing though, does she still want you?" I ask scared of the answer because I don't know if I could fight that bond they seem to have.

"No not like that. She understands I'll always be here for her, I have to be, but my heart belongs completely to you Iz."

I put my arms around his neck and kiss him deeply after those words. Seriously, this guy is amazing. He's gorgeous through and through and I love him even more for caring. And I do know without a doubt, that I can trust him despite his past and despite his involvement with Lina. The heavens suddenly open and rain starts to pelt down. I shriek and Declan turns around as I grab onto his back, accepting the piggyback ride as he runs inside, but not before we get absolutely drenched. Laughing out loud he takes me straight upstairs and we quickly rid ourselves of our clothes and jump under the duvet. I cuddle into his strong arms as he rubs my back, trying to warm me up, as he's careful not to touch my new tattoos. I suddenly feel exhausted and start to drift off.

"Love you Declan. So much," I whisper.

"Love you right back babe." He kisses the top of my head and I sigh in pure pleasure before I feel sleep catching up with me.

I wake with a start and realise I'm crying, the tears furiously running down my cheeks. I try and untangle myself from the duvet and Declan's arms as I feel smothered and trapped, my breathing erratic and laboured. Losing my patience, I shove everything off me and rush over to the loft window, frantically trying to unlatch the old rusty window clasp. My useless efforts making me cry even harder.

"Shhh calm down Iz, I've got it." Declan moves in behind me, opening the window wide as I lift myself up on the chair and stick my head out into the cold night taking deep breaths. Declan still stands behind me and I feel him put his arms around my middle, resting his cheek on my naked back, which feels like ice except where his hot breaths touch me. My breathing slows and I relax into his arms looking up at the stars in the night sky.

"You're freezing Izzy, you ready to come back to bed?" Declan asks hesitantly.

I'm shivering from the cold and the remnants of my dream so I nod my head as he lifts me into his arms and carries me back to bed.

"You have a bad dream?" he asks, as he gathers me into his arms and pulls the duvet up to cover us both.

"Yeah," I whisper, not wanting to let the words out into the space around us so I leave it at that.

"You okay now?"

"Yeah."

"Okay," he says and squeezes me tight as if afraid I'll disappear on him. I lie here in his arms for what seems like hours, unable to fall back asleep and I know Declan's doing the same but neither of us speaks another word.

Declan

I have no clue how long we lie here in silence, just breathing, not a single word spoken. Izzy scares the shit out of me at times. She's definitely coming to terms with everything but these moments of extreme distress make me so fucking angry at what she's been through. I just want to make it all go away. But I feel bloody powerless. Knowing what to do or say…argh…fucks sake. I know there are no words that'll take it away, every single one useless against a memory so strong and fierce. I know, because no words ever made me feel better when Dad lost it with Mum. And I know no word ever made Lina feel better either. Only strong arms and silent understanding did it for me, so that's what I give Izzy, hoping it's enough, hoping it's what she needs. I stroke the hair away from her face and kiss it, hugging her to me as tight as I can without hurting her. Her breathing slows down and I feel her relax as those cute little sleeping noises she makes, start up. I have no idea how long I lie here listening to her breathe, stroking her, kissing her, trying to chase the memories away from her dreams, her nightmares.

Chapter Eighteen

I blink my eyes open to the strong sun streaming through the loft window. It's finally the weekend and I can't be arsed to get up and out of bed, I'm shattered from last night's dream. I check the alarm clock on the bedside table and realise it's already eleven am. Declan must have gotten up a few hours ago to go to work. Aiden and him both work at the same restaurant during the morning rush hour. Max got me a job in the old record store in town that he manages, but fortunately I only work week day afternoon shifts or week day evenings, so the weekends are all mine. I burrow back under my duvet and decide to stay in bed where I do my best thinking.

The last month; the days and weeks are passing me by so quickly. I can't believe it's less than two months till Christmas. I guess keeping my head down, getting stuck into my coursework and my continuous visits to Dr McGrath are keeping me busy, my mind occupied. Dr McGrath and Declan are my rocks, encouraging me to understand that what's happened was out of my control, that it was a tragic accident. I still hold my Dad partly responsible; for what happened, where I am right now and for Zack, Mum too I suppose.

I ring Mum every day to check up on her. She's still on her own most days, and I can always tell by the easy relaxed tone in her voice when she picks up the phone that she is. She's still recovering and wants to be left alone. I fully realise that she's pushing me away in order for me to create my own life away from drama and subsequent pain of hers.

On the days I ring her and she doesn't pick up the phone I know he's home. Those are the days where I struggle more than others as a part of me wants to go home and check she's okay. But that would upset her and I suppose me at the end of the day. Once she's ready I'll be here waiting.

I must have fallen asleep again because when I open my eyes, I'm lying on my side with Declan's arms around me. He must've finished his shift. I can't see him but his steady and gentle breathing tells me he's fast asleep. I quietly scoot out of his arms and sit up on the edge of the bed to look back at him. It's been two months now and even though my confidence grows daily, I still can't believe he's mine. He makes me smile, laugh and yeah…I blush at how amazing he makes me feel. I leave him to sleep, wondering how long he stayed awake last night as I pad downstairs to the kitchen for my first cup of much needed coffee. Sofia's sitting at the kitchen table furiously scribbling in her notebook.

"Hey Sof, what you doing hun?"

"Writing Taylor, the knob-head, a letter," she answers without looking away from what she's doing. "I need him to send me a reference letter from the school we volunteered at so I can pass it on to the Head of Oak Farm School. They've been really good letting me start without it really..." She sighs and face plants the table. "All I want to do is bloody rant at him for breaking my heart after all those years, for not even trying to fight for me." She looks up at me with tears in her eyes. "I'm worth that right Izzy?…Worth fighting for?"

I immediately put my arms around her, my sweet and funny best mate who's always been here for me when I needed her. "Yes hun, yes you're worth fighting for, and then some. He's lost the best thing he could've ever possibly had when he did what he did, and he knows it. Hiding away in silence like this, choosing the coward's way. I actually can't believe he hasn't come back for you, after all those years together. I wonder what he's thinking?" I say as I stroke her long curly hair.

"Thinking with his knob that's what." She gives me a sad smile. I squeeze her hard and a give her a kiss before I go back to making coffee.

"How's your Mum doing?" she asks me as she puts her papers away.

"Not really sure to be honest." I sit down at the table warming my fingers by curling them around the hot coffee mug. "I was thinking about going back tomorrow to check up on her. Apparently she's started seeing a new therapist. I'm hoping this one will work out for her, though what I wish even more that she'd see Dr McGrath. He's such an amazing and brilliant man."

"He really is," Sofia says, beaming at me. "I got you back didn't I and, look at you hun, you're doing great."

"Yeah, I think if I haven't heard from her, I'll go check out how she is tomorrow. I really miss her." I make a coffee for Declan and top up mine before I go back upstairs to see if he's woken up yet. Balancing the mugs I nudge the door open with my foot as I hear the gentle sound of Declan playing his guitar. The sight that greets me melts me to the core. Declan's sitting in the middle of the bed, cross legged and dressed only in his fitted boxers. His hair's a tousled mess as he sits there playing with his eyes closed. I can't move or breathe as I literally eat him up with my eyes, listen to his husky voice, watch his long fingers stroking the guitar strings. My insides melt. As he gets to the end of Coldplay's *'Fix You'* his eyes open. They look haunted and a chill runs through me. I know that look, recognise it and wonder if I've caused him to remember things he's buried deep inside. I wish I could help him, as he's helping me, and decide from this moment to make it my mission to do just that. I know he needs me as much as I need him. Declan starts playing *The Scientist*, closing his eyes again and singing really low. I still haven't moved, I can't. Just as he can't seem to stop playing. I'm scared to break the moment so I stay where I am, listening to him, thinking back to when I first saw him.

My first impression of Declan was need, want and pure lust. He's gorgeous, looks *'filthy'* in the sexual sense, rough and cool, cocky and cheeky. Anyone would want to be in his space, have him smile at you, protect you with his strength, look at you with those dark eyes. You'd never know there was hurt and vulnerability hiding underneath. I finally move from where I've been rooted to the spot and place our mugs down on the bedside table. I carefully lie down next to him, not wanting to disturb him as I listen to the rest of the song. Closing my eyes, I drift away to the tune of the chords he releases into the room. His voice envelops me and I feel it in my heart, making it ache and all I want to do is cry but I don't. Instead I listen and I wait.

Chapter Nineteen

Declan

I feel Izzy's warmth next to me and it's as if I can hear the questions running through her head, I know what they are, but I keep playing, not really sure I want to stop to face them. As I wind down the song, I feel her hand on my back. Her palm flat against me, her fingers spread, as if she's marking me with her palm print.

"I got you a coffee," she says.

Turning around I see her bright smile that doesn't quite reach her eyes. I stand up and put my guitar back on its stand running my hand through my hair as I turn to face her. She's lying on her side, resting her head on her arm, her long hair spread out around her like an angel. She's so fucking perfect and I wish I could capture her as she looks now, but I'm no artist and could never do her justice. I walk over to the bed and sit down next to her, running my fingers through her hair.

"You're so beautiful Izzy. I'm never going to be able to tell you enough. You astound me every day."

"Declan..." she sighs, her face turning beet red.

"So fucking cute too," I smile, I can't help it.

I wonder what she wants me to say, how much I actually want to tell her so she knows I understand, that I *get* her. That I knew her the minute I saw her eyes, the minute I saw her soul, mine recognized hers. I don't want to fucking disappoint her, so I try to explain myself to her, wanting to convince her.

"I've always thought it strange how they say love's blind," I pause trying to choose my next words carefully. "I never really understood that saying. I see everything that makes me love you. Love's not instantaneous. Love comes when you move past the initial attraction." I reach down and tuck her hair behind her ear.

"What attracts can start as superficial in an instant, even sexual, then you see what's in the eyes, what's hiding behind them. It draws you in. When you see what lies beneath, *then* you fall in love." I place my hand over her heart; feeling it pound so fast beneath it. I feel mine against my chest trying to out race hers as she looks at me with those big blues.

"The heart may start out hollow and empty, just waiting and biding its time, but then it builds and builds and you take what you believe is yours and give in return. You hijack the soul that sees yours, sees the other half of what completes it, the part that's missing, making it whole. Your heart is blinded by another, as if it remembers and knows it can't live without it."

I take her hand and bring it up to my mouth kissing each finger noticing how she closes her eyes after each one. I'm stalling, wondering how I can get her to really understand how I feel. I keep looking into her eyes. She starts crying silent tears, I made her fucking cry again and right this minute I feel like a bastard for it, but I need to explain and can't help but think I'm making a piss poor attempt at it. I kiss away her salty tears as I continue, "I never went through what you did, but you know I saw it, shit like that leaves scars and it takes fucking years to come to terms with seeing your Mum reduced to a scared shell of a woman. Her soul leaving her eyes when the *one* person who should be lighting her soul up, who should be making her eyes shine brightly, is the one who ultimately destroys it and extinguishes that light. Her dreams were stolen and her spirit was broken by him. You start to wonder how you stay alive, how your life did a U-turn and what was right, suddenly turned so wrong." I feel Izzy grab my hand squeezing it tight over her heart, not letting go as I continue.

"When Dad left, Mum told Finn and I that we helped put the light back in her eyes and we both had to promise her there and then, to always put the light in the eyes of the ones we love. Always make sure the light is maintained, so strong, it lights the whole fucking world up Izzy." I stop talking because I suddenly feel exposed. I've never been so open and honest with anyone before and it's fucking freaking me out. We just look at each other and I'm willing her to say something, anything to convince me I haven't just made a complete tool out of myself or worse, sounded like a fucking pussy despite meaning every word I said. She suddenly pulls me down to her and kisses me hard with her soft lips.

"You did that Declan," she says. "You gave me my light back, only you, just you and I'll always love you for that."

My fucking heart feels like it wants to jump out of my chest. I laid it all out there and whether I deserve her or not, she's mine. She's literally under my skin, in my heart and I'll fight anyone or anything that tries to take her away from me.

"I'll fight every day to keep that light burning in your eyes beautiful girl, with everything I've got," I say before my body shows her how much I meant every bloody word I just said to her.

Chapter Twenty

Later that afternoon after making the decision to try and help Mum, Declan and I are sitting in his car, parked next to my parent's house. The sun is setting and the sky has that pretty pink and yellow glow it gets as the late autumn evening draws in. I'm looking at the house shrouded in this eerie glow, a flickering light in the hallway window. I suddenly get chills.

"You sure you want to do this Iz?" Declan takes my hand and rubs it between both of his.

"Yeah, I just need a minute; I need to make sure I'm as ready as I felt a few hours ago."

"Sweetheart," he sighs and turns my face so I'm looking at him. "You don't need to do this today; we can turn around right now. But you know you can do anything Iz. I've never met such a beautiful and strong person as you. You shine Izzy. So fucking bright, strong and beautiful, you *know* you can do anything." He leans over and I melt into his arms opening my mouth under his as he shows me his love and gives me some of his strength to reinforce my own. He rests his forehead against mine on an exhale, "Go and do what you need to do, and don't forget Iz, anything…you can do anything." He grabs the back of my head and looks so deeply into my eyes that it makes me want to crawl into his lap and never leave. "I love you Izzy, so fucking much. Never forget that." He looks so serious when he says this, making a point. I start grinning, I just can't help it because yes, I can do anything, but with Declan's love I feel like I can do even more, I can do everything.

"I love you too Declan."

"Now go, before I turn this bloody car round and take you home to show you just how much I love you Izzy," he growls at me. "And don't forget to ring me when you want to be picked up okay. Even though I'd feel much happier staying outside in the car, just in case." He looks at me as if he's seriously debating whether to let me go or not.

"I know, but I'll be fine Declan, please just go and I'll ring you." I really won't be able to do this if he's sitting outside. I'll be worried Dad will see him if he suddenly comes home. His face looks so serious while he's having a mental debate with himself on what to do. I'd rather do this on my own, not only because I need to, but because I don't want to feel ashamed or embarrassed. I burst out laughing at his expression and quickly scoot back to my side of the car and open the door.

"You ring me the minute you want me to come for you Izzy. Say it, say I promise to ring you Declan."

"Yes Sir, I promise to ring you Declan. Sir," I smartly respond and hide a grin when this makes him growl even more in frustration. I step out of the car and slam it shut, then I kiss the closed window just to tease him even more. I start the walk towards confrontation but look over my shoulder one last time and wave at him as I get to the front door of the house. I let myself in and walk down the candlelit hallway towards what looks like the only light in the house, a candle flickering in the lounge. Mum's always preferred candles to electric lights. They can hide the truth, and sins can hide in the shadows leaving a blur that's unable to be distinguished as anything real. Electric lights expose too much, everything laid out, naked to the eye with nowhere to hide. As I pass the office door I see that there's a sliver of light coming from underneath it. Shit, I think to myself. He's home, I wasn't banking on that. I'm debating whether to quietly leave. Pretend I was never here. Instead, I tip toe past his door and walk into the lounge where I see Mum asleep in her chair, a chain of tea lights flickering on the mantelpiece next to her.

I crouch down next to her, wondering if I should wake her up. Forget about my plan which is pretty much shot to bollocks because he's home. No way can I sit and have the conversation I want, with him in the house.

"Izobel," his voice booms into the quiet room making me literally jump out of my skin. I stand and turn to look at him.

"Dad."

I can't think of anything else to say as I look at him standing there with a cigarette in one hand, his other in the pocket of his neatly pressed work trousers. His shirt is wrinkled though and his tie is hanging loose. His hair is dishevelled as if he's been raking his hands through it in frustration. Dad is a very handsome man who projects power and money. One look from him can silence anyone into submission out of fear and respect.

"What are you doing home Izobel, you're not supposed to be here tonight," he says walking over to the bar and pouring himself a scotch. I stare transfixed at him, wondering how many he's already had. It's always so difficult to tell unless you've been able to count from when he started. If I'd been able to count them, I'd know how to approach this situation. I'd know whether to run the fuck out of here or stay. His words sound odd, I think to myself. I wonder what he means.

"I wanted to come over and check on Mum, that's all." My voice is breaking, I know why. The fear has set in.

"Why do you think she needs checking on?" he asks as he slowly walks over to where I'm sitting perched on the arm rest of Mum's chair, not even realising. He takes a long deep drag of his cigarette as if contemplating the situation in front of him, before exhaling dramatically. Every hair stands to attention. My body instantly knows and is already preparing itself for what's sure to come, any minute now. A deep fear grabs me, chills me to the bone and suddenly I understand. I lean back and gently try to rouse Mum with a hand behind my back so as not to give anything away.

"Izobel?" Mum calls out, her words slurry, as if drugged, and trying to move but failing. "Oh no Izobel…no darling, you shouldn't have come, not tonight," she whispers and turns her face slowly towards me. This is when I actually get a good look at her, see the blooming start of a palm print stretching across her check. Bruise upon bruise I think to myself as I look into her bloodshot eyes.

"You've gotten careless," I say in a whisper, turning around to face him head on. My nerves are shot and my pulse is throbbing in my neck. I can literally feel myself shrinking in front of him.

"How dare you?" he roars coming towards me with a menacing look on his face that only he can perfect.

"Izobel…" Mum cries out in fear, her flailing arms trying to move me behind her small body as if that's going to protect any of us. Dad pushes her out of his way and, as if in slow motion, I see her fall and hit her head on the mantelpiece. Her hand tries to grab the surround to stop herself from falling, knocking over a tea light on her way down.

"Ironic darling…I was meant to do that, set things right," Dad's chilling words aimed at Mum wrap themselves around me and I feel the hard grip of his fingers on my arm as he pulls me closer, leaning down into my face, sneering with his hot alcohol fuelled breath,

"I never should've had any kids, nothing but a disgrace and an embarrassment. Both of you," he shouts into my ear. A sharp pain follows and I immediately feel something strong course through my body, as if strength now burns through my veins. I stand up straight and look him up at him, directly into his eyes.

"How dare you Dad…you're the disgrace…you are…" The pain comes before I realise he's raised his hand. I should have expected it really I think to myself as the pain explodes behind my eyes; in my head. I don't know why I thought I could stand up to him. For about one second I felt strong, empowered. Suddenly I smell fire and feel him shove me to the other side of the room. Landing hard and awkwardly on the floor with him covering me. And then everything goes black….

Chapter Twenty-one

Declan

As I drive back home, leaving Izzy to talk to her Mum I wonder if I've done the right thing, or whether I should've stayed. I park the car and just sit, tapping my fingers on the steering wheel in time to the music on the radio as the thought runs through my head. Fuck, I wish I knew what to do. I rest my head against the side window of the car and look out as the rain suddenly starts to pound the streets. I don't know what's the best thing to do right now. Will Izzy get pissed at me for interfering? I feel like a bloody chick, sitting here debating with myself about what to do. All I can hear is the sound of heavy rain, but when the beginning of *'Watch Over You'* by Alter Bridge starts to play, I know what I need to do. I need to go back and check she's okay. It's as if the weather, this song, is trying to tell me something. Something I already feel.

Fuck....Shit....Bollocks.

I crank my car back to life and drive at stupid crazy speed back to her Mum's house, hoping there's no police on the roads tonight. I'm such a fucking idiot to leave her, I should've stayed, pretended to leave then parked round the corner. I start slowing down as I come to the corner of her parents' road. A fire truck passes me with its sirens blaring and the lights cast a freaky blue glow across the white bungalows lining the road. My stomach drops when I round the corner and see the truck come to a halt outside Izzy's parents' house. There's a crowd of people forming already, a police car parked to the side, an officer shouting into a radio. My mind's trying to take it all in, but doing a piss poor job of it.

The flashing lights are everywhere and I pull the car to a screeching standstill, as close to the scene as I can get. This is like something out of a movie and it's bloody surreal. I rush out of the car and start running towards the house shouting Izzy's name from the top of my lungs. The fire that's blazing almost hugs the house, as if it's giving it a warm all-encompassing embrace. The crowd of people part as I run up towards it. The heat hitting me as I get closer, giving me a snap-shot into what Izzy went through, what she's going through now….again.

Fuck.

I run towards Izzy, but I'm stopped by a fireman, his arm pulling me to prevent me from going in. "Sir, you have to stand back."

"Let me the fuck go….let me go…I need to go in there," I yell at him in desperation.

"Sir, my men are in there doing what they can, I suggest you move back a safe distance and let them get on with it."

The heat inevitably makes me move back to the pavement anyway and I shudder as I hear, then see, two ambulances come speeding towards the scene, where I'm standing feeling completely helpless, fucking useless. I just stand here, the guilt of leaving her, gnawing at my heart as I stupidly start to think I'll never see those eyes again, that smile. I want to fucking punch something. I pull my beanie off and rake both my hands through my hair in frustration as I crouch down, suddenly feeling like I want to throw up.

Someone puts their hand on my arm, so I look up and see an elderly lady who must've walked over. She tries to wrap those small fingers covered in paper thin skin around my forearm but not quite succeeding. She doesn't look at me as she starts talking.

"The rain will help lad, the rain was sent to help those brave men. Help the Jerome family."

"Do you know them well?" I ask her, needing some sort of connection with reality as I stand back up, wondering how the fuck this happened, how I suddenly stand to lose the first girl I've ever loved. I feel so fucking helpless and I'm counting my breaths as I pinch the bridge of my nose.

"No not really dear, they haven't lived here long. I of course see Mrs Jerome out and about every day and we exchange pleasantries. Now the young girl, Izobel, no I don't see her as much. I fear that family has seen a lot of tragedy. Betty down the club said there was word going round that there used to be a young man in the family too, but sadly he was taken from them. Don't know about that lad, they keep to themselves mostly," she shrugs yet refuses to take her eyes away from the scene. "Now, as for Mr Jerome, well he's a remarkable man. Always so stern, quiet and stoic I suppose. Don't see him much either, no. I say hello like, and enquire to his health when I see him in the road." Her eyes still haven't left the carnage in front of us, as if she may miss something if she looks away just for a second. She's starting to piss me off and I know it's an irrational feeling. Counting my breaths I look up into the darkened sky feeling the rain pelt my face as I close my eyes. A momentary chuckle escapes my lips as it registers that this tiny old lady called me lad as if I couldn't fit her in my pocket.

I suddenly hear someone shouting and my head immediately snaps to attention as I see a stretcher being taken out of the house. I want to run over and follow them, see who they've found. As if sensing my thoughts, the old lady tightens her fingers on my arm. Fingers that I didn't realise were still attached to me. My body must be as numb as my mind. It feels as if a fucking hour passes before the stretcher is rushed to one of the waiting ambulances. I hear a paramedic shouting to the waiting driver so wrench myself loose from the crippling fingers and run as close as I can get. My heart drops when I see Izzy's Mum's face covered in an oxygen mask, black from the fire, quickly being placed into the ambulance. As it drives off I'm hoping Izzy's already been taken away, hoping she left the house before this fire took hold. Just hoping…

One of the firemen's radio comes to life and I, and everyone else hear of another body being recovered. A stretcher flies past me again to the side of the house, and I know. I just know the sight I'll be forced to face next, will be one I'll never forget. I know it as strongly as I know that I love the girl who will pass me any minute now. With a fucking painful heart, I know this.

As if in slow motion, the stretcher comes back into my line of vision and I see her. She looks as if she's sleeping, peacefully. My first thought is that strangely, I can't see much trace of fire except for her long blonde hair, which is blackened as if it was caught in the blaze. The oxygen mask on her face immediately gives me hope and I run to her side.

"Izzy…Izzy baby, I'm here, you're not alone and I promise you, I'm not going to leave you again," I keep shouting random shit at her as I follow the stretcher hoping my voice will wake her up. Hoping she can hear me and won't feel scared.

"Sir, are you family or friend?" the paramedic hurriedly shouts at me as he loads her onto the waiting ambulance.

"Boyfriend," I answer as I attempt to climb in with them. For one minute, I think they aren't going to let me, but they do and I take a seat by her feet whilst they bang on the closing door signalling to the driver to take off to the hospital. The paramedics immediately start working on her as I watch in silence. I have to sit on my hands or I might just grab her and pull her into my lap. Their medical words and questions thrown at me, go way above my head and I haven't got a fucking clue what's going on or what the right answers are. The ambulance suddenly comes to a stop and the doors spring open, waiting medical staff standing on the other side. The paramedics reel off a load of shit and then wheel her out of the ambulance and through the doors, into the hospital. My legs feel like dead weight and I can't move. But I do and I start to half run so I can catch up with her.

I follow Izzy until they won't let me come any further. I feel as if I'm on a boat caught in a storm, the axis of the world swaying, combined with a rushing noise in my ears that Izzy once explained to me, reminds her of the sea. I recognise heart break, it's staring me right in the fucking face. A nurse looks at me sympathetically and shouts for everyone to take a second, for me to touch her or hold her, I don't know. They respectfully look away as I take her limp, cold hand in mine and hold it up to my heart.

"Remember me…come back to me," I plead with her as I bend down and kiss her sooty cheek. It probably lasts a fraction of a second before they move her through a set of swinging doors that needs a code to open. Her white face and pale lips are the last image I see, but I can't see if the light has gone from her eyes, they're closed. I'm frozen to the spot watching the doors swing furiously behind her until there's no strength and effort left and they gently close. What the fuck do I do now? I feel around my jeans pockets for my mobile and realise I have no reception in here. Walking outside the hospital I write a quick text message and send it to Sofia and Aiden. I quit smoking a few years back, but in this moment I wish I had a pack on me because my hands need something before I punch a hole in the wall. It's freezing outside and the rain's still coming down heavy. My t-shirt it soaked through but I don't care; all I want is to hold her in my arms, taste her and see her smile.

"Declan!" I hear shouted as Sofia and Aiden run towards me. Sofia doesn't stop running until her body hits mine and she starts crying.

"What happened Dec?" Aiden asks as the three of us walk back inside, I check the signs for the floor I need to get back to as I quickly fill them in on everything I know, which is basically fuck all.

"I'll go find out what's going on, I'll pretend to be family," Sofia says giving me a sad smile as Aiden and I go find some empty seats in the waiting room.

"Why the fuck do they put the most uncomfortable and small plastic chairs in a room that has people waiting for hours?" he says as both of us shift in them awkwardly trying to get comfortable, not knowing how long we'll be sitting here.

"I don't even know who to call Aiden," I say, rubbing my hand continuously over my face as I scrunch my eyes tight and try to forget the last image that has tattooed itself onto my eyes.

"Has Izzy ever mentioned anyone else, any other family?" Aiden asks.

"No, never," I sigh.

"Maybe Sofia knows," he says, getting his phone out. "Max is just parking the car, he dropped us off."

As I look at Aiden I suddenly realise that Izzy and her mum may not make it through this. And the only people who know and care, are us, a bunch of strangers in the grand scheme of things. There should be a room full of loved ones, family here for them. They deserve that, Izzy deserves that. Sofia comes back into the waiting room. Her face is so pale I immediately stand up and walk over putting my arm around her. I pull her to the spare seat next to mine and we sit down.

"Izzy's father died…he died in the fire." She doesn't cry but looks as if she may pass out. My stomach drops and for one whole minute…sixty seconds…I feel sorry for him. But then it's only Izzy I feel sorry for. Not him, not a man I never met, but who on face value, I despise. How's she gonna feel when she finds out? No matter what's happened, what he did, he's still her Dad, or was. They are still related in name and shared blood running through their veins.

"Hey Declan," Max comes into the room and stirs me out of my thoughts. "Any news?" he asks us, sitting down next to Sofia. I look around and here we are, the four of us sitting in a neat little row and none of us have a bloody clue about much of anything.

"I just checked," Sofia answers, her voice shaking and tears streaming down her face. "Izzy's Dad died at the scene, the nurse said something about percentage of burn coverage and inhalation." Sofia stops and wipes her tears before continuing, "Both Izzy and her Mum are being treated for inhalation of smoke and carbon monoxide. They also suffered second degree burns, but apparently her Mum's suffering from partial thickness burns which are more severe. I don't know what it all means really. You'd think I would. I've been in a room like this before waiting for Izzy to wake up."

"Life's one huge fucking ironic satire at times," Aiden says, as he stands up and walks over to the large window that overlooks the park and the Thames. I look to the door when I hear it open, hoping it's a nurse with information on Izzy, but it's Connor of all people.

"What are you doing here?" I ask him as he walks over to Sofia.

"Sofia sent me a text telling me what happened and there's nowhere else I should be but here. I care about Izzy, as a friend, a great deal, so please don't start anything Declan, it's not the time or the place, okay?" He pulls Sofia up by her hand and sits down taking her with him so she's sitting on his lap in his arms. Yeah right, 'cause there's no other spare chairs in the room.

"I can't believe this has happened again," she murmurs over and over. For a brief second, I wonder if there's something going on between them but it's quickly forgotten as a nurse walks into the room and towards us. She stops in front of Sofia to acknowledge her and the pair of them leave the room. I sit here in stunned silence for a minute. What the fuck? I quickly jump out of my chair and follow them out. The nurse and Sofia are talking in hushed tones and then the nurse walks away, back through the double doors that swallowed Izzy up.

"She's going to be okay," Sofia tells me as she grabs my arm trying not to collapse. "They're transferring Elizabeth to another hospital with a better equipped burns unit, but Izzy is okay Declan…she's okay." Sofia bursts out crying and I hold her in my arms as I feel heavy breaths leave my lungs, a ton of bricks lift of my heart.

"Can we go see her?" I ask.

"Yeah, Karen, the nurse assigned to Izzy said she'd come and tell us when she's been moved to a different room." We walk back into the family waiting room and the guys and I decide that everyone should go home. There's no fucking way I'm leaving though, neither is Sofia so we stay and just wait. It seems like hours pass before Nurse Karen comes back in to see us.

"Izobel's sleeping but you can go and see her for just a few minutes at a time, each of you," she says in a stern and practiced voice, even as her eyes look sympathetic. I stand up ready to go, as I look pleadingly at Sofia, knowing by right, she should be going first.

"It's fine Declan, go and see her," she says sitting back down, rubbing her hands together nervously but looking less frightened. Karen takes me through those same double doors into a darkened hallway that reeks of antibacterial wash, sickness and death. She pushes a door open and I hear the steady pumping noise of the oxygen machine and the high pitch beeping of a monitor before I see her.

"Just five minutes," she tells me as she leaves the room quietly.

I walk up to the bed, staggered by how small Izzy looks, her skin as white as the hospital sheets. Her long blonde hair is charred and black at the ends. She looks like an angel after a battle and I can feel my anger increasing when I see bruises on her face. I sit down on the edge of the bed and pick up her hand, trying not to wake her while I make an inventory of her battle wounds and scars. Other than the bruises to her face, the partly burnt hair and a couple of blistered burns on her arms, she looks undamaged. I tell Izzy how much I love her and how strong she is, how she's a survivor and that I'm here, always, waiting for her to wake up so I can take her home. My heart is her home and hers is mine. Without it, everything feels hollow. And even though my voice is strong, as I tell her all of these things, inside I'm breaking. I lean over and kiss her forehead, the only place I feel safe doing so. It takes so much bloody restraint not to grab her and squeeze her tight. My emotions, everything I'm feeling right now, it all feels as if my skin's too tight to contain it, as though it's being stretched to its full capacity. I want to yell, scream or fight. Instead, I stand up and reluctantly walk back out into the dimmed tunnel of hushed whispers and smells of despair, and make my way to the family waiting room.

I wait as Sofia goes in for her turn, to see with her own eyes that Izzy really is okay. She's not gone long before she walks back into the room looking knackered, but relieved. She's silently crying but she has a tiny relieved smile on her face. "Are you staying?" she asks me, getting her phone out.

"Yeah, I'm never fucking leaving her again," I say angrily.

"Listen Declan, this isn't your fault, you're not responsible okay." She stops messing with her phone and looks at me with fierce determination, which is kind of funny considering how small she is compared to me.

"How are you getting back home?" I ask pulling her into a quick hug.

"Connor said he'd pick me up," she answers, looking down at the floor.

"Connor, hey," I wink at her.

"Fuck off Declan," she laughs as her phone beeps. "Right I'm off, tell her I love her and that I'll come back tomorrow okay."

"Will do Sofia. Oh and tell Connor thanks."

She waves as she walks off and I sit back down, wondering when someone will realise I'm still here and kick me out. As the night really draws in, the fluorescent lights are turned off and whatever light remains is dimmed. An eerie silence sets in, only to be suddenly broken every so often by running feet, crying and monotone announcements over an intercom. No one comes in and even though this puzzles me, I'm thankful. I walk over to the dark corner underneath the window and sit down on the floor, pulling my leather jacket tight. I rest my head against the window pane and look out, feeling like shit as I bite on my lip ring. I let Izzy down, I should've stayed and then this would've never happened. I fucking hope this hasn't broken her again, I've watched her cry and kissed her tears away. I've watched her sleeping restlessly, and heard her nightmares in her screams. I've felt her fears and her doubts, but more than that, I've seen her smiles, seen the light in her eyes, her spirit getting stronger. Fuck, I love her.

The room is getting bloody cold, so I pull my beanie back on. I notice a discarded notepad on the side table and get a pen out of my pocket, automatically writing down words to help unscramble all the thoughts in my head.

Chapter Twenty-two

Declan

I must have dozed off, as I come around to a hand on my shoulder, which is trying to rouse me awake. I open my eyes and see the nurse from last night trying to tempt me with a coffee from Costas. "It's okay, I knew you were in here but I left you to it. What the duty manager doesn't know and all that," she says with a wink. "I don't know how you take your coffee so I got a white no sugar."

I give her a genuine smile to show my gratefulness and how much I appreciate her discretion. "Spot on Karen."

"Family visiting hours start soon and as I'm on shift, I'll let you in to see your girlfriend as soon as possible."

"Thank you again, I really appreciate this," I tell her, genuinely grateful for this kind hearted nurse.

"Right, well I best get moving, I'll come get you when it's time."

I watch her leave thanking the lucky stars that Izzy got such an understanding nurse. I drink the coffee, trying to quench my thirst but scalding my mouth in the process, before I go to the bathroom to freshen up. I pop a mint ready to see her; hoping she's awake so I can look into those eyes of hers again. For some reason seeing those eyes and checking for that light is all I can focus on right now. Nothing's more important. My neck and shoulders are killing me, a trapped nerve from falling asleep on the floor. I try and massage it away while I wait. Needing something to do with my hands, I leaf through the old and out of date magazines on the table. The selection is shit as usual. Not only are they over a year old, but unless you have an interest in fishing, interior decorating or gossip that has lost all meaning, you're pretty fucked.

I stand up to stretch my legs as I realise what a fucking mess this all is. The last twenty-four hours have played out like a bloody soap opera. Lightening never strikes twice right? It's a cheap strike by some fucked up hand delivering a blow for a blow. Take the life that took another; an eye for an eye. If I'd seen this play out on the big screen, I would've laughed and thought it was bullshit. Unless the guilty hand that played the fate, dealt?

I push my hands through my hair as I sit down again, my head hanging down between my knees. I really don't want to disappoint Izzy or let her down. I'm hers and she's mine and I'll make bloody sure she gets through this; I just hope my love is enough. There's no way we'll be over before we've really begun. This is our fate, she's mine, and this, this right here, what happened, will not take her away from me, I'll make damned sure of that.

I pick up the pen and paper again, as my thoughts go on a bender, words furiously expelled from my overcrowded brain.

"I remember when we used to be the ones who were too blind to see the way

When times were tough and all went wrong we showed them all that we belong together

In the end it's just you and me and that's the way we'll always be

You're my evidence....

That there is a way.... to realise our time is now....just Breathe.

No matter what life throws at me

You and I will always be...

We just need to realise...

And....Breathe"

"You ready to go see her Declan, she's just waking up?" Karen asks, coming into the room and taking me out of my thoughts. I look up and see her standing in front of me. I didn't even hear her open the door.

"Yeah, thank you, lead the way," I say, standing up. Taking a deep steadying breath, I put my beanie and my leather jacket back on, folding up the songs and sticking them in my pocket for later. Just as she's about to open the door to Izzy's room her hands pause and she turns around to face me.

"I'm sure you'd like some time with her before the old bill turn up, they'll be here soon to take a statement from her."

I nod and take a step into the room, ready to see my beautiful girl.

Chapter Twenty-three

I wake up with a horrible metallic taste in my mouth, I try and swallow it away, noting my scratchy throat and the smell of burning in my nose. I daren't open my eyes, as long as I haven't greeted the light of consciousness, I can pretend. I remember everything and I know exactly where I am. I remember the nurse who came in to see me in the night when I rang the panic button, I remember her kind face and I know what my injuries are. It's déjà vu of the most horrific and soul destroying kind but this time without the permanent scars. My memories of yesterday are hazy but I can remember understanding what was happening, what I walked in on. It remains, as if burnt into my soul; that suspicion, which I'll never voice to anyone out of fear of recriminations.

I hear the door open and I smell him immediately. His mixed scent of man and aftershave, permeating through the acrid burnt smell, fighting away the memories of last night and winning.

"Izzy?" he asks cautiously. I want to answer him but I just don't know what to say. I hear the high pitched scratch of a chair as it's dragged across the hard linoleum floor before he sits down next to me, his clothes brushing against the bed sheets. It's odd how you can have your eyes closed, yet still see shadows through the darkness. I know he's leaning over me before I feel the heat and softness of his lips on my forehead.

"Light up for me Iz, open your eyes, I know you can hear my voice," he whispers quietly in my ear. I feel the tears force themselves out beneath my closed lids and as soon as they fall, I feel his thumbs picking them up.

"Open your eyes sweetheart, I need to see your eyes."

His voice sounds urgent and pleading as his hand squeezes mine, as though to give me the strength I need, while his other hand cradles my face, almost afraid to let go. I open my eyes and look straight into his. Both of us jump slightly when they meet, the intensity of this moment bigger than any words could ever be.

"Hey," he says with a cheeky smile that's both relieved and unsure at the same time.

"Hi," I whisper in a strained voice that takes a lot of effort from the pain. He suddenly gets this torturous look on his face.

"I'm sorry Izzy," he starts, but I stop him. I know where he's going.

"Don't Declan, just don't even go there. This right here, what happened, is not on you. No way is this on you. I never want you to think this is in any way your fault, I don't need your apology." My voice sounds like it's been cut by sandpaper and Declan obviously realises as he reaches over for a glass of water, helping me take some much needed sips.

"So Izzy, the police will be here soon to ask about what happened…do you want to talk to me about it first?"

"I know he's dead Declan….*I know*….because he saved my life," I break off shaking in fits of tears and feeling overwhelmed by the fact that last night, I lost my Dad. Yes I feel devastated, even after everything that happened. He protected me when it was clear we were trapped and I remember his last breath as he said sorry, before going very still and heavy on top of me. I close my eyes as I remember how we all ended up on the floor and how he moved so his body covered mine, right till the end, right until I heard the voices of the brave men that came to save us. Then everything went hazy and black. And now, my Dad is dead and where the hell do I go from here?

"How's Mum?" I finally ask him, as if prolonging the news that would be the final straw breaking me.

"They've taken her to a specialist burns unit at another hospital. She got hurt real bad Izzy, but the nurse said she'll be okay with time."

I release the breath I didn't realise I was holding and reach up to touch his face, watching as he closes his eyes. "I love you Declan."

He wraps me up in his arms, and even though I feel some pain, I refuse to acknowledge it as right now, being in his arms is the only place that feels right. I welcome the pain that reminds me I'm still alive.

"I love you so fucking much Izzy, I can barely look at you without my bloody heart hurting from the way it's trying to beat out of my chest. You have my heart, you own it; it's yours."

We are interrupted by two police officers coming into the room. They ask me all the standard questions, which I remember from last time, I explain what happened, calling it for what it was, an accident. I'm a good liar, I've had plenty of practice, years of practice, which makes the lies roll off my tongue so eloquently, they are executed…perfectly.

They tell me about my Dad, his injuries, his cause of death and give me the details I'll need to plan his funeral. They make him sound like a hero for saving his daughter's life. I'll give him this one, his last attempt at being a father; when he gave me my life, by offering his. I can't reconcile all this in my head right now though, so I store it away for another day. Before they leave, they inform me that they'll go talk to Mum to take a statement from her and will come back to us once the fire investigation report has been completed.

Once they've left the room, I'm in floods of tears again, thinking that I do nothing but bloody cry. But for fucks sake, how tragic can it all get. Me and Mum, we're all that's left now. We have no other family, well that we see or speak to anyway. I turn to Declan who's been watching me without looking away even once, since I woke up.

"I feel really numb Declan, I'm relieved it's all over, but at the same time, I never wanted him dead, I just wanted him to leave us alone. There was always that hope that he would change, you know?" I close my eyes wanting some of the pain to go away. Wishing for the numbness to set in.

"I think that's pretty understandable Izzy, no one would think badly of you for that, and *no one* would ever think you'd want this ending."

A nurse comes into the room, the same nurse who came in to see me in the night. "How are we doing Izzy?" she asks as she carries out her checks. "Any pain or dizzy spells?"

"Just tired and a sore throat really, a bit uncomfortable," I croak back at her.

"Well, seeing as the injuries are quite superficial, you should be okay to go home tomorrow once we've gone through some last checks and shown you how to treat your burns." She fusses around me and just before she leaves, she tells Declan that he needs to get out of here soon. He doesn't look at all happy with this information.

"I'm so tired Declan, and you look knackered too. Why don't you go home and come back tomorrow to pick me up?" I exaggerate a yawn to try and get my point across, as he really does look tired, his eyes blood shot with black circles underneath them. He still looks gorgeous though. My Declan. He hugs me tight and I cling to him as hard as I can, wishing I could crawl into him now and be taken home.

I smile at him, trying to reassure him that I'm fine, which all things considering, I am. "I'll see you tomorrow Declan, I love you."

"Love you too sweetheart. I'll see you in the morning once the doctor's done the morning rounds." He gives me a soft kiss and I watch him as he disappears through the doors. Once he's gone I close my eyes and try to remember every detail from yesterday.

I think back to the moment I opened that front door. Trying to visualise everything, see if there were any clues or whether my overactive imagination is making me see or feel things that were never really there. My head and my heart hurts from watching it all play out. The slurring of her words, the candles, the tension and her words *Izobel you were not meant to be here*....

I feel like I'm facing directly into the wind, trying to run uphill, trying to find answers that will no doubt hurt me in their knowledge. What do I do? Let sleeping dogs lie, safe in the unknown, or wake the angry rabid beasts that'll take bites out of you until you have nothing left, until you cease to be? I have no idea what the correct answer is and I have a feeling that I'm going to go crazy trying to figure it out. I do worry for Mum and the statement she'll give the police but I know that the fire investigation report will come back with *accidental* stamped on it. It was an accident as far as I see it, but how easy is it to set that scene with everyone none the wiser. It happened before. The one person that can answer these questions, my Dad, is no longer able to.

I sit up on the edge of my bed and turn to face the window overlooking the hospital park and the river. Standing on shaking legs I walk over to watch the world get on with their life as I'm yet again, stuck in a room, a disturbing consequence of Dad's violent and destructive behaviour. I place my palms on the window pane, resting my forehead against the grimy glass and try to connect with the world I see outside. The leaves on the trees have that blinding bright hued orange, that makes every artist and photographer's fingers itch to grab the camera or palette. The park is stunning, the leaves blowing off the trees in a haphazard manner, so vibrant, they're lighting up a sky that's quickly turning grey.

The overwhelming cruelty of what's happened hits me as I stand here. All the victims of his actions either broken or no longer breathing, him a victim too in the end. How can the hurt that's bleeding through my veins feel so intense, the skin covering them so tight, I can't fit within it. My soul wanting to escape on the wings that were broken when I was a child. Falling to the ground and lost for so long that crying myself to sleep became my nightly prayer. The reason to fight has gone but we're still victims fighting for the hurt to fade from our souls. I feel so alone in the world, I can't help it. I know I have Declan but I'm one person standing alone with no family ties to bind me to anything. No roots firmly planted. No home to speak of that calls me back to experience memories of the good old days; that tug at the heart, giving you that lump in your throat before bringing a tear to your eyes.

I think the only way for it all to fade, for the hurt that rests just beneath the surface to stop, is to reclaim my soul. Sounds dramatic sure, but then it really is. When I leave this room tomorrow with Declan, I leave the past right here. What I've been searching for, for so long, is to mend the broken and reclaim the light. Take myself out of the past and bring myself in to the future where my skin fits, my wings have healed and my veins no longer bleed hurt. Celebrate my life in recognition of what was lost in the fire, the burning and the senselessness from the hands of another broken soul. My Father.

I pinch my left arm as hard as I can to recognise and remind myself of the physical pain. I feel it and it's a pain so different from the one you feel inside when you have to fight a fight alone. I look at the two bandages I have on my right arm. It's all I have to show from it all. I can smell the fire on my hair and wish I had some scissors to cut it out. The light is fading outside but I have nowhere to go. I feel so alone. I walk into the bathroom and thank the lucky stars that it's an en-suite and I don't have to leave my room, as all I'm wearing is a knee length slightly see through hospital gown tied at the back. I pull the long cord with the big handle on the end, the kind that can only be found in a hospital, and turn on the dimmed toilet light that casts more shadows than it lights up.

I look at myself in the mirror and I immediately see what it is that was killing me. But despite everything, I see me, not a shadow of me or a changed me. Just me. Well if you discount the blackened bits in my hair and the bruises on the left hand side of my face. But my eyes look the same. They don't look any different. I would know, because they did last time. I close my eyes, wait five seconds then open them again. Nothing seems darker. What I see doesn't make me want to run. I repeat the process until I'm absolutely sure I've lost my mind. I have no idea how long I stand here for, but the shadows become longer and the only light I see behind me in my room is from underneath the door to the hallway and the square window at eye level.

I climb back into the bed and pull the sheet over me trying to get comfortable. I feel physically shattered but my mind is working overtime, though none of the pictures or thoughts are making any sense. It's more like, they're jumping from one image to the next with no rhyme nor reason, a mind scramble.

Chapter Twenty-four

I wake up feeling the heat and comfort of a hand cradling my face, a thumb stroking ever so gently across my bruised cheek. I open my eyes and look straight into those unusual dark eyes. I smile at him as he smiles at me and I know in a heartbeat, that he's the one who's going to keep me safe, he's my home. I want to hold him so I sit up and literally climb into his arms, burying my face in his chest. The smell of him is achingly familiar and I breathe deeply, savouring him, feeling safe as he helps rebuild what's broken inside me. His arms tighten around me as if sensing my need, speaking with actions rather than words. We sit here like this and slowly, but surely, the numbness and heavy loneliness seeps out through broken cracks, to be replaced with what I can only describe as relief and contentment. I know I shouldn't be feeling like this but I do, whether it's rational or not.

We're interrupted by a knock as the Doctor on rounds, walks into the room. As he checks me over, Declan paces the room flicking a guitar pick between his fingers. This startles me as I've never seen him do this before and it makes me worry.

"Well I'm happy to sign your release forms, so once that's done one of the nurses will come and let you know and you can go on home," he says. I thank him as he shakes my hand and walks out the room.

"I picked up some clothes and stuff for you Izzy," Declan mumbles as he picks up a back pack from the floor. I'm not sure why, but the childish thrill of him selecting my clothes and not having a clue what he may have picked, makes me laugh. He laughs right back knowing exactly what I'm thinking. "Yeah, just don't okay. At least if it's wrong you're only getting in the car and going back to the house. Oh and I never said I was a personal stylist." I pick up the back pack and start walking into the bathroom to change.

He stops me by taking my hand and pulling me in front of where he's still sitting on the bed. "No, let me help you."

"Someone might see me though the peephole Declan," I blush, as he puts his hands around me sliding them underneath the hospital gown.

"I'm not doing anything sweetheart and I'll cover you, I promise." He pulls out a clean pair of knickers and I close my eyes in total mortification as I feel the heat in my cheeks. He's only gone and picked out my jokey Hello Kitty ones that Sofia bought me.

"How could I not," he laughs enjoying my embarrassment. He reaches underneath my gown and slides his hands over my bum. "Wasn't sure," he winks at me and slides my paper hospital underwear down, his eyes never leaving mine, as he asks me to step out of them. He bends down and lifts one leg after the other as he pulls up my Hello Kitty knickers and we both burst out laughing. I can't help but worry what the hell else he's brought me.

Next come a pair of cropped black leggings, which again he insists on putting on me. He stands up facing me, shielding me from the door as he unties the gown at the back and slides it carefully off me, so as to not disturb the bandages on my arm. His palms stroke down my front as he picks out a fitted black tank top.

"Hold your arms up sweetheart," he says as he pulls them up sliding his hands with them to make sure I do as I'm told. Despite the fact that his actions are how you'd treat a child there's something intriguing, even sensual, yet comforting about what Declan's doing. He puts the top over my head and pulls it down. I'm standing there like an idiot still with my arms up in the air and don't realise this till he bursts out laughing. "You can put your arms down now."

"Oh yeah…umm sorry," I stutter coming out of the trance he's somehow put me in. He pulls out his own hoodie, the one I wore for a whole weekend once, refusing to take it off, claiming complete ownership of it. Again he puts it on me, carefully making sure my hair doesn't get stuck.

"Sit down on the bed Izzy," he says as he crouches down and slides one foot out of the hospital slippers I've had to wear.

"Oh no Declan, not the matching Hello Kitty socks," I groan in shame.

"Yup, doesn't stuff have to match somehow or did I not read the 101 guide right?" he tries to say without laughing, hiding his face by pretending to concentrate on putting the socks on me. I can hear the supressed laughter in his voice. He pulls out my Converse and I slip them on and tie up my laces.

"There, we're good to go, want me to go check at the nurse's station how long they think it'll be?" he asks, looking at me with such love, I can feel the heat of his eyes.

"Yeah that'd be good," I smile at him wanting him to leave me for a minute as this moment has completely overwhelmed me. I pick up his back pack from the floor and place it on my lap, sitting completely still and ready, on the edge of the bed, my legs still not able to reach the floor. I'm not sure why, but that always makes me feel younger than I am and somehow fragile too, which pisses me

267

off. I sit here looking out of the hospital window, unable to focus my eyes on anything in particular. I'm looking for a feeling, any feeling. I know I should be feeling something right now but for the life of me I'm not sure what, so I keep on searching. This moment feels momentous; it should be marked somehow as the end. This right here is me, crossing the finish line of a marathon in which I was an unwilling participant. The marathon lasted twenty-two years and I'm tired, so very tired but I completed it, gave it everything I had. Even when the route became hazardous, and obstacles were placed in front of me left right and centre. Not everyone managed to finish it; some lost their way or lost their lives from their efforts.

The race meant something different to each and every one of us. I try and search for the meaning behind this marathon but I'm not really sure I ever will. I should celebrate my victory, but right now is not the time. There will be plenty of time for that later. Scarred both on the inside and on the outside, right now this small victory seems bittersweet.

I cling to the comfort I've had ever since I was a little girl, a memory of my grandmother trying to explain death to me. She said that, each and every one of us is represented by a candle in the sky. I close my eyes and visualise a field of candles as far as my eye can see. The blinding white pillars of candles, some very tall, some not so much, a myriad of different sizes, the flames on the taller ones bright with a powerful warm glow, the smaller one's with flames less discernible, but still fighting to stay alight. I feel sorry for them.

As the fading flame fights on, the light in the soul starts to fade. The sudden line of black smoke coming from the tired wick signals another life extinguished. What the soul gave in life, it will carry on to its next destination, no matter how broken the body was; the force of the extinguished flame sends it onwards. The candles for my brother and my Dad are no more, yet Mum's and mine burn on. We survived the marathon. I'm roused out of my thoughts as I hear

Declan coming back into the room.

"You're good to go sweetheart," he smiles at me, as he comes to stand in front of me his eyes searching my face. "Where did you go Izzy?" He bends down and cradles my face in his hands, gliding his lips over mine, so gently I barely feel them.

"I didn't go anywhere Declan, I arrived," I reply with a smile.

"Right, well let's go home beautiful girl."

He takes my hand and gently pulls me off the bed as though he's scared he'll break me. We walk to Declan's car in the multi storey car park and every time I catch my reflection in a window, I wince. In the daylight my face looks white as a sheet, and even in the glassy transparency of a car window, I can see the purple bruises of fatigue under my eyes, the yellowing bruises on my cheek. My hair looks dead and tangled with black burnt into the ends.

As if Declan realises where my thoughts are going, he pulls me into his side and picks up the pace of his long strides as though to rush me out of here. The drive home takes forever. I feel like chanting are we there yet in impatience. I'm so desperate for a bath and to get Sofia to cut my hair. I can't face going anywhere else; there'll be too many questions. Declan and I sit in silence the whole way home, the only sound is the haunting melody of *'Dream On'* by Aerosmith coming from the speakers. Declan's hand, every now and then, gives my thigh a reassuring squeeze or grabs my hand, stroking me with his thumb. Once the car is parked, I walk out of my breathless bubble of self-reflective bollocks and back into reality. Along the way, I shrug off the heaviness that's always kept me from enjoying life, worried that it'll be taken from me, grieving it's loss as another strike is etched into the wooden trunk of a tree, marked forever.

"You okay Izzy. You're so quiet?" Declan takes my hand as we walk up the concrete steps to the front door, getting the keys out to unlock it.

"Yeah just reflecting a bit and counting the seconds till the bath I can't wait to sink into," I say, feeling tired. We walk into a house with no music playing; no TV or radio on, it's completely silent. I guess everyone's either at work or at Uni.

"I'm going to go run a bath; will you stick the kettle on please?" I ask him taking my hand from his and giving him a confident smile that hopefully shows I'm not going to crack, that in fact I'm okay.

"Yeah I'll make you a coffee and bring it up Izzy." He kisses the top of my head before I walk upstairs and into the bathroom where I immediately crank the taps. Pouring about half of the bath crème into the bath, I start undressing and sink into the still running water making sure my injured arm stays out of the bath. I close my eyes and sink down as far as I can go, covering myself in the copious amounts of bubbles that are thankfully overpowering the stench of burnt hair still embedded in my nose.

I'm turning off the tap with my foot just as Declan walks into the bathroom with my coffee, closing the door behind him.

"I don't know why but that's so bloody sexy and just reminded me of that Cadbury chocolate commercial on telly years ago."

"Mmmm chocolate," I sigh closing my eyes again and wishing I had a Snickers bar.

"Hang on, be right back." Declan disappears again down the stairs. I drink some of my coffee and feel more relaxed than I have in a long while.

"Nothing says I love you more than giving you my last Snickers bar," he laughs as he comes back in.

"No it really doesn't," I grin in pure happiness as I make a grab for it splashing him in the process. I laugh as I quickly put my coffee down to un-wrap chocolate heaven and take a huge bite. I close my eyes and sigh loudly in pure enjoyment as I have everything that makes me happy right here in this room. I have Declan, the man who carries my heart in his, a hot bath, my coffee and my favourite chocolate bar.

"Bloody hell sweetheart, that sound you just made, you naked in the bath taking a huge bite, I think I just came in my jeans," he chokes on a groan.

I burst out laughing, feeling myself blush as I take the last bite of the Snickers bar before I submerge my head in the water. When I surface and open my eyes he walks over and crouches beside the bath. He has that look on his face, which makes me feel like I'm about to be ravished and I immediately start to tremble. He bends his head down and catches my bottom lip with his teeth; his tongue slowly licks a path, raining kisses up my jaw ending with a bite and a tug of my ear lobe. I shiver and feel desperate for his touch. His hand slowly and barely touching me, brushes down my neck until it rests on the middle of my chest, where it stills.

"Tease," I moan to him and I hear and feel his chuckle, somewhere near my collar bone.

"Just relax Izzy, let me take it all away for a moment and just feel."

He starts skimming his fingers across my breasts, alternating between strokes and soft pinches. My head falls back as I close my eyes in pure bliss. Moving his hand slowly down over my stomach, it dips under the water and he pushes my legs apart lifting one leg up and over the edge of the bath. I feel his palm stroke a slow sensuous path from my foot, up the inside of my leg until it stills, cupping me under the water. One finger starts to work me, another dipping inside and I tense as I feel weightless, yet grounded by his strong hand. I can't open my eyes, they're forced shut by the sensations of his strong guitar-calloused fingers. His mouth devours mine as he takes me right to the edge and over, swallowing my moans as I shake in the water. The come down seems to last forever and a warm blanket of fatigue wraps itself around me. Declan starts stroking my hair whilst raining butterfly kisses all over my face.

"Let me take you to bed Iz." He stands up and walks over to the cupboard to get me a clean towel. I pull out the plug and stand to get out the bath. Declan smiles as he looks at me reverently.

"Just beautiful." He wraps me in the towel and puts his arms around me, rubbing his hand up and down my back. Back in our bedroom I climb under the covers exhausted and as soon as I close my eyes I fall asleep.

Chapter Twenty-five

It's completely dark when I wake up and I realise I've been asleep most of the day. Stretching, I get out of bed just as my stomach decides to complain, wanting food. Pulling on a pair of black joggers and a fitted black tank top, I pad downstairs to search the fridge for some food. As I round the stairs, Sofia's there with her arms around me in floods of tears as she inspects almost every inch of me.

"How are you feeling Izzy, are you coping hun?" She pulls back to look at my face trying to gage if I'm going to feed her a lie.

"Sad, happy, relieved, devastated Sofia. You name it, I probably feel it, but right now it's too overwhelming to analyse, so I won't. Instead I want to eat and drink, alcohol preferably." Sofia nods and I know she understands. We walk into the kitchen and I sit down.

"Okay," she says, coming to stand in front of me with about ten take-away menus in her hands. "Pick a menu…any menu."

I scrunch my eyes as I look them over, licking my lips, while my stomach groans yet again. "Mmm Indian, yeah definitely an Indian. The butter chicken and some coconut naan bread and poppadums please," I say, my mouth watering in anticipation.

"Right, let me go ring them, you open the wine," she says, as she goes to get her mobile. I check out the fridge for wine and find a bottle of white, which I open and pour into the nearest glasses. No proper etiquette needed, I fill them to the brim. I stick my iPod in the docking station and put on Biffy Clyro. Only when the mind is as scrambled as much as mine do their lyrics make sense, actually, maybe not, but I love them all the same.

I empty half my glass and although it's chilled, I feel the warmth of the wine, coat my insides. Opening the kitchen drawer I take out a pair of kitchen scissors, waiting for Sofia to come back.

"So I've rung them, the food will be here in forty-five minutes, hey what are you doing with the scissors?" She stops what she's doing, looking at me all confused.

"I want you to cut my hair Sof."

"Why hun?" she whispers, as if scared of the answer.

I pull out the hairband from my hair and shake it out showing her the dead blackened ends.

"Aw shit, that's quite a chunk to take off, are you sure you want me to do it?" She lifts up the ends that reach half way down my back.

"Cut it straight across above the highest burn mark please," I tell her as I sit down, just wanting it done. Sofia has cut hair before. She used to work in our local hairdresser after school, and although she mostly swept floors and made tea and coffee for Gemma's clients, she started helping out, getting trained in the basics. Sofia gets her hairbrush out and places a tea towel on my shoulders. She starts brushing my hair free of as many knots as she can find without hurting me, then gets the water spray we use for the potted plants and wets my hair.

"I have to take your hair up to about where your bra would sit Izzy." She sounds so apologetic and upset.

"It's fine Sofia just do it."

As she starts cutting and I visualise the black patched hair hitting the floor, I feel a sense of relief, almost like Sofia's cutting out all the bad, all the fear and the worry. Cutting off the obedient side I had to adopt to stay out of harm's way. It so freeing and I feel weightless.

We talk about my Dad and Mum while she fixes my hair. I explain to her that there's nothing I can do until what happened has been investigated and signed off. I don't voice my nagging suspicions that something seemed off that night, that I walked in on something I shouldn't have. It sounds too unbelievable and as there's no proof that I know of, I want to keep these thoughts to myself for now.

"Umm yeah so I got a bit carried away here Izzy, but it looks the dog's bollocks, if I say so myself."

I laugh at her as I stand up to go check it out in the hallway mirror. I'm gobsmacked, Sofia's managed to not only cut out the bad, she's cut long layers into it as well. But my hair is still long and to top it off, she's given me a sweeping fringe.

"I bloody love it Sof, thank you so much hun, but how on earth did I not know you were this talented?" I run my fingers through my hair in wonder. I've never really changed my hair style before. I get it trimmed when it needs it and that's pretty much it.

"You're very welcome Izzy, I'm a woman of many talents, you know that. And now, I declare, wine o'clock."

As Sofia sweeps the floor I take our wine glasses into the living room, balancing the half-empty bottle under my arm. I half lie down on one couch as Sofia takes the other, savouring the chilled wine as we wait for our food.

"Oh I heard from Taylor, did I tell you? Turns out that twat-bag bint left him," Sofia laughs, but I hear the strain in her voice.

"And, is he trying to worm his way back in with you?" I ask her.

"Yeah, but I told him to bugger off. It's too late Izzy, he acted like an arsehole, I can't forgive him and I swear I won't ever be someone's second choice, which is what I became when he let that munter suck him off. Anyway, I think his biggest problem is that he feels like billy no mates at the moment because everyone's pissed off with him and he's so pathetic he needs me." She takes a huge gulp of wine and despite her words I know she's more upset over Taylor than she says.

The doorbell interrupts us and Sofia runs to get our food as I start sticking some plates and forks out. We sit in complete silence for ages while we devour our meal. It's been a long time since I've felt this hungry. The evening flies past as we eat and drink, both of us getting more pissed by the minute as two empty wine bottles stand on the coffee table. Currently we're lying next to each other on the lounge floor, in the dark, holding hands and listening to Caleb's haunting voice as Kings of Leon belts out *'Closer'*. There's just something about lying in complete darkness and listening to music. I think when you remove all of your other senses the music affects you so much more, literally crawls into your soul and makes a home there, invoking whatever feelings you associate with that song. I've always believed that other than your written memoirs you can have a musical one too. Music is, without doubt, one of the most effective ways of telling someone how you feel or what you went through. It heightens your emotions and makes you feel them so much more.

I have no idea how long we lie here but we're taken out of our thoughts when the front door slams open and the lads come home. I can hear Declan, Aiden and Max come into the room.

"Yo pissheads," Max shouts so we can hear him over Caleb's voice.

"If you're not going to join us on the floor, piss off you dozy gits," Sofia laughs.

I refuse to open my eyes but I sense the lads coming in and joining us. And a hand wraps around mine as Declan lies down next to me.

There is complete silence through another song until *'Sex on Fire'* comes on, and as if on cue, all five of us start belting it out, trying to over sing each other. We sing the whole song, getting louder and louder and burst into laughter when it finishes.

"Right kids, I'm off to bed." Aiden stands up and comes over to give me a kiss and a cuddle before bounding upstairs. Max soon follows, carrying a drunk and fast asleep Sofia up to put her to bed. Declan and I are the only ones left as we listen to a few more songs in the darkness.

"You ready to go up sweetheart?" he asks, stroking my face with his hand and running his fingers through my hair. I hiccup very loudly turning my face to look at him laughing.

"I'll take that as a yes shall I?" he grins, standing and pulling me up by my hand. I sway as I stand there trying to focus on him but everything is starting to spin.

"You're bladdered Izzy," he says as he lifts me up into a fire man hold and takes me upstairs.

I'm thinking this isn't such a great idea as the blood rushing to my head is starting to make me feel sick. I start smacking his arse yelling at him to let me down. He stops and guides me into the bathroom.

"Right, go have a wee and brush your teeth, then come to bed madam," he laughs.

"You said wee," I say, and can't stop laughing as Declan shakes his head at me. I close the door and sort myself out, getting ready for bed. As I walk into the bedroom, Declan's sitting on the bed strumming on his guitar. I crawl under the covers and get comfortable, wrapping myself up in the blanket. "Play me a song Declan?" I ask him.

He looks over at me, shifting to sit so he's facing me with his legs crossed. There's something about the way he's sat there in just his t-shirt and boxers that makes my heart skip a beat.

"Will you play me one of your own songs?" I plead.

"Yeah…sure." His brows furrow deep in thought.

He starts playing a slow mesmerising tune, his fingers moving effortlessly across the strings and frets.

"With You

When you are low/I'll be your high

You are my mountain/I'll be your sky

When you are weak/I'll be your strong

You are the words/You are my song

When times get tough and you can't find the words to say…

I need you now no matter how

You know I'd fight for you/do anything you asked me to

I'd crawl a thousand miles to hold your hand to be with you

You know I'd die for you/sell my soul to be with you

I'd tell a thousand lies and make them all believe it's true...just to be with you

When I am wrong/You'll be my right

You are my day/You are my night

When I am lost/You'll be my way

You are my words/When there's nothing to say

When times get tough don't think you're all alone...I'll be there...Everywhere

You know I'd fight for you/Do anything you'd ask me to

I'd crawl a thousand miles to hold your hand...to be with you

You know I'd die for you/ Sell my soul to be with you

I'd tell a thousand lies and make them all believe it's true...Just to be with you.

When walls start shaking and fall to the ground...I will

be building them back to keep us safe all around. All you need to do is ask me to...

You know I'd do anything just to be with you....Be with you."

As the song slows down and finishes, he opens his eyes and looks straight at me.

"Come to bed," I whisper to him, feeling this moment as something monumental. Declan stands and walks over to place his guitar back in its stand. He walks back towards the bed just as the clouds part from hiding the moon and it shines like a spotlight through the skylight. I sit up and pull my hair band from my hair, shaking my head to release it. Declan's eyes widen and I swear I hear him gasp. I slowly pull my tank top off and sit up on my knees. Pulling down my joggers, I wriggle out of them until I am completely naked sitting on my knees on the edge of the bed.

Declan walks over to stand right in front of me. "My amazing Izzy," he sighs, as he reaches over to touch me.

"No, don't, let me do this." I push him back and run my fingers up and under the edge of his t-shirt. Trailing my finger over his skin just above his waistband. Touching him with my palms my fingers spread wide, I softly glide them up, pulling his shirt with me. He pulls it the rest of the way throwing, it into the corner of the room, his arm muscles flexing as he does. I lick my lips as the strength in his arms makes my mouth dry. I run my hands over every bit of his exposed skin, my fingers trailing over every inch of his tattoos.

"Beautiful…sexy…amazing Izzy, I need to be inside you." His breathing is erratic and it's an unbelievable heady feeling to think I'm the cause of this.

"No, it's my turn," I reply, as I start to kiss and lick every muscle, every groove and every inch of his tattoos. I just can't get enough of him. I grab his hips as I kiss down the trail that disappears beneath the waist band of his boxers. I kiss the hardness through the material before pushing them down.

Looking up at him, my eyes connect with his and the intensity with which they look at me, is like a burning brand, and I shiver as they mark me. Still looking at him, I close my hand around him as I grab his arse with my other one. I start to move my hand slowly, still looking at him. His breathing accelerates and he pushes one hand roughly though his hair.

"Jesus Iz, you drive me crazy," he groans as I speed up my hand, licking up the length of him before putting him in my mouth. His hand moves down to gently cradle the back of my head, no pressure from him at all, letting me set my own speed. The sounds he makes spur me on and I'm rubbing my thighs together as I too get worked up making him feel good. He suddenly pulls me away and gently pushes me onto my back on the bed, pulling my legs over his shoulders, as he decides to play the payback game. I squirm and grab the headboard under the onslaught of emotions from what he's doing to me. Just as I'm about to come, he climbs up my body and penetrates me completely in one forceful move that has me shouting in desperation for him. He stills, so I grab his arse and wriggle, trying to get him to move. He does, but these are not slow or languid thrusts. This is possession and taking, this is complete submission to him as he takes what's his, what he desires, so hard, so forcefully. He buries his face in my neck and bites me, making me fall over the edge and come so hard I scream his name.

"That's right Izzy *you are mine*, only mine and it is my fucking name you scream when you come."

He slows down but he puts so much force behind his slow thrusts until the last one makes him shake and growl my name in return before collapsing in a heap on top of me. I'm savouring the heavy feel of him, covering every inch of my body, so I wrap my arm around him and just hold on for dear life.

This man saved me from pretending any more. He knows pretty much everything there is to know now. The details will come later. For now, I'm safe and I feel secure. I can face anything. The relief of not having to pretend anymore is overwhelming. As if knowing where my thoughts are heading, Declan holds me tighter against him and whispers in my ear… *"**Always.**"*

Epilogue

It's snowing. Not the normal freezing and horrible sleet kind though, it's the proper big fat snowflake kind; the silence of cotton balls dropping from the sky is deafening. It's beautiful. Strangely it doesn't feel cold at all. I thought it would but all I feel is the beauty and the silence as we wait for the coffin to arrive. We arrived early, wanting to be here before the funeral director got here with Dad's coffin. I'm savouring the silence, closing my eyes, tilting my head back to feel the flakes on my face. Weightless. The only feeling is the soft wetness as they melt the second they touch my warm skin.

Declan squeezes my hand. A silent question asking me if I'm okay. I squeeze it back, yes, yes I am. I look to my side and squeeze Mum's hand asking her the same thing. Mum smiles at me. She's okay. The tears silently falling from her eyes tell a different story, but I would struggle to interpret it. Max, Aiden and Connor stand behind us with Sofia. All in black; the only colour in a line of black is Sofia's pink bobble hat, scarf and gloves. It's been just over a month since Dad died. Once we received the Coroner's report and the fire investigation report, Dad's body was released to the funeral director hired to plan his last journey. Mum was still recovering at the time so I was left to make the decisions and register his death. Sofia helped me choose the coffin, hymns and flowers. Dad will be buried in his parent's family plot near Oxford. As an only child he'll be buried with his parents.

Mum left hospital a week ago and despite looking frail, she'll make a full recovery with only scars to remind her. There's a fighting spirit in her eyes and I know who put that there. The same man who helped me find mine, who set me on the road to live again by letting me come to terms with what's happened. I owe so much to Dr McGrath. I'll be forever indebted to him.

The hearse arrives at the village church and draws up next to us by the wooden archway with the wonky gate, separating the path from the road. We are in the middle of nowhere; right in the heart of the English countryside. The country lane has been iced and gritted though and I wonder if this is in preparation for the funeral today.

The church bells ring us in just as the snow stops falling. The grey sky stays though, as it waits for the next storm to pass. The atmosphere is eerie but then, so is the occasion.

Declan tightens his hand in mine as the driver steps out of the car and walks over to us. He nods and shakes everyone's hands and then Declan, Aiden, Connor and Max follow him to the back of the hearse. No one could have been more overwhelmingly surprised than me when the lads offered to carry Dad's coffin in.

I was sitting one night with Sofia in the kitchen, going through the checklist and wondering out loud who'd carry him into the church and to the burial plot. Dad didn't have any friends; we have no family to speak of so when I said there was no one to carry him in, the guys stepped up. They all knew the kind of man he was, so I knew this offer was them doing something for me; wanting to show *me* their respect and their friendship I suppose. I still remember the lump in my throat and my difficulty speaking as I hugged every single one of them. They roped Connor in too and I was amazed when he agreed.

To the sounds of sombre melodic bells and freshly fallen snow, Mum, Sofia and I follow behind Dad as he's carried into the church on four strong shoulders. The service is short. There's not much to be said and the echoes of the ministers voice as he reads the Lord's prayer in an almost empty church, bounces off the walls and stained glass windows.

All of us stand up to sing '*Ave Maria*' and then the service is over before it really began. I requested *'Jerusalem'* to be played as Dad's coffin is carried out. This song has always had a very special place in my heart. Zack loved it too. I get goose bumps and the hairs on the back of my neck stand up whenever I hear it; it squeezes my heart.

We walk to the family plot where the open grave is waiting. Funerals are emotional for anyone. Even if you don't really know the person, you can't help but cry or at least feel that shiver and lump in your throat. I'm standing between Mum and Declan just staring at that hole in the ground. I'm burying my Dad today. People talk about what they want to get out of life. All I ever wanted from life was love and no pain. I wonder what Dad's answer would've been when he was my age. When you bring it back to basics, what is there to life? At what stage do we forget our way and change? Do we not realise we've changed until we recognise it's lost?

Declan tightens his arm around me and I lean against him, resting my head on his chest as I see the coffin being lowered into the grave. The minister is chanting as the coffin disappears, until we can no longer see it. He signals for us to come up and place our offerings into the grave. Mum chose rosemary tied in a lilac silk ribbon from her wedding bouquet. I understand her sentiment. A remembrance of a better time. I'm up next. Walking on unsteady feet I reach the edge and look down. This moment is bigger than me and I feel dizzy. I gently drop my bunched thyme and say goodbye. Declan pulls me into him and we walk back to Mum. I notice the grave diggers leaning up against a nearby tree. Waiting for their turn.

It's over. It's the end of a life lived in fear and pain. It's done. Does happiness follow? I really hope so, I wish it for Dad too. Maybe finally. The taxi's we booked earlier are waiting in the lane outside the front of the church, ready to take us to the village pub for some much needed brandy. In the past, when I've been to funerals, people will go to the pub after the service and over a ham sandwich and a pint they'll reminisce about the loved one or friend who passed away. Well, I'm sitting here in complete silence as is everyone else, around a worn and scratched wooden table. It's awkward and uncomfortable and I hate it. I stand and walk over to the waitress station to get some menus because I'm sure everyone is getting hungry and I want to feed the lads for everything they've done for Mum and me today.

We all order food and after a while, once everyone has a few drinks in them, we get talking. Not once does Dad get mentioned though. But he's still on my mind; like a persisting ticking clock.

We all get a people carrier taxi to take us the hour drive back home. I managed to get a great deal and this way everyone could have a drink. We've just arrived outside Mum's, as she's being dropped off first. Rather than get out she looks behind from the front seat at us.

"Izobel, I need to give you something, can you come inside with me for a minute before you go on home?" I wonder what it is as I follow her into the house. Mum had an industrial cleaning company come and clean up after the fire. The back is still sealed off as it needs to be rebuilt before she puts it on the market. Mum wants to move and I can't say I blame her. I'm going flat hunting with her as soon as she is ready.

"So honey, I'm not sure you're aware but I've been sent papers and personal belongings from your Dad's solicitor. It seems as though he had a new will written and some things put aside in the event of his death."

She passes me a brown box which has been sealed with heavy duty duct tape. On the top of the box there's a label that clearly states: *For Izobel* on it in Dad's handwriting. My heart skips a beat.

"Take that home with you and open it in your own good time darling; I have no idea what's in it, so I can't prepare you."

"I wonder what it is Mum?" My voice is barely audible.

"I don't know honey but I'm right here if you need me once you've opened it. Thank you for planning today my lovely girl; your Dad despite everything, would have been proud. I was proud. I love you Izobel."

"I love you too Mum; I'll ring you okay," I say, as I leave and go back to join the others in the waiting taxi. We get home and as it's still early evening, everyone but Declan and I go down to the local for a last pint. Declan and I go upstairs and sit on the bed with the box in between us. I wonder if this is how a bomb disposal team feel like. I have no idea if this parcel is dangerous or not; what it'll do to me; what it is.

"Are you going to open it?" Declan asks, taking my hand and gently stroking it with his thumb.

"I'll be honest and say I'm freaking out here Declan; I'm too scared to."

"Well, there's nothing to say you have to open it now Izzy, you can wait till you feel ready, there's no rush." He reaches over to pull my face to his, giving me a heart stopping sweet and gentle kiss of reassurance.

"No…no, I'll never be ready and it'll always be here, so I'm going to open it now." I begin to peel the tape back; achingly slowly and I'm sure I'm annoying the hell out of Declan for it. Once I have all the tape removed I slowly unfold the cardboard sides and immediately my insides hurt. I feel sick. Running to the bathroom with my hand clamped across my mouth I empty the contents of my stomach into the toilet. All this time….he had it all this time.

"Shhh sweetheart, it's okay, you're okay. I'm going to go get you a glass of water okay?"

I sit down on the floor in the bathroom and wait the dizziness out. Declan comes back in with a glass of water which I down in one before I stand up and brush my teeth to get the horrible taste away.

"Did you look in the box Declan?" I ask him when I've finished.

"No, if you want to show me then you will, it wasn't my place to." He pulls me in for a hug and buries his face in my hair.

"Let's go back upstairs; there's something I need to show you," I say to him with a shaky voice. My hands feel clammy and sweaty; I've always wondered how you can feel so hot yet be covered in a cold sweat from pure adrenalin. That's what this is; what it feels like; the adrenalin spikes through my veins as two nights collide and come back to haunt me. All that is left of it, currently sitting in a cardboard box on my bed.

I sit down in the middle of the bed next to the box. Declan moves to sit behind me so my back is resting against his front; his long muscular legs on either side of me acting like a barrier.

"Before I open this Declan, will you listen to something for me? I haven't got the strength to tell you myself, so will you listen to my story instead? This'll make so much more sense to you then."

"I'd do anything for you beautiful, you know that but I'm not sure I know what you mean," he says sounding almost frustrated.

"Dr McGrath taped a session where I told him all about the night Zack died and what's in that box is what sparked it all, but it's so very precious to me and I thought it was broken and lost forever."

Declan goes to get his dictaphone from his music case and I find the tape for him to play. We get back into the same position but as my voice from the tape fills the room he leans his head down on my shoulder and nuzzles my neck, his arms getting tighter and tighter around me, the further along in my story we get.

Hearing my own voice re-telling my past is incredibly surreal. It doesn't sound like me at all. My voice is weak with no affectation. Declan's breath speeds up and his hands close into fists around me.

I'm so glad I can't see his face right now because the shame fills me up to the point of bursting. As soon as the tape is over, I press stop and move the dictaphone to the bedside table.

"My strong, brave and beautiful Izzy, come here sweetheart." He pulls me back into him and rains kisses on me like he can't get enough, like he can't get close enough to me. "I love you so fucking much Iz, my heart can't bloody stand the fullness of it. I'm sorry….so fucking sorry you had to go through this. But listening to this tape right here; I'm bursting with pride over your strength."

I reach behind me to pull his face down. "I love you too Declan, and you gave this strength to me when you gave me *you*. I began my life again the day I met you. You saw me and gave me the butterflies back, my smile and my laughter, you gave me everything that had been missing, but most important of all, you gave me my strength, because you saw me and I understand that now."

I slide the box closer with my fingertips, take a deep breath and on my exhale I pull out my 'Fairy tale' snow globe. It's not broken, the sparkles still fall, the fairy still looks as if she's floating. There are black marks running along the bottom and the glass is yellowed which I guess is from the fire. I can't believe it survived; my 'Fairy tale' survived and I have it in my hand unharmed, unbroken.

"I don't understand why he had it, he actually had it all this time. I thought it got broken and lost that night." I move out of Declan's arms and place the snow globe on the bedside table. I got a bit of Zack back tonight. Zack's last gift to me, it survived.

With a deep shaking breath I remove the box from the bed and go pick up Declan's guitar.

"Will you play something for me Declan?"

"Always Izzy, always. I'd do anything for you beautiful girl."

While Declan plays *'Chasing Cars'* by Snow Patrol I take my funeral clothes off under his watchful eyes and walk over to his chest of drawers to get one of his t-shirts out. I hold it up to my face for a second before putting it on. Declan smiles at me as I walk back to the bed and get under the covers. Lying here, I can't help but think that this is the second time today I'm experiencing a moment that's bigger than me; bigger than anything and everything. I love this man; he understands and he knows everything there is to know and he still loves me; he didn't run. He didn't let me run.

I start to feel tired and Declan realises I think, because he puts his guitar back and strips off his clothes before getting into bed with me.

"Come here sweetheart." He moves me into his arms so my back is to his front. Moving my hair aside he kisses my scars now covered by beautiful script. I love this man, *my* Declan.

"You and me Izzy…*Always*. You're *Mine* now beautiful girl."

To Izzy, you have my heart

Your Declan

"You fell into my arms and then into my heart

And bound us together never to part

Those scars that you have left you broken in two

Now you are mine, I'll wear them for you

Stare at the sun which burns as we stand

Then we'll run through the fire as you take hold of my hand

Together we stand forever in time

And space the in between is all that is mine

I'll be your strength when you're weak in your bones

The glass in your house to stop all the stones

You're the blood in my veins and life in my air

I promise to stay and always be there…

……For You"

THE END

Thank You

There are so many important people in my life and I want to thank each and every one of you for your encouragement, your faith in me, and your patience when I went missing in action. The fact that you are still here with me means the world. You know who you are and you know I love you for being in my life and for putting up with me.

I want to thank every musician and songwriter for giving us an escape and a place to go. For soothing us, making us excited and rejoice, making us strong, happy and sad. You bring us the world.

Thank you to every Author whose words have found a place in my heart. For making me believe and feel.

I also wish to thank every reader who picks up Broken Fairytale from the bottom of my heart. Izzy's story was and is very important for me to tell and I hope you enjoyed reading about her journey.

For every voice, is an ear willing to listen.

"Life isn't about waiting for the storm to pass...It's about learning to dance in the rain."

~ Author Unknown

About the Author

Nikola Jensen has always enjoyed reading and creating stories in her head. She finally decided to take the plunge and put her first story down on paper and independently published Broken Fairytale.

Nikola lives in the UK and is an avid music lover and when not reading or talking to the characters in her head, she can be found dancing around her lounge room to her favourite band, with iPod in hand.

Nikola would love to hear from readers and can be contacted through her Facebook page or email. You can also find her on Goodreads.

Printed in Great Britain
by Amazon.co.uk, Ltd.,
Marston Gate.